Blood and Fate

T.K. Holmes

Table of Contents

Coming Soon

Fate Be Damned

This is the exciting second novel in the Blood and fate series.

Many other books in the works, so please stay up to date with my

Facebook page and website.

Fatespinnerarts16.com

Special Thanks!

Thank you to my Husband, Darrell Holmes, for being my sounding

board and letting me bounce millions of ideas off of him repeatedly and

at all hours of the night. Thank you to my Wife, Sarah Clark; you give

me confidence in my ability to craft a story worthy of the masses. Thank

you to Leah Guinan for her services as an Editor and friend. Thank you

very much to Britney Messick for the beautiful photo that became my

book cover. Special thanks go out to everyone who helped to make this

book possible with their donations to my GoFundMe page: Katroma

Dana, Jennifer Williams, and Mark VanHaelst.

Dedicated

To every single one of my English teachers who told me to prove all of

the people who doubted me wrong. Without you pushing me past my

comfort zone, I would never have been able to do this.

Blood and Fate

"I'll be fine. You worry too much." She kissed him on the cheek. "Take care of her, she looks awful."

"Okay then. Logan and the others will be here later this evening, maybe after midnight. Johnny, I command you to be sure that she comes to no harm." Michael told him.

"I will sir, you can count on me." He sat down on the floor in front of where Kayla was sitting.

"Okay Penny dear, let's get you taken care of. I'll carry you to a place where you can feed safely." He picked her up and disappeared out the door.

Kayla stood up and went into the kitchen, noticing that Johnny had followed right behind her.

"You can't follow me to the bathroom, okay; other than that, thanks for watching out for me."

"I'll take good care of you." He said quietly and she went about getting herself a snack. She felt a sharp pinch in her right shoulder and turned around to see him holding a syringe that was empty. It took only seconds for the sedative to black her out.

The house smelled different. It was missing the warm, almost spicy scent that he had come to recognize as Kayla. Michael knew in that instant that something was terribly wrong. He snatched his phone out and hit the speed dial for Logan.

"Yes?" Logan asked in a muffle that sounded like he was stuffing his face with food again.

"They've snatched her!"

"Though my soul may set in darkness, it will rise in perfect light,

I have loved the stars too fondly, to be fearful of the night."

Sarah Williams

Chapter 1

The stool under her was losing its cushion, and the rough edge was digging into the backs of her thighs, she was sure there would be lines there and even a few splinters maybe. The drink in her hand had long since gone flat; Kayla had every intention of drinking it anyways. She didn't even remember what type of beer it was. The clock on the wall behind her, one of those name brand alcohol advertisement ones, showed that it wasn't even 9:00 pm and she was already about as drunk as she could get without vomiting or passing out. Give her a few more drinks and a little longer and she would probably do both of those things. It was just your typical night for her, walking the streets, looking for drugs, and praying that things wouldn't actually get any worse.

She knew deep down that she had hit the bottom and somehow, some way, she had to drag herself back up. If she could just get clean, then she would be able to get a job at a fast food joint. She had been so

determined that she would be better than that when she had first gotten

here, that she had turned down fast food jobs. Now, looking back, she

berated her past self for being a fool. A job like that could lead to better

things, being a hooker led you nowhere, quickly.

She didn't even glance around to see if there were any "clients"

for her. Most of the men she was with these days were regulars that

came here and they would find her if they needed her. The atmosphere

here was not as bad as one would expect. It was a little run down, its

paint chipping, its floors scuffed and sticky, but not a complete hell

hole. The owner even overlooked her and the other "working" girl that

came in here to find customers.

The big fans up on the ceiling clicked, and wobbled and some of

the lights had blown out, while others had that telltale buzzing noise

that meant they were on the way out the door, one foot in the grave. To

be honest, that was exactly how Kayla felt. All she knew was that it was

Wednesday, it was ladies night with half price beers and that she was

not likely to find a John, with all the women here competing for male

attention.

Her brain was muddled with the need for more; more drink,

more drugs, just . . . more. The Xanax from earlier had worn off, letting

all the harsh emotions back in. It worked great to numb things, but

when it cut out on you, it was all at once, leaving you desperate for

more and floundering in emotions that you weren't ready to handle.

That blank slate of numb unfeeling brought on by mixing whatever

prescription meds she could find, was what she truly craved, not the

high, not the rush that so many others hungered for. She wanted to be

numb; without it she would never be able to do what she did for a

living, or forget the things that had happened to her both as a child and

since she had moved here to Savannah. Later tonight, she knew she

would have the money for more drugs, but she wasn't sure if she had

the strength to make it until then. She would have to get more of

something before the shakes set in again leaving her almost unable to

function.

Just hold it together girl; you have a stash in your purse. She thought to

herself. Looking around the bar room in desperation. She was glad she

had even remembered to carry her purse. These days her brain felt like

Swiss cheese; there were so many holes in her memory, and you could

drive a big rig through some of them. Too many pills, too many drinks,

and even a few too many knocks to the head from bad John's could do that to a person. She wondered if her mind would ever go back to normal. Was there some kind of super pill out there that healed the kind of damage she had done to herself?

In all honesty her stash was minuscule, but she would take almost anything at this point, even some of that weird stuff she had gotten the other day from some guy in the street. She wasn't too keen on that though. There was a giant blank spot in her mind; it started from the time when she had taken it, until much later the next day. Unfeeling was one thing, but amnesia was way too dangerous. She knew better than to try and find him to ask what he had given her. He was likely to get offended and give her a knife the hard way, point first. That was just the way it was on the streets and no one spoke about it in the polite society of Savannah.

This was supposedly a good Christian American Southern town, those kinds of things only happened in bad places, like New York. She wanted to scream at them to open their eyes, but she just didn't have the energy to do a damn thing about stuck up southern idiots. The things
that they didn't know about their own town would have given most of them ulcers and some of them heart failure. Like the fact that just last

night, a thirteen year old hooker got gang raped by four thugs who took

all her money and drugs and left her broken and bleeding in an alley.

It had been Kayla that half dragged, half carried her into the ER

and told them where she had been found. Kayla only hoped that the girl

had survived the trauma. She had been slurring her words and bleeding

from the nose when she was left at the ER; who knew what kind of

head injury she had sustained.

Kayla had seen dead bodies, witnessed muggings and had been

the victim of a couple of John's that just wanted fun without having to

pay for it. She was not exactly sure she would call it rape at that point.

They did give her some good drugs before pinning her down to the bed

to have their way. It was almost a fair trade.

There was a nauseating burn in her stomach that she knew was

the first sign that she needed to slow down on the drinks. She stood and

wobbled to the bathroom for the third time. She took out some pills

she had stashed inside a compact and took all three of them, dry

swallowing, not even caring what they were or what they were for. She

had gotten them out of the bathroom at the neighbor's apartment. That

lady wouldn't miss three little pills, and Kayla could mix whatever they

were with the cold pills she had lifted from the drug store. That was one way of getting a decent high if she didn't have the money for good pain

killers; mix several types of medications from where ever she could lift

them. She dragged her fingers through her half matted mop of black

hair. She looked like hell and she knew it. Once the pills kicked in she

wouldn't give a damn how she looked. She sighed with relief, knowing

that in a few minutes she would feel the effects, hopefully before the

shakes started. She got back to the bar and started sipping her beer

looking for a good mark, even though she knew it was probably

hopeless.

She watched as someone from out of town came strolling in,

looking like a dark god from some of the books she used to read. She

knew better than to even think of approaching him. His clothing

screamed rich, his walk whispered power and his looks, ah well, she

would at least have pleasant dreams about him. He was probably lost

and just wanted directions. It was pretty shocking when he took a seat

in a dark corner, ordered a drink and started looking around with

interest.

There was no way he would pay for a low class hooker when he

could probably afford an escort of much higher quality. She watched

him for what felt like hours and all he did was sip the one drink he ordered and watch the people.

Her mind played through scenarios where he actually spoke to her, wanted to meet her. Even thought up scenes where it became a whole unlikely romance. Boredom mixed with drugs could do some awfully strange things to your imagination. She turned her eyes away every time she thought he might be looking in her direction. She did not want to see that handsome face scowling at her with disgust, or worse, pity. Her beer was running out, but she didn't have money for more, so she just played with the bottle while trying to watch the stranger covertly.

Finally one of her good regular Johns came in and headed straight for her. He was a decent man, single and lonely. He always paid well and was clean and polite in spite of his unattractive pockmarked face and swarthy complexion. He paid his regular fee and she left with him to get into his car. He drove them to his normal flea bag motel, where they completed their transaction. As usual he left in his car while she was forced to walk back to the bar. By the time she returned, the handsome man was gone. It was rather disappointing; she had been enjoying trying to figure out what he was doing and what he wanted.

Closing time rolled around without any other "clients" looking for her. She did keep the number of beers below double digits, which

was a minor miracle for her on a bad night like tonight. She made a last

trip to the bathroom to swallow two little pills that she had found in the

ripped lining of her purse. It took a few minutes for the feeling of

lightness to kick in. By the time she hit the door to leave she wasn't

quite as sharp as she should be when walking home alone in an area like

this.

The money in her purse felt like it was on fire. She knew it

wasn't far to her dealer's house and she knew if she offered him her

services for a while that he would cut the price of her drugs way down.

He got the girls he pimped out, to go to the clinic and say they had

depression and anxiety troubles. Those girls brought home their

prescription pills and he sold it to people like Kayla. He also sold

Heroin, but she avoided that stuff. Now that she had used the last of

her stash, she made a straight line to his place not really paying attention

to the world around her until the blue flashes burning into her retinas

made her stop and look around in worry and fear.

Standing across the street from the dealer's place she saw more

cops there than at any one place other than the local doughnut shop.

Obviously she was not going to be able to make any purchases from him any time soon. A raid on a drug house put that dealer out of

business for a very long time, if not permanently.

"Well shit." She said out loud and kept walking as if she was just

interested in the show and not the building or the people in it. She knew

she would have to hit her hidden pills at home in order to just make it

through the night. She hadn't wanted to dip into that stash, because

some of them were harder drugs that had a lot of side effects. Still, there

was no way she would make it through the night with nothing.

She saw movement out of the corner of her eyes and thought

she noticed a dark shadow in the alley to her left on the same side of the

street that she was on, but she had seen things in the past when she was

half drugged, drunk and itching for more. She convinced herself that it

was nothing and picked up the pace. She sighed with relief when she

had made the trip to her apartment without any other incidents. She

would need to work double hard tomorrow night to get the extra

money to go looking for a new supplier. She was sure that hers was

going to be dead or in jail by morning, and new dealers often charged

you double if you weren't a new user they were trying to hook.

The after image of the young woman walking past and staring

almost directly at him startled him. She was beautiful under the makeup and mistreatment. Jenna had been right, even though he had doubted that he would find what he was looking for in this forsaken southern hell. He was not a big fan of the south and Savannah sang an off key dirge about the death of the Old South that nearly made him gag.

This young woman maybe in her early twenties, was the only bright spot here in the city. It was unfortunate that she was so terribly tarnished; he would have to see to it that she was shined up to all her glory before he let them become involved. He knew that one day he would hold her in his arms, for if Jenna could be so right about her being *here* of all places, then the rest of what she "saw" must also come true.

He lifted his head to the night wind and sniffed; smelling the path of her cheap perfume on the currents of air and feeling her vibrations like a trail that he could follow to where she was living. He decided to take the risk and do just that. Caution be damned, he was going to gather as much information on this particular woman as he could find. There was not a snowball's chance in hell that he would let this turn out the way his other attempts to find a mate had turned out.

He had seen her in the bar that night, but it wasn't until he had gotten a closer look at her and had been close enough to catch her scent

that he knew that she was who he had been searching for. She was

exactly what he needed in the beginning stages of his depression, a

distraction at the least and at the best, who knew?

When he got to the ramshackle apartment building with two

stories, boarded windows, graffiti walls and missing bricks, he shook his

head in dismay; how could people live this way. He swung around to

the back of the building where there was a fire escape of sorts, really

just a metal ladder bolted to the wall, and climbed up to an open

window. Luck was with him and her scent was wafting out of it to hit

him in the face. The young woman was asleep, or so he thought at first,

on a much abused mattress on the floor in the corner, her arms and legs

flung out

carelessly in her drug induced state. There was an empty bottle of pills

and a spilled bottle of liquor lying next to her.

He leaned in closer to her and could hear the stumbling rhythm

of her heart. Something was very wrong. Throwing caution to the wind,

he crawled into her room, sat her up, and lightly tapped her cheek. He

could tell by her breathing and heartbeat that she must have taken too

much and if he didn't get her to a hospital, she would not make it through the night.

He couldn't let her die, not now that he had found her. His brain whirled in a hundred different directions. He couldn't drain this kind of drug out of her system; most of it was still working its way from her stomach. He tore part of his sleeve off and ran it under cold water then started wiping her face and neck with it as he carried her to the window.

He took her out of her apartment the way he had come in and then not caring if anyone saw him he took to the rooftops and used his speed and power to make the best time to the nearest hospital. Taking a car or a cab would have taken much too long. Even an ambulance would have been slower.

Once there he found the emergency entrance and carried her through with her head slumped back over his shoulder and her arms dangling uselessly. He quickly turned her over to the skilled nurses and doctors. He explained that he had found her on the side of the road and brought her here. The nurse thanked him for being a caring citizen and just shook her head at the state of the young woman. He left with his mind full of desperate confusion and worry.

He hated the south, he hated Savannah, there was nothing here for him but her, so he wandered aimlessly his mind turning again and again to that young woman. Morning was creeping up on him and he made his way back to his hotel with its very dark curtains, still feeling her skin beneath his hands, her softness against his chest. He lay on the bed staring up at the ceiling with his heart pounding. Thoughts of eternity not spent alone and lingering, but of feeling truly alive within the night, raced through his mind.

He nearly wept; to be this close, and to have it possibly snatched away from him. Even with the knowledge that Jenna had told him he would have her, he was worried. He had never known her to be wrong before, but he simply could not shake the vision of her pale as shifting fog under the lights of the ER. He knew without her, that perfect completion to his spirit, he would never make it through eternity.

All Vampires had to deal with the lonely exhaustion that came with living for far too long a time. He hadn't thought that he would start to feel that for at least another forty or fifty years, but it had crept up on him suddenly. He needed her, and her life hung in the balance at the local hospital. He lay all day, not truly resting, but laying like a corpse on the bed waiting impatiently for the sun to sink below the horizon. Hours turned his worries into knives that dug viciously into his heart.

He knew he would be very tired the next day, but none of that mattered

to him as he lay there ignoring the impulse to sleep, that the sun being

over the horizon brought to all vampires.

His brain kept wandering through what had brought him here to

Savannah. Each vampire had a blood parent, the person that changed

them, his was Jenna. Each vampire had a general list of abilities brought

on by the change, but each also his or her own special capabilities that

came with age and experience. He for instance had the same mental

abilities of all vampires, but it was much, much stronger in him and he

could do so much more with it. Jenna's ability was precognition,

knowing things before they happened. It was random, she couldn't

focus it to find anything specific, and she would just get a flash of the

future and know it would happen.

That was why he had come here; he had felt the first chill of

loneliness and was moping around his home when Jenna had returned

from one of her trips. She and her mate Roland were always traveling;

she said it helped to keep her from getting bored. She had hugged him,

and then whispered in his ear that he would find what he was looking

for in Savannah. He had asked her what he would find and Jenna had

simply said. "Her."

With a deep heart wrenching sigh he flipped over on to his side, a position that he used to always use when he had been human. It was something of a comfort in times of stress. The clock on the small table next to the bed glared at him and seemed to mock him with its slow progress. If only he could have fallen into the sleep of the dead as he normally did, he would have woken the minute the sun was below the horizon without all of the stress of this damnable wait.

He remembered the first time he had failed to listen to one of Jenna's premonitions. She had been visiting his home at the time and they were in the middle of watching a private concert by a newly turned musician. Many of the vampires that were turned had some kind of lyrical talent or were exceptional with the written word. He himself liked to write horror stories and documentaries.

Jenna had stopped in the middle of the concert, her eyes going blank and her mouth making an exaggerated "O" while she stared off at nothing. Just as suddenly as it had started, it had ended and she turned to him with a warning on her lips. "She is not the one." Shortly after that he had met Eliza and wrapped up in the mystery of a new romance he had ignored Jenna's warning. Now Eliza had become one of his greatest regrets.

The clock counted down the minutes and then the seconds until sundown. Once it was finally dark enough to be safe for him, he was up and out of his hotel room like a shot from a gun. He ran across the roof tops like a phantom; silent and unseen. A few streets away from the hospital he dropped to ground level in a darkened area and walked to the ER entrance he had used last night. His heart was pounding in his throat like a hammer on an anvil and agitation showed clearly on his face.

There was a different nurse at the main ER station, one he had not seen there the night before, and he asked her quietly about the woman he had dropped off last night. She had no clue who he was talking about. Luckily a janitor from the night before remembered him and told him that the woman was alive and had been discharged already, after having been treated for the overdose.

"Well as alive as any of *them* are when they leave here. She's probably out trying to find another hit or a John for more money. That's just the way it is these days." The man said to him turning away and going back to mopping the floor.

The vampire simply turned and walked out not staying to thank any of the staff. He had to make it back to where he could check on her for himself. He made it to her apartment just as she was walking

unsteadily out the front door of the building. He followed her, hoping

that she would make it to the bar *without* stopping for drugs, or having

any other incident that could harm her or kill her.

When she had come to in the hospital bed, Kayla knew that

things had hit rock bottom. The nurse told her that she had been

brought in by a stranger due to an overdose. They had injected

medication to counteract the drugs, pumped her stomach and then

pumped her full of I.V. fluids. Kayla just nodded and listened to the

nurse say that a counselor would be in to speak with her. There was a

tray on the table in front of her with eggs, bacon and orange juice. She

tried to eat some, but her stomach was not happy with her. She settled

for crunching on some ice chips, and scratching absently at her arm

around the site of the IV.

She remembered getting home and finding the bottle of pills

stuffed into the side of her mattress where she normally kept her extra

money. Then she had grabbed the half bottle of vodka from the tiny

fridge and started swallowing, alternating between pill and booze.

Sometime after that she had blacked out, she couldn't even remember what type of pills she had been taking.

The counselor knocked on the door, just as the nurse was taking out her IV and having her sign discharge papers. She was an older female, wearing thin wire framed glasses and she had hair that was died this very strange blue gray. She looked at Kayla over her glasses as if assessing her for more flaws than those written in her charts. There was nothing this woman could tell Kayla that would change anything and she and Kayla both knew it.

"It seems that you have gotten yourself into some trouble. I'm going to tell you right now, that if you refuse to speak with me or to participate in treatment there is nothing I can do to stop you. The hospital is already discharging you; you will be on your way and on your own again. Are you going to co-operate or are you a go your own way kind of girl?" She pursed her lips and Kayla could see her lipstick bleeding into the wrinkles around her mouth. It made her want to scrub the woman's face with a wash cloth for some strange reason.

"I just want to go home and shower." Kayla said quietly.

"I figured you would be that way. I've seen your kind too many times lately. Good luck miss, and if I may say one bit of advice, get some form of help from somewhere before there is nothing the ER can do to save you." The woman left, her warning hanging in the air like a cloud of noxious gas.

The nurse came back in and handed Kayla a bag containing some scrubs. The hospital kept them on hand for those who had been brought in with little to no clothing or had to have theirs cut off of them. Kayla had been in a ratty t-shirt and her underpants; those were not in the bag. She left Kayla so that she could get dressed. The hospital paid for her to get a cab and sent her on her way. There were too many other people who needed and wanted help in the ER and they were not going to waste their time on one junky that refused treatment.

By the time Kayla made it home it was nearly four in the afternoon. It was starting to feel like autumn, and the borrowed clothing she was wearing certainly didn't do anything to ward off the chill. When the cab dropped her off she was shivering. She made it up to her apartment and collapsed into the bed not even caring that she had wanted a shower.

She woke with a start after sundown, feeling odd and unsettled, like something was about to happen. She rubbed sleep from her eyes to look at the cheap clock on the floor near her bed; it was almost seven in the evening and she needed to get ready to head down to the bar and find a John or two. Her rent would be due soon and she was not going

to get kicked out and end up on the streets like one of her friends that

had disappeared. She took a semi-clean wash cloth and ran it over

herself and washed her dark hair in the kitchen sink with stolen

shampoo from the hospital, she had grabbed it on her way out. She

barely dragged the brush through it, making a token effort to tame the

midnight tangle.

She slipped out the door not too long after eight and wobbled

her way to the bar. She knew she should just give up and go back to her

apartment. She wasn't sure if she would make it through the night.

There was unsteadiness to her feet and her head felt like the skull was

splitting open right down the middle. Maybe she would feel better after

a drink, but she doubted it. She slipped onto her normal stool at the bar

and ordered a beer; she didn't like the taste, but it was the cheapest

thing she could get drunk on. She sipped it and watched the crowd not

really expecting a John at this time of the evening. She took a cold pill

and a single pain killer from her purse and swallowed it with a mouthful

of beer. She had found one of her other stashes in the bathroom before

she left the apartment. She had nothing left in her purse or in her

apartment now. She should have been desperately hunting for a John for money for drugs, but she just couldn't pull up enough energy. She wanted to lie back down on her bed and just stop trying. Eventually she knew that the need would replace this terrifying lethargy.

It was at times like this that her mind began to work high gear, as the drugs numbed the inevitable pains of her body and dulled the ache of her most horrid memories. *How, exactly did I end up this way?* Kayla thought to herself. She really didn't remember much of the past year or so. There were patches of horror in those memories that she really didn't want to delve too deeply into. She knew she had really fallen low from her lofty dreams of being a singer. Now she would be happy just to lead a somewhat normal life. Greatness was no longer within her reach; she just prayed that normalcy was something she could accomplish.

The last truly clear memory was from before she started hooking. She remembered the trip had started from middle of nowhere deep south to Savannah in hopes of finding someone to back her singing career; that was about five years ago when she had been 16 and idealistic, beyond the norm. Now those dreams had been flushed down the toilet, along with most of the food she ate; drinking too much did that to her. She resolutely turned her thoughts away from those things and put her mind back on getting the money she needed for more

drugs, preferably Xanax or something like it.

Hopefully a John would come in and not be too offended by her

overly drunk state and her aroma of too much perfume. She used that

to cover the smell of marijuana and other things that she was slowly

poisoning her body with. A crappy jukebox in the corner behind her

blared metal tunes into the smoke filled air, and Kayla, was just about to

give up and leave. Something kept her there, beyond hope, probably

beyond help.

She kept feeling like her body was going to give out on her.

There were more and more days were she couldn't even get out of bed

because of the shakes and the nausea. She chugged the last of the beer

she had and pushed her money across the bar to the bartender who

took it and handed her another bottle. She left it where it was to go to

the bathroom. At this point it didn't matter if anyone slipped her

something, hell it may even do her some good considering the shakes

were starting again. She was starting to crave oblivion with such fervor,

that if she had been coherent enough, she would have been frightened

sober in an instant. She stumbled half blindly down the short hall to

where the restrooms were and somewhere there must have been a higher power that smiled down on her, because she wasn't mugged in

the hallway, like had happened once before.

The black clothed stranger shook his head in utter

bewilderment. He could see just how close the woman was to collapse

and still she struggled on. He had gotten between her and her dealer

with a tip to the cops and he had saved her from her overdose, now he

needed to fix her broken soul. He smiled as one of his favorite songs

came on the jukebox; Amaranth always got his blood pumping.

The woman was named Kayla; he had picked the name up from

her thoughts. *What a lovely name for what should be such a lovely young woman.*

He watched quietly as she stood from the bar and half stumbled half

walked to the bathroom leaving her drink all alone and unprotected. A

quick use of his *don't see me* abilities and he slipped to the bar next to her

seat. Then he stabbed his thumb with the fingernail on his first finger,

drawing a thin dribble of blood that he held over her drink. You

couldn't even tell that he had done anything to her drink with the brown

bottle that the cheap beer came in. He remained nearby, knowing that

she may need help when his blood took effect, which would be very

quickly indeed. He also knew that the tiny taste of his blood would help

him to track her anywhere she went. It would enhance her receptiveness to his advances for a few days before wearing off, but what he was really using it for, was to help her detox.

He knew there was not much life left in her with her in this state. He had to get her off the drugs. If he needed to, he could slip her more blood at another time, but once was usually enough. Had she been on something stronger, rather than just being a candy popper, he would have had a much more difficult time getting her to detox. He saw her come out of the bathroom and stumble into the wall, stubbornly hauling herself up and after looking around to make sure she was going the right way, she hobbled back to the bar.

Chapter 2

Kayla was dizzy as she stumbled back to the bar and her drink. Once there she blindly chugged it and slid the empty bottle back to the bartender who just shook his head sadly. The last of the money in her pockets gone, she turned to watch the room for a John, but it seemed that they were all out somewhere else tonight. She figured she may as well get up and go home. She still felt like there was something wrong with her body that the beer and pills were not fixing.

There may be a few more pills at home, if she could sober up enough to track them down. She wanted Xanax, more of her personal hell. She had to leave to go check her home for more pills; it was driving her mad with need at this point. All hope of finding a John for money went right out the window. Kayla stood up, slipped, stumbled and went down in a tangle of legs, arms and what was now left of her bar stool.

"May I help you up, my lady?" The male voice was soft, warm, silky even, and it sent shivers up Kayla's spine as she shoved her slightly matted black tresses out of her face to see who had spoken to her.

There was a pale hand held out to her, it looked almost unreal in the bar

light. That hand was attached to an arm in a very nice black button

down shirt and above that in the darkness, a pale face with two of the

most glorious deep blue eyes.

"I think I had one . . . a few too many. I'll make it. I've done this

before." The man looked at her strangely and she hoped that she had

spoken somewhat coherently. She tended to slur her words so badly

when she was drunk that it sounded like a whole new language. She

recognized him as the handsome man that she had been watching the

other night, and a strange tingle ran down her body.

"I'll help just in case." He smiled at her, giving her more shivers.

She wasn't sure how much of what she was seeing was the drugs and

booze and how much was real. For some reason Kayla thought that she

saw sharp canine teeth peeking out from behind his upper lip. She

really didn't have time to think much, because he swooped down upon

her and picked her up as if she weighed nothing.

He moved her too quickly and she felt her head pounding and her

heart thumping wildly. The room began to spin and her stomach

threatened to vent its frustrations on her in serious fashion. "Down

please, sick." She managed to squeak out before she had to dash to the restroom. She nearly collided with the corner of the bar and just barely

avoided disaster. She made it to the woman's room just in time for her

toes to try and claw their way up out of her stomach. When she came

back out she looked for the stranger only to find that he was gone.

Drunk, sick and now just a little bit freaked out, Kayla decided it was

definitely time to go home.

She hadn't found a John and she certainly had not found anyone

to supply her with more of the drugs she craved, but at this point she

was so sick that she had to stop at four trash cans between the bar and

her apartment to throw up. She was sick enough to not care about

getting drugs, which was a first, in a very long time. She was pretty sure

she was empty, but her stomach told her differently.

Her apartment was little more than a single room for kitchen,

living, and sleeping, with a tiny bathroom attached. The bathroom only

had a toilet, a sink, and a stand up shower. She was just glad she had it

all to herself; this would be impossible to explain to a roommate with

the state she was in. She threw herself into the bathroom as soon as the

apartment door was shut behind her and emptied the last of her

stomach contents into the toilet and flushed it down. Digging out her

stolen mouth wash, she rinsed her mouth out three times before the foul taste of stale alcohol faded. She grabbed her one plastic cup from the bathroom counter and drank several cups of ice cold water at full speed.

She was shaking so hard she could barely walk to her battered mattress on the floor. She was not proud of her apartment, but she was very glad to have it. The last of her tiny savings had paid for the apartment's rent for a while and all the second hand furniture. She tumbled into her tattered blankets and pillows and fell asleep before she could even get her eyes fully closed. Dreams of blue eyed saviors who turned into demons haunted her the rest of that night and she was not surprised to find herself crammed into the corner of the mattress against the walls with her pillows and blankets knotted around her when she finally woke up.

That morning she was more sober than she had been in a very long time, and looking around her apartment in dismay she felt an overwhelming urge to clean it or burn it. The idea to clean it won out and she dragged herself out of bed to start. The first thing to do was to separate her clean and dirty clothes into two piles. There was very little that was clean and once all the dirty clothing was tied up into a black garbage bag, she could go down to the ground floor of the building and use the communal laundry. There was usually free detergent down there

for her to borrow. She lugged the bag downstairs and it looked like her

luck was with her for once. No one had urinated on the floor lately so

the smell wasn't nearly as bad as normal, and indeed someone had left a

bottle of detergent that she could use.

She really noticed a change in herself when she was *folding* her

laundry before carrying it back upstairs, but she shrugged it off as she

returned to her apartment. She walked to the sink in between the fridge

and the stove against one wall that served as a kitchen, and began

washing her very few dishes in stolen soap. She set them up to dry once

she was done and then proceeded to make her bed and sweep the dirt

from floors, the whole place was cheap linoleum, into a dust pan and

throw it away. Once done with those things, the place didn't look quite

so bad.

Her skin felt like it was going to crawl away from her at that

point, so she took more stolen soap, shampoo, conditioner and a stolen

towel into the bathroom to shower. Sitting on the toilet after shaving

her legs she realized just how long it had been since she had done

anything to take care of herself and her place. That was when she took

her abused brush and literally attacked the matted state of her hair. In the mirror she could see dark circles under her eyes. She called her eyes

shit brown, but one of her John's said they looked like dark amber to

him; he was one of the nice ones.

Have I really been out of it for so long? She added up the days and

weeks she could remember and came to the shocking conclusion that

she was very messed up. *I'm still going to have to hook for some time to earn the*

money to do something better. I am definitely going to get tested for ST D's as soon

as I can and I am going to use protection from now on. What about withdrawal from

the drugs? She walked into the main room and sat down on her bed, her

legs starting to shake so badly that she couldn't stand. That was when

the crying began and she kept crying for some time, knowing that at any

moment the need would take over again. She still didn't understand how

it was that she hadn't started craving it already. Hours later she got back

up, having cried herself out, and rested for a while. She wiped her face

on her blankets and stood up, looking at her clock.

Well, it's almost dark, I have to get down to Shade's Bar and see if I can

pick up a John. Rent will be due and I do not want to get behind. Now where did I

put my gear? Kayla dug through her now clean clothing for a skin tight

black mini skirt and an even tighter light blue tank top. She threw her

leather jacket over the tank and pulled her stiletto boots on over a pair of fishnets that weren't too tattered. She ran the brush through her hair

again and was out the door, this time actually remembering to carry a

pack of rubbers and her pocket knife in her tiny purse.

Shade's was nearly empty when she came in, but there were at

least two potential John's who looked up at her and smiled as she came

in. *At least they are both regulars and decent. No kink stuff with them.* She

turned to head over to the big blonde one first. He paid more and was

very quick with his business. As she moved forward, a shadow seemed

to separate itself from the wall and slide in front of her. She couldn't

help it, she let out a half scream and took a step back. The beautiful pale

man from last night held out his hand to her as if to shake hands.

"I'm Michael. How much would you charge for your company,

my lady?" He smiled and his eyes pierced into Kayla enough to make

her shiver.

"It's Karaoke night. I'm here to listen and maybe sing. I don't

sell my company, and I sure as hell am not a lady." Kayla lied, thinking

he may be an undercover cop and tried to walk away. A gentle hand on

her shoulder stopped her and she turned to look at the man again.

"Did I offend you? I would just like to have a friend for the evening. I know you were going to sell your time to the man in the

corner. I assure you I can pay any amount. You wouldn't even have to

remove a single article of clothing. I just want conversation." The man,

Michael, pulled a money clip from his black suede jacket pocket and

handed her two, one hundred dollar bills. "Will this cover conversation?

I will also cover the cost of all your drinks." He smiled a very charming

and certainly disarming smile. She blushed, but she couldn't exactly

explain why.

Faced with the amount of money she normally got after

spending at least one night of hard work, and just for conversation this

time, she couldn't refuse. "I suppose, but if you try anything funny, I

carry a knife." She let herself be led to a table near the tiny Karaoke

stage in the corner. The waitress hustled over and set two drinks in

front of them. Kayla was surprised that when she raised hers to her lips

that it was nothing more than a cola.

Michael chuckled at her look. "I assumed you had enough to

drink for the rest of the week last night. If you would like to have

something stronger, feel free to order it." He took his jacket off and

leaned back into the chair, carefully. Here at Shade's you always treated

the chairs carefully, you never knew which ones had barely made it through a bar fight and might collapse at any moment.

"Actually I think this is fine. I'm just not really in the mood to get smashed." She went silent for a bit, but almost immediately blurted out the first thought in her head. "By the way, what makes a man like you pay a piece of trash like me two hundred dollars for conversation?" Kayla couldn't stop the words that poured out as if her tongue had a mind of its own. She mentally kicked herself, thinking she had just insulted this man.

"Well, it really is the salt of the earth that has the most interesting stories. I'm writing a book about the lowest of the low, no offense intended." He smiled again and Kayla felt that tingle in her groin that said she would be happy to give him more than words without any money involved.

"If I wasn't the lowest of the low I would not be here doing what I normally do." She said with a sigh. She turned to watch the owner setting up the karaoke machine and trying desperately to get it to work properly this time. Last time they had karaoke it had been acting up and only worked on three songs, none of them very popular. They had scrapped it after the third rendition of "There's a tear in my beer", thank gods.

"So what is the beautiful name that goes with all that gloriously

dark hair?" He reached out a hand to brush a stray lock away from her

face and goose bumps spread like wild fire across her flesh. She had to

take a sip of her drink just to clear her throat and slow her heart down.

"It's Kayla." A blush reddened her face. She turned away and

looked to the stage where the first Karaoke singer was standing up.

"He's not too terrible. I have certainly heard worse. It's best to leave

when he gets drunk though. He replaces the words with curses at that

point. It's funny the first song, but after that it gets old pretty quickly. I

sing sometimes, when . . . well when I'm not plastered." She shrugged

her shoulders and turned back to watch the stage again.

"And will you sing for me, Kayla, my sweet?" He turned her

chin with a gentle finger so that she was looking into his eyes again. He

could feel electricity between them and he was sure that Jenna had been

right.

"If you wish." She felt hot and cold all over at the same time

and she knew she was blushing like a school girl. How was it that she,

with all she had seen and done, could still blush in the presence of this

man?

"I most certainly wish it so. Pick something with lots of

emotion." He leaned back into his chair and it was then that Kayla

noticed how out of place his clothing really was. She had assumed it was

expensive from a distance, but up close she could see that it was a real

suede jacket, and probably a real silk shirt. Everything had the look of

something that had been tailored to fit him and him alone. He didn't

wear any jewelry, but he almost smelled like newly printed money.

The man on stage finished his rendition of some heavy metal

80's song and then ducked off the stage to the cheers of his group of

friends. He accepted the pats on the back and a beer from one of his

friends. Kayla cringed when he took a sip, the idea of having a beer held

no appeal to her for some reason.

Kayla had already tucked the money into her purse so she kept

in slung across her body and went up to the stage. She chose "Bring Me

to Life" by Evanescence, one of her favorite songs. She knew just how

fitting the line, *save me from this nothing I've become,* was for her. She

watched the pale faced Michael out in the crowd watching her. She

wanted to see his reaction to her singing, but as always the feel of the

music became so powerful to her that she closed her eyes and gave

herself over to the song. When she opened her eyes after the song the

table where they had been sitting was empty of everything but her glass of cola. She went back to the table thinking that he had slipped off to

the restroom. After waiting for a while it became obvious that he was

not going to come back, and she wondered just what she had done to

drive him away.

Kayla was on the stage and he knew just what the song was with

the first few notes of music. He smiled at her song choice and knew just

how appropriate that song was for what she was going through. He

certainly did intend to bring her to life, in several very important ways.

She began to sing and he was shocked almost out of his seat, she was

not just good, she was amazing. Even he, who had heard some of the

best of his kind singing, was impressed. He watched fascinated as she

closed her eyes giving in to the emotion of the music. Her pain hit him

like a blow to the chest, he tried desperately to hold off what he knew

was coming, but he was forced to leave before things started going bad.

Heavy emotion often allowed the Hunger a chance to break free. He

did not need to lose control over himself in this setting. She was too

important to him for him to treat her just like some average meal. If he

didn't get himself under control he would feed from her, even if he

knew it was the wrong thing to do.

He dashed outside and made a scrambling leap for the edge of the roof; hauling himself up and over. He sat back on his heels up on the roof of Shade's bar breathing deeply with his eyes closed. *Dear Gods above, I haven't had a reaction like that to anyone, EVER. She makes what I've felt before seem like nothing.* He thought to himself. Several moments of deep breathing exercises and he was almost ready to behave rationally again. In the middle of her song his body had reacted to her outpouring of emotion, by becoming Hungry, saddened *and* aroused; not a good combination for one of his kind. He desperately wanted to drag her away to someplace safe and keep her for his very own for a very long time, but he knew that would have to wait.

He had to set things up so that she would want him as much as he wanted her. For now he was going to drop money into her lap and help get and keep her clean. Tonight he would watch her and protect her without her knowing he was even there. He slipped back into the bar to begin; he stayed there until she left, watching her from the shadows and keeping her from seeing him with his abilities.

He hated that she kept looking around for him and that there was disappointment in her eyes. She seemed so very lonely at that point. He would have liked nothing more than to go back to her and comfort her in so many ways, but he knew she could not handle what he was,

not yet. He wasn't sure he could handle all that it would mean to have

her in his life the way he wanted her. She was a searing light within his

soul; it made all the dark places inside him feel dirty, like he should take

the time to set his life to rights before becoming involved with her.

For now he would worry about the immediate. He fully

intended to follow her home and keep her safe from the other predators

out in the dark. Those predators, so human, so soft, would never stand

a

chance against a lion of the night.

Kayla spent two more hours at the bar after Michael had left,

listening to varying degrees of skill, or lack thereof, singing. She sipped

her cola and then ordered another, wondering the whole time if he

would come back. When he didn't show, she just decided it was better

to leave, in case any withdrawal symptoms kicked in. The walk home

was the same as always; she kept her knife in one hand and her little

purse with its chain strap wrapped around her other hand. She had even

more reason to be cautious tonight; she was carrying more money than

usual.

When she reached the building with her apartment in it, she

went straight to the manager's apartment to give him the two hundred

dollars. She hardly cared at all that she was probably waking the man up.

He was angry at first, but stopped fussing the minute she shoved the

money into his hands. She could do without more food for a day; she

could not do without a relatively safe place to lay her head to sleep.

Besides she had some bread and cheese that she could toast up on the

gas stove like she would over a campfire, not that she had ever gone

camping. She wanted to go bed after eating and cleaning up, but she felt

unsettled. She couldn't pinpoint the reason either.

She puttered around the apartment for a few hours. It was

earlier than normal for her to have returned home. When she did finally

go to bed, it took her a few hours to get truly comfortable and drift off.

She kept getting the feeling that she was being watched. She got up

several times to double and triple check the door locks and the

windows. After a while she just gave it up, thinking it was the paranoia

that came with quitting drugs cold turkey. When sleep claimed her, she

slipped into dreams of richly dressed men and women dancing at a

grand ball. She saw her strange pale skinned client from tonight there;

he kept holding his hand out to her and asking her to trust him. She had these dreams as child a very long time ago, but the stranger had never

had a face before. Tonight he took on all the aspects of Michael and

somehow the dream seemed that much more real because of it. Dreams

had been an escape to slip into during all the terrible things that had

happened to her. The dreams took her away to happier times and

happier places, where nothing bad was happening to her. When all else

had failed she would curl up in her bed at home and pray to sleep.

Michael crouched next to Kayla's bed, his hand itching to touch

her, his arms aching with the need to hold her. When he had gotten to

her building he had climbed the fire ladder to wait on her to fall asleep.

Once she was lost to dreamland he had used his mind to open the

window lock and then slip inside silent as a breath of wind. Looking

down on her, laying there in just her underthings and a tank top he felt

his body respond.

He wanted to feel her next to him, it was so hard to resist. He

knew he could use his mental abilities, given to him by the change, to

make her sleep even more deeply. Deep enough to allow him to slip

into bed next to her, to hold her close, so he did just that. He refused to

give in to his Hunger with her, no matter how tantalizing she smelled.

He wanted her to accept him as he was and allow him to feed willingly.

For now it was almost enough to hold her and smell the skin of her

neck; he sternly told his Hunger and *other* parts of his body to calm

down. He knew if he was careful that there would be time enough for

both things later. There had to be a way to make things turn out the way

he wanted, and what he wanted was her for now and forever. She had

to be his partner, there was no other way he would accept things.

He lay with her all night, watching her breath, hearing her

whisper nonsense in her sleep. When it was almost dawn he snuck out

of her apartment leaving things exactly as he had found them, including

locking the window behind him. He turned toward the sky line and saw

a lighter shade of purple at the horizon. He knew it was time for him to

go, so he went back to his hotel room feeling as though he had sated a

different sort of hunger by lying next to her. It's like he had needed her

warmth, her human scent to remind him what it was to be and feel

alive.

The sun was just below the horizon, he could still smell her on

his clothes and it made him mad with Hunger and desperation. He

knew that as soon as he had left, she would have started to come out of

the deep sleep he had put her into. He pictured her, waking up, looking around confusedly, and wondering what had happened. He sighed as he rolled over onto his back in the bed of his hotel room and quickly succumbed to the slumber that was brought on by sunrise each morning. Tomorrow, things would be different for him tomorrow.

It took a lot of eye rubbing confusion for Kayla to realize that she was actually at her own apartment in Savannah when she woke. She felt like she should have been in a big four poster bed with dark curtains. She thought she could almost smell some very expensive male cologne on her blanket next to her. It was a scent that made her feel very warm and comforted. She took a minute trying to get a better sense of what or who it reminded her of. Then she gave up and shook her head thinking she was being silly. *Good grief, I didn't think withdrawal caused hallucinations.* She got up and showered, making it two days in a row that she had actually taken the time to do so.

Not knowing what to do with herself at this hour of the day, normally she would be asleep still, she decided that she would try and make her home a little more presentable. She dashed next door when her stomach started growling at her and borrowed two eggs from Mrs. Little-old-Lady in the apartment next door. She made a small breakfast with a piece of toast and the eggs. It was pretty unbelievable that it was

before noon and she was both awake and sober. Her hair had gotten

really long and she could tell by the fuzzy parts at the end that it was in

desperate need of a trim. She didn't have the money to go get it

trimmed, so she did the best she could to trim it herself with a pair of

old scissors she had found a few weeks ago. Once that was done she

tugged it up into a sloppy bun and threw on some sweatpants and a t-

shirt and started in on the cleaning.

This time she scrubbed the bathroom with borrowed bleach

until it no longer smelled like a port-a-potty. Then she borrowed a mop

and bucket and went to work on the floors. The older ladies on either

side of her were only too happy to let her borrow things as long as she

stood around for a while and listened to them tell stories about how

their lives used to be. She was so intent on getting things cleaned that

she even pulled down all her curtains and took that along with her

bedding and washed and dried all of it before putting everything back

up.

Mrs. Lipstick-on-her-teeth, who lived next door on the opposite

side from Mrs. Little-Old-Lady, let her have some dusting supplies, so

she dusted. She had one shelving unit with some much worn, and often read books, and a few movies, a small coffee table, a much abused bean

bag chair, and a TV stand with an ancient television that only had two

channels, News and Hispanic News.

She went through her tiny dorm room fridge and threw out

anything that was fussier than it should be and took the trash bags from

both days of cleaning out to the dumpster in the back of her apartment

building. It seemed her luck was with her, because she found a cheap

metal bed frame that was in decent shape and a plastic outdoor chair

that with a pillow may actually be comfortable.

She lugged her prizes up the stairs to her room one load at a

time, praying no one stole any of the extra pieces while she was carrying

up the previous load. She managed to drag everything up in only three

loads. She set the chair across from the TV not knowing where else to

put it and then went to work on the bed frame. She got it all together

with a few borrowed tools from the apartment manager and then

flipped her mattress to the nicer side and put on her now clean bedding.

Once that was done she was exhausted, but very pleased with how

much nicer her tiny apartment looked.

Now if I can only get a good paying John for tonight, I may be able to buy

some food and supplies for the house, instead of stealing them. She plopped down into the chair and was only there for five seconds before she realized

that she had yet to have any really bad withdrawal symptoms. She had

the shakes a few times and the paranoia and hallucinations, but nothing

so bad that she had gone out hunting for a free hit of anything. She

shrugged. *Maybe my system is stronger than I thought.*

She tucked her feet up in the chair and rested her chin on her

knees for a bit. After all the cleaning, it was closing in on sundown and

she should really be leaving to go find a John, but she just didn't feel like

changing out of her comfy clothes. She couldn't remember the last time

she had stayed in and just watched a worn out movie on her yard sale

VHS player.

But I need more food in the house and maybe I can get some more clothes

from goodwill. Better get up and go. Maybe I'll just wear my corset with some jeans

and my boots. That should be enough to turn someone on. I have a pretty nice ass in

jeans.

The thought was parent to the deed, and she found herself

halfway to Shade's in no time at all. Somewhere between her apartment

and the bar the sun started sinking below the horizon and there was a

chill in the air that said winter in the south was on the way. Luckily her

fake leather jacket was just enough to keep her from being chilled.

She always went back to Shade's, they never asked too many

questions, and they had been nice enough in the past to let her have a

tab when she was running short. She got a seat at the edge of the bar. A

small band was setting up on the stage and she ordered a cola hoping

they would sound better than they looked. The bartender gave her a

strange look when she ordered, but she ignored him. She half expected

her strange client to show up again tonight but she saw no sign of him.

The band was marginally good and she had nothing but a couple of

cola's before leaving the bar to go to her sure fire, get a John corner.

There was a bus bench nearby and a phone booth as well, just in

case the weather turned for the worse. She felt like she was being

followed, possibly more paranoia from quitting. She had no clue that

Michael was following silently behind her, or that he had also lifted her

wallet from her tiny purse while at the bar. She didn't know that even

now his jaw ached from clenching it so tightly trying to deny the

Hunger.

She didn't know it was him that sent her a wordless notion to

stop into the dollar store that was part of the way to her home, in order

to keep her from running into the police. She didn't see him as he was

waiting for her to come back out. He was invisible to her as he slipped into the phone booth on her corner. Years later, maybe she would hear

the story of how he had slipped a roll of twenties into the change slot

and dashed back into the shadows as he sent her an image of someone

else leaving the booth. She felt him urge her inside, her mind showing

her an image of someone following her, maybe even a cop car, which

was in fact, just a regular old white sedan. Another gentle suggestion

had her fiddling with the phone, especially the change slot.

Chapter 3

Kayla stepped into the phone booth as a police cruiser drove past. She watched it out of the corner of her eyes as she acted like she was making a call. She slipped her finger into the change cup digging for change that might have been left and to her amazement she pulled out a roll of cash. She stuffed it into her purse without even counting it. The way her life was these days, you didn't question good luck when it fell into your lap. She waited for the cop to pass and then left the booth. Even if the roll was only a few bucks it was enough for food for a day or two. With the unexpected windfall, she decided to skip finding a John and treat herself to a night off. She got to a safe spot and took the cash out and counted it. *Sixty Dollars? Who in the hell leaves sixty bucks in the change slot of a pay phone?* She smiled to herself, thinking who ever had done it was going to be mad that it was gone when they got back.

She decided to splurge and so she walked an extra block to the nearest fast food place. She tugged out some cash from her purse and walked into the florescent lit Taco Bell and grabbed a few soft tacos. She kept thinking that there must be some patron saint of street walkers looking down on her and smiling for once. She hadn't had anything bad happen to her since the night she had gotten so sick. That was when she felt the eyes on her again, like she had in front of her ex-dealer's house and her apartment a couple of times over the past few days. She spun around to look as she left the Taco Bell with her food.

I'm losing it. I've been out here too long. Paranoia may be the worst symptom I'm having from going cold turkey.

She could feel her skin crawling and her shoulders getting tight with strain as she hurried back to the apartment. She knew she must look half-crazy as she dashed up the stairs, slamming and locking the door behind her. Her shoulders immediately stopped feeling tense and she heaved a sigh of relief making her way to the coffee table to sit. She had just un-wrapped the first soft taco when there was a knock on her door. She didn't have a peep hole, but she unfolded her knife and left the chain on the door so it would only open a crack. She about dropped the knife when she saw the blue eyes of her strange client, Michael.

"I'm sorry to intrude Kayla, but you seem to have left this behind at the bar tonight." He handed the tiny wallet that held her I.D. to her through the crack. Her body tingling as his hand brushed hers. She stepped back a little, not even worried that she was opening the door for him.

"I don't even remember dropping it. Thank you. You scared the devil out of me." She sighed deeply and leaned against the door frame. There was magnetism with this man; she didn't know where it came from.

He on the other hand could see that the reactions were, at least in part, caused by his blood.

"There is no devil in you, and you are very welcome. Will you be at the bar tomorrow? I am sorry I missed you this evening." He was smiling at her as they stood in the doorway, all her normal caution completely forgotten.

"Probably, I . . . work that area. Would you . . . uh . . . like to come in?" She was shocked at herself for even suggesting such a thing, but something about him seemed so safe and familiar. It was almost like she had known him for a very long time.

"If you are comfortable with that, I will gladly accept your invitation. I wouldn't want to impose." He smiled at her again and she felt weak in the knees. She had never been nervous around men before, especially considering her current profession.

"No, it's no trouble. Please excuse the house. You don't mind if

I eat do you?" She let him in and shut the door behind him, reattaching

the chain.

"Please go ahead. I'm not in the mood for fast food. I do love

the smell of Tacos though." He chuckled pointing at the bag in her one

and only chair.

Kayla finally got a truly good look at him in the fluorescent light

bulb hanging from her ceiling. He was not much taller than herself,

maybe 5'10" or 5'11" to her 5'8". He had dark brownish hair that came

down to just pass his shoulders, but was brushed away from his face.

Oh what a face it was; high cheek bones, a mouth that smiled easily, a

nose that while attractive looked to have been broken once, and those

eyes that could melt and freeze her all in one moment. They were deep

and piercing, the pure crystalline blue of glacier waters. There was a

look of sadness in those eyes that she doubted many people noticed.

She could tell that there was good strong muscle under the expensive

clothing and the way he moved reminded her of a panther stalking

through the jungle. Her instincts said that this man was probably very

quick and agile; definitely not a muscle covered lunk head.

He solved her dilemma of only one chair by gracefully folding

himself down to sit on her bean bag on the floor. "Many years of martial arts sometimes makes me more comfortable sitting like this." He

told her chuckling.

"That explains the way you move." Kayla spoke again without

thinking and realized that maybe she needed to staple her tongue down,

since it was acting all on its own these days.

"Ah, I must give you credit, most people are not that observant.

You see what I meant about the ordinary people sometimes being the

most interesting. So since I am here and you are here and there is not

much to watch on TV these days, would you agree to finish what we

started the other night? I will pay you for the interview of course. We

really didn't get to speak much the other night. I must apologize for

running off like that. I got a business call that I had to answer. It turned

out to be an emergency with one of my businesses." He smiled and

pulled out a small digital recorder clicking some buttons and then

placing it on the coffee table between them.

"I wondered why you had disappeared. An interview is fine I

suppose. I have nowhere to be and I have enough hold over money to

keep me from having to go out tonight; especially if I get paid to talk to

you." Kayla found herself smiling at him and could see his eyes light up,

she hoped that it was with pleasure and not something much more sinister. She had never allowed a man into her apartment. Hell, she had

never even allowed anyone in here except for her next door neighbors,

and a temporary room mate who was long gone.

"Same fee as before? You don't have any objections to another

two hundred dollars, do you?" He let her finish her last bite of taco and

wash it down with a sip of water.

"No objections at all. What would you like to know about me?"

She threw another pillow on the floor across the coffee table from him

and slipped out of her plastic chair to flop down onto it, propping her

elbows on the scarred table surface.

"Well, names will not be used in the book, not full ones anyway,

so I will write you in as Kayla from Georgia. Hopefully that is okay with

you. I can change your name if you wish to remain anonymous. What I

really want to know about is your childhood and what has brought you

here to Savannah and to your . . . um . . . current occupation." He

looked like he should have been blushing, but just didn't have the skin

tone for it.

"You mean how I ended up a hooker. That, my friend, is a very

long and difficult story. Would you like me to start from the very

beginning or from when I first got here?" She was cringing inside at the idea of telling him everything, but two hundred dollars was a lot of money for her and she wasn't going to pass it up for being squeamish about her past.

"The beginning would be best." He stated, there was a subtle calmness in his voice, a quality of patient waiting, like he knew that this story would not be pleasant, but he absolutely had to hear it. She wondered why anyone would want to hear about her life.

"Alright, I'll start at the very beginning then. My Mother, has, at last count, been married five times, been with lord only knows how many men, and now has twelve children from some of them. I was the first child. My dad was a Marine, sniper I think, and died when I was three, doing something in some other country that they couldn't tell anyone about. I wish I could remember him more, all I know is he used to sing to me and he had the strongest arms. The only respectable man my Mom was ever with by the way. I think his death broke her. She was just never the same after that. She started sleeping around and getting drunk a lot.

She was remarried after a while. I was six at the time. Husband number Two got her pregnant with baby number two and then started his nightly visits to my room. I won't go into detail, but by the time I was eight and he and my mother divorced. I was no longer a virgin and I knew more about the male anatomy than any child under fifteen should.

Husband Three came along a year later and got Mom pregnant with twins, children three and four. She married him after they found out she was pregnant and then he turned into a drunken batterer. He hit her and us kids all the time, for the smallest things. When the twins were born, Mom went back to drinking with total abandon. It was like she wanted to be completely smashed all the time so she didn't have to deal with things. Because of that, I was stuck raising the kids. Husband Three was killed by soon to be Husband Four when Three walked in on my Mom having sex with Four in the bed that Number Three paid for. It was a rather sordid gossip fodder going around our really small town. Mom was the laughing stock and she was way too drunk to care.

I was ten when Number Four was killed in a drug deal gone badly. Mom was pregnant with child number five at the time. Then along comes a fiancé, and honestly I'm kind of thankful that mom killed him in her drunk driving car crash before she could marry him. He was a complete waste of oxygen. The bad news was that she was pregnant with twins again, number six and seven. I swear that women could look at a man the wrong way and end up pregnant!" Kayla paused, taking a few deep breaths. She was trying to not let all the hurt and pain make her cry and it was very hard.

She had Michael sitting across from her, his eyes looking equal parts, sad and angry, like he wanted to run out and hurt anyone for treating her badly. It made her feel somewhat better, but it also brought her walls close to crumbling.

"Let's just hurry this along shall we," She said instead of bursting into tears and crying, all while hoping he would hold her. "By the time that I was sixteen, Mom had all twelve of us, a full hysterectomy, and was on to Husband Five. He also decided I was fresh innocent juicy pickings for him. I never gave him the chance; I packed up all my things and left. I took my college fund and all of my clothes and self-recorded music." Kayla sighed again, taking a long pause to still her nerves before she continued.

"I've always wanted to be a singer. I used to use music as an escape. I moved out of my home town, here to Savannah in the hopes of getting discovered. The only discovery that was made was that it is almost impossible to get discovered here. I used what little I had saved up in a college fund to get this apartment and began selling the only thing I had, my body, because I refused to go back to my Mom. The only thing I would go back for would be to save my brothers and sisters.

I've been here for about five, six years I guess. I lost track of time for a while there. Some John got me into alcohol and a different one got me hooked on prescription meds. I'm in the middle of a cold turkey quit, and I think I'm hanging in there pretty well. I've had the shakes a few times, some paranoia I think, but I'm dealing. It's been damned hard. Life dealt me a hand of nothing and I still built a ramshackle house of cards out of it." Kayla stopped again not sure how to go on, so Michael changed the subject to different things for a while.

They found themselves talking about musical interests, movies, and books. Somehow they even began talking about government and laws, and even a touch of religion. It was strange to her that she would have so very much in common with someone of such a vastly different financial level. Eventually the conversation turned back to Kayla's life.

"Well, that is certainly one heck of a story Kayla. I can't imagine how difficult things have been for you. I mean how do you stay safe on the streets?" His sad eyes said more than his words did, that he would like to help her.

"I have a knife, and I try to be as cautious as I can be. It doesn't always work. I've been beaten, raped, and stabbed once. I got shot about a year ago. It was only in my side, and it missed everything important. A friend of mine wasn't so lucky two months ago. She ended up with a psycho John and was murdered. They found him a week ago. He'd been killing hookers up and down the east coast for months. I overdosed a few days ago. Still not sure how I ended up in the hospital, they think I tried to kill myself. It must have been one of the neighbors or someone that took me in. I'm pretty lucky to be alive according to the ER nurses. That's why I'm going cold turkey I guess. I never wanted to be a drug addict; I just wanted to forget how terrible things were, for just a little while." Kayla stretched and looked over at the clock, trying to hide the tears in her eyes. Michael watched her stretching and mentally pummeled his body into submission as the Hunger crept to the surface again. "It's almost four in the morning. I'm sorry to have kept you awake for so long."

"Don't be. I'm much more of a night owl anyway, but I should probably be leaving now anyway." He stood up as gracefully as he had seated himself and Kayla got a glimpse of the line of his muscles under his shirt. That sent her heart thumping for sure.

"You don't have to go if you don't want to. You could stay here with me. I know the place isn't what you are probably used to, but, well . . . we seem to . . . I mean, I seem to . . . feel safe with you." She blushed to the roots of her dark hair as she stood and straightened up.

"What a very nice thing to offer, and to say, but I really must go. My hotel is quite a ways. Can I meet with you tomorrow evening at the bar?" He left a folded bunch of twenties on her coffee table between them.

"I would like that Mr. Michael." Kayla followed him to the door to let him out. Her heart was already sinking that he wouldn't be staying. She was sure it had something to do with her profession.

"Please, if I may call you Kayla, then you must call me Michael." He brushed a stray lock of her hair away from her face again and then without warning planted a quick kiss on her cheek. "You smell delicious by the way." He whispered into her ear, and her body rocked with shivers from head to toe.

"Hotel shampoo . . . they smell pretty decent." She stammered feeling so flushed that she knew that her face must be glowing red.

"Then I will see you tomorrow. We can have more interview time, so wear whatever makes you comfortable. You won't need to find any other clients." He smiled then, something almost hungry in his eyes, and slipped out the door.

"Good night, Michael." She said in a half sigh as she closed the door and leaned against it. She had never felt like this about anyone, and she wasn't sure if she should be feeling this way about someone who was essentially still a stranger. She had only just met the man and already he had been in her home, seen her ID and knew her full name. She walked around her home for a few minutes trying to sort things out. *"What am I doing? Asking him to stay, where is my caution and good lord what kind of silly school girl is he turning me into, blushing like that?"* she stripped down to a t-shirt and panties and then tumbled into bed.

She wanted to stay awake and think more about things, but exhaustion crept over her and she was sleeping soundly as soon as her head found the pillow.

He heard her whisper 'good night Michael' as she closed the door, and he smiled. From his hidden spot on the roof of her building he listened to her climb into bed and then the gentle noise of her breathing and muttering softly in her sleep. His enhanced hearing had no trouble picking up some of the words she mumbled and he was pleased to hear his name among them. *Who says one of my kind can't be*

aroused, intrigued or fascinated by a mere human? He smiled at the thought.

He kept a watchful eye and open ears out for trouble near her

building until just before true dawn and then he made a series of long

high jumps from building top to building top until he reached his hotel.

He slipped inside the room put the "do not disturb" sign up and pulled

the light blocking curtains closed. It was safe enough for him to sleep in

a hotel. He always made sure that the curtains were dark enough and

with his strength he could handle a little sun much better than most of

his kind. He could still smell her scent all around him and he was nearly

mad with Hunger and need. He could understand how she had fallen to

where she was, but a woman like her deserved so much better. He could

see that there was strength in her, but she had been rendered hopeless

by her situation. He didn't want to force her into anything, and he knew

that he would have to stay around long enough to make her want him

without the influence of his blood. A few more days and that would

purge itself from her body along with the remnants of toxicity left by

drugs, alcohol and poor food. He already felt so very possessive and

protective of her. She should be his and his alone, for no other man,

human or other to lay their hands upon.

She was already beginning to trust him, asking him to spend the night. It had been so hard to say no, but he knew that she was not yet ready for what he was. He had to have her trust and he had to build her desire for him as well. When he was intimate with a human and his emotions got all built up sometimes it was not possible to resist the urge to feed. The Hunger had a mind of its own in those times.

When he had come to Savannah it had been at the request of his blood parent, Jenna. She told him that she felt he should be there, and that someone was waiting for him. To this day he had never ignored one of her bouts of intuition, since the last catastrophe. So he had come and wandered the streets at night looking, feeling, sensing, and smelling. Nothing had struck him and he had almost been ready to return to his home up North. He decided on a whim to go "slumming" as an old friend of his called it. He found the local area where street whores, pimps and drug dealers wandered the streets, places he usually hunted when the Hunger became too much.

That was when he had seen her walking into the bar. She wobbled as if she had been drinking since early morning and her scent was rank with drugs and booze. The face, the body, the spirit beneath it all made him stop in his tracks. She was not meant to be here, to be this way; she should have been healthy, so that her beauty could shine. He had felt his body react to the way that she had looked in the low light of the street tonight when he had followed her home. She had cleaned herself up physically on the outside, and his little slip of blood into her alcohol before she had fallen from her bar stool had helped to clear her system of the main taint of drugs. She was simply amazing. Her hair now looked like midnight silk falling nearly to her waist instead of the tangled black mass that it had been. Her eyes were brilliant amber with golden flecks in it, were so very sad. Her body, *a body to make a saint sin,* lithe, yet strong, curved perfectly in every place that it should. The thing that drew him the most was her lips. They were soft, kissable and helped give her a smile that lit up the room.

Michael could feel the sun slipping up over the horizon as he lay in the hotel bed thinking of her, and the drowsiness that usually came with dawn crept over him, but as he began to sleep he dreamed for the first time in a very long time, about haunted eyes and glorious midnight hair.

Kayla sat up, awake all at once. She could tell that it was completely dark outside. She didn't know what time it was, or what had woken her, but something told her to grab her knife. She sat in the pitch

black room in total silence with her heart thumping in her throat. There

were all the normal sounds outside and she strained to hear anything

unusual.

Bam bam bam. Someone thudded on her door and she nearly

wet herself, she was so startled. She scrambled out of the bed nearly

breaking her neck getting untangled from the blankets.

"One second." She called as she held her knife in her teeth and

tugged on her jeans, trying not to fall and hoping if she did she wouldn't

stab herself. She ran for the door and made sure the chain was on.

Keeping her knife in one hand she cracked the door open. "Who is it?"

"It's Michael. Did I wake you?" Michael's voice asked from the

other side of the door, he sounded concerned and there was worry on

his face as she peered through the crack in the door. "I went to the bar

and you weren't there. It's nearly eight o'clock, are you alright?" He

peered at her through the crack in the door and she almost giggled

because he looked kind of silly that way.

"Oh good grief, I can't believe I slept straight through the whole

day. I'm so sorry. Come on in." She unhooked the chain, relief flooding

her system and making her nearly faint. She shut the door behind him and went to straighten the bed. She was glad that she had pulled on her

jeans, but she felt a little awkward that she wasn't wearing a bra yet.

"Your body must be recovering from . . . well . . . from things.

I'm sorry to wake you. I did bring you some Taco bell. I got hungry on

the way over and ate mine in the cab." He took his seat in front of the

coffee table again and set the food between them as she went into the

bathroom for a moment to get dressed properly and then resumed her

seat from the night before.

"Oh my gods, I could kiss you, I'm starving!" Kayla dug into the

soft tacos, alternating bites with sips from the cola. She glanced up at

him after a while and he had a bit of a strange look on his face. "What?"

she asked.

"Oh nothing really, just been a while since anyone kissed me."

He looked a little chagrined at that. She blushed as images of her

pressing her lips to every part of him flashed through her mind.

"Someone is going to have to remedy that at some point." She

said quietly and was pleased to see him smile at her.

Michael took out another fold of bills and set them on the table.

"We may as well have the interview here if that isn't a problem." He had

been smiling at her quite a bit and each time was like he set butterflies loose in her chest. She felt completely safe with him, but in spite of that she suddenly got this strange feeling that something was not exactly as it seemed.

"Why are you really paying me this much? A book isn't worth this kind of money for one interview and you said it was about more than just me." A look of suspicion crossed her face as she saw the slight look of guilt in his face.

"Mostly for the reason I told you. I do need research for a book. I have, as you can tell, quite a bit of money to do research of any kind I wish. The second reason is of a bit more selfish nature. I just cannot stand to see something beautiful waste away. You were doing yourself quite a bit of harm wouldn't you say? With the money from a few interviews you can possibly buy the things you need to help you get a better job and get away from this area." He chuckled because she looked shocked and he took a sip from his own soda.

"You're some kind of rich do-good person aren't you?" She rolled her eyes. "I really never thought I would end up as a charity case." She laughed a little at herself and the situation she had found herself in.

"You could say that. Has the money I've given you already

helped?" His hand was lingering on the edge of the coffee table.

Impulsively she laid her warm hand atop his surprisingly cool one.

"You have been so much help that it scares me that you may

want something bad." She felt a spark between their hands and she

pulled hers back. Michael's eyes went wide, startled, but he covered it

quickly.

"I will not say that other things have not crossed my mind,

nothing bad I promise. You are a very attractive young woman, but I

would like more than anything to just be your friend for now." He

replied quietly. Looking sad again and somewhat frustrated. She plowed

ahead and kept talking, praying that she wasn't digging a hole she

couldn't climb out of.

"So you have thought about it too? I did offer last night; no

charge." She tried to grab his hand again, but he pulled away fast,

almost too quickly to believe. Now that she had questioned him and he

had done a good job of setting her mind at ease all the attraction she

had felt for him flamed to the surface again.

"I think I should refrain from giving in to my temptations at this

point. Please, let us just talk. Tell me more about what you have gone

through here on the streets. That is what will be best for my book." His hands he kept folded in his lap for the rest of the evening. He didn't act

any differently and he smiled the same, but she could feel a subtle

tension in him as if he had to hold back something.

For his part he felt like he was a guitar that someone had strung

way too tight. He had to pull out all of his old meditation techniques

just to keep himself from dragging her to the floor with him and making

his desires, reality.

They talked about what she had experienced, about stories she

had heard, and about crimes she had witnessed. She confessed that she

had been raped four times by John's not wanting to pay for her services.

She told about the time she had been mugged at knife point, and the

time that she had nearly been kidnapped.

"I told you I was shot in the side and stabbed. Would you need

photos of the wounds?" She stood up before he could even stop her

and lifted her shirt almost to the bra line. He bit his tongue until blood

flowed as his groin tightened, painfully. She had such soft beautiful

curves with a hint of muscle underneath and he wanted nothing more

than to explore them at great length.

He coughed once or twice, took a sip of his soda, mental

throttled himself and then he spoke. "No, no pictures necessary please continue." He did notice the two small white scars from her injuries and that made him very angry.

He expressed shock at her tone throughout the details of the rapes, and fury at the fact that nothing had been done to the criminals who had hurt her. She may have sounded calm to him, but inside she felt all the hurt and shame all over again. She wasn't sure she would ever truly get back those pieces of her spirit that had been shattered and stolen with each violation. Duct tape couldn't fix everything.

"It's life on the street. I've heard it's worse than that in larger cities. I knew three different girls from here that have all just vanished. The last girl lived here with me for two days. All they found of her was a shoe. I knew it was hers when I saw the picture of it in the paper. Not many people have orange tiger striped stilettos. Here you're tough or you're dead. I can't just go crying back to my Momma I've done what I've had to do to get by. I don't enjoy this life, I don't want this life, but I will do what I have to just to survive. The worst thing is missing my brothers and sisters. I wish I could have saved them, but I was barely able to save me. I'm tired of talking about me, tell me something about you, anything?" She stretched trying to get her back to pop and noticed that hungry look on his face again as he watched her body move. The only thing she could think was that he looked like a tiger that she had seen at a zoo once right at feeding time. It made her shiver and she wrapped her arms around her knees as she sat on the floor.

"It's getting late again. I should probably leave." He stood up and turned to the door, as if he wasn't even going to say goodbye. Her heart felt crushed by an iron grip. She felt like she couldn't catch her breath, she knew what she was about to do was going to take a lot of courage. She plunged in.

"I'll give you one of these hundreds back to stay with me." She stood and reached for him again, only managing to snag the end of his sleeve. She couldn't explain it, but there was a magnetic pull that drew her to him. She wanted him to hold her and to touch her gently even if nothing more than that happened.

"You need that. I have to go. I'm getting very . . . sleepy." He pulled away from her again, very gently this time. "I promise you will see me again, but I may be away for a while. Good night Kayla." He brushed a gentle kiss across her forehead and he was out the door before she could say anything.

"Damn it all to hell." She kicked the door closed and latched it. "He probably thinks I'm a walking STD farm. Why would a man like that want anything to do with me?" She dropped back down in front of the coffee table to add up all the money she had stuffed into her tiny purse. Every bit of money she had at this point was from him.

Oh my gods there is Eight hundred dollars here. How the hell did I end up with that much? He must have over paid me. Bless him for being so kind, but I would almost give it all back just for one night with him. I have never had anyone make me this crazy.

Michael sat on the roof doing deep breathing exercises again and reminding his body that he had already fed and reminding certain parts of him that he did not need to do *that* at this point in time.

She has me and she does not even know it. He opened his mind and ears and brought her into his awareness. He could almost see her sitting on the edge of her bed hugging her bare knees and crying. *Damn it. I did not want to hurt her. I don't want to feed from her yet. If I had stayed things would have moved too quickly. I want to see her more, but I don't know how much more I can take without giving in. She has to know first and I have to know that she will not reveal the secret. I have to get away from her for a few days.* He paid attention to her long enough for her to crawl under the covers. The minute she began to dream and mumble his name in her sleep, he left; heading for his hotel room. Tomorrow night he would go take care of a plan that

had invaded his mind while she spoke of her family and how much she

missed her brothers and sisters. Then he would go to speak with Jenna

to get her opinion. He would leave a note and more money behind. He

had already been planning on introducing her to a lawyer friend of his in

the area that needed a file clerk. Getting her that job would be the first

step in getting her away from this. He could only hope that she would

stay clean and stay away from her current profession.

Chapter 4:

Michael woke the next evening and went looking for Kayla's relatives. He couldn't do anything about her right now, so he went to do what he did best, rescue people. He spent a long time hacking into any and all information that he could find about Kayla and her family. Kayla's Mother and siblings were the easiest to locate due to the recent death of her Mom.

It seemed that her Mom had died in a drunken car crash only a few months ago. The oldest son, Henry, who was 18, had taken custody of the other children. According to the state's records every home visit since then had been excellent and it seemed that no more visits were needed. He felt good leaving the situation as it was. If her brother was doing a good job making sure everyone was well taken care of, then there was really no need for him to get involved at all.

What he did not expect to find was a curious mystery surrounding the supposed death of her father. It was obvious that everyone assumed he had been killed in action, but no body had been found. That wasn't terribly strange, considering his line of work, but what really set off the alarm bells for Michael was that sometime after he had supposedly died, someone had gotten into his storage locker and taken some things. Michael went over the list of missing things three times, and it only made sense if her father was still alive somehow.

None of the keepsakes, even the ones worth money, had been taken. None of the jewelry had been disturbed. The only things taken were surplus military clothing, weapons, ammo and a small one man tent. No thief in his right mind would only take those things, but a man pretending to be dead and going on the run certainly would.

He would have to have a very long talk with his former military friend Logan to see if he knew anything that may be of use to Michael in solving this mystery. From the way she spoke, Kayla may not have remembered her father very much, but she missed his presence for sure. He would do what he could to find him.

He returned to Savannah to leave Kayla the money he had decided to give her and a note. Also he wanted to feed there once again in an attempt to frighten off any rival vampires. If it looked as if he had claimed the area, the others would hopefully leave.

Michael walked into the bottom floor of the apartments and slipped the note with the check and money into the mail box that belonged to Kayla. He had already spoken with the lawyer at the firm

and Kayla had a guaranteed position if she showed up. He was debating

sneaking in to see her, and that was when the scent of another of his

kind hit him. It was drifting down the staircase, which meant that it was

inside the building. He darted back outside and around to the back

where the fire ladder was. He climbed it and looked into Kayla's

window. She was asleep in a nest of blankets in front of the TV.

He heard a gurgle from the window to his left and saw the

vampire making a glutton of himself with Kayla's neighbor inside the

bathroom. The vampire looked up from his bloody feast and stared

right at Michael, a blood drenched smile spreading across his face. He

was naked in the shower of the tiny bathroom with the old woman, also

stripped down, and pressed against him in a completely lewd fashion.

The shower was on and the blood that he wasn't licking from the huge

gash in the woman's throat was being washed down the drain.

Michael snarled in hatred, these were the fiends that he spent his

time tracking down and killing. This would just be one more in a list

that grew longer every year. He smashed the window with his fist and

crawled through. The other vampire finally realized that he may be in

trouble. He dropped the body and dashed for the door out into the rest of the apartment building. He didn't make it; Michael placed his hand almost lovingly around the beast's neck and twisted him around so that he could face Michael. He glanced down at the older lady and couldn't hear a heartbeat; she was already gone beyond saving.

"You have been found guilty. I am your Judge, your jury and the executioner of your nightmares." Michael whispered as he wrapped a pink bath robe around the murderer. He did not want to drag this vampire through Savannah in nothing but his skin. It was bad enough that he had to touch him at all; it made him feel even angrier.

He made a quick exit from the apartment watching around in the darkness to make sure that no one was watching. He knew the way to a safe spot out away from town where he would not be disturbed. It was just before dawn and he knew how to deal with this piece of vampire trash. It took him no time at all to get there. The small clearing in the woods was perfect for this sort of thing.

"Have you anything to say for yourself?" Michael asked as he stood over the other vampire. He always asked, maybe this once he would find one worthy of redemption, but he doubted it. The other vampire only hissed and attempted to bite him. "Then take your punishment." A blade came out from the waistband of Michael's pants and slit the throat of the other vampire, much the same way that he had

slit that poor woman's throat. Then Michael proceeded to pull the

vampire limb from limb leaving a pile of twitching parts that he quickly

set ablaze. When you burnt a vampire, nothing was left but ash, thus

ensuring that their secret remained secret. Random not so human

bodies led to a lot of unwanted questions that were not easily answered.

He felt sickened all over by having to do this, but there was no

other choice. Vampires like this, threatened all vampires. When he

turned to leave he caught movement out of the corner of his eye. It

seemed that he had been followed by someone.

He had to find out who was following him and if anyone had

sent them. He had enemies, that did not believe the way he did and if

the main one, Nicholai, had found him here and found Kayla, there

would be no chance that he would be able to keep her safe.

Kayla was his number one priority and he would do everything

in his power to keep her safe. That's why even though he could have

followed her to her temporary hotel room and then on to where ever

she found a place to stay, he didn't. The last thing he wanted to do was

lead whoever was tracking him to her.

There was an annoying bird singing outside her only window in

the morning around ten o'clock so she dragged herself out of bed and

into the shower. It had been too long since she had seen Michael, only a

few days, but it felt like forever. She realized that she should probably

take some of the money she had and go shopping for things she needed

for the house. She also wanted to get a few things for herself. Maybe if

she looked nicer when he saw her again he may not be so quick to turn

her down. She took a cab to the nearest Goodwill store and picked out

some nicer clothing than she had owned in a long time, including a

pretty emerald green dress and a pair of nice black heels. She picked up

a new purse to match the shoes, a new movie, and nicer newer bedding,

then paid for her things and got back into the cab heading for the

corner store just down from her apartment. Once there she picked up a

folding table, two folding chairs and some food supplies. She still had

around two hundred dollars left when she got home, so she stashed it in

a bag that she stuffed between the mattress and box spring.

Now what do I do? I don't need to go out tonight. I've got dinner and some

money stashed away. My rent is paid for the next two months. I can watch my new

movie. "Bran Stoker's Dracula" At least it was something that she had

not watched before. So she curled up into her old blankets on the floor in front of the TV and pressed the play button. Sometime between

when the Mina character met the splendidly dressed Prince and when

the overly annoying Lucy died, she started drifting off.

She never got to see the end of the movie, but woke to find the

tape had self-rewound and the really late news was just coming on. The

anchor man was talking about a rash of strange late night animal attacks,

so far all of the victims had survived, but exhibited confusion, gashes

from teeth in random spots on their bodies and weakness due to blood

loss. She just sighed. *What is this world coming to? Don't they have animal*

control officers for that sort of thing?

She couldn't help but wonder where Michael was. She kept

remembering how strong his arms were when he had picked her up.

The scent of him when he had kissed her those two times still drove her

nuts. She hugged her own arms and sighed. *I'll probably never see him again.*

That thought made her cry again. *The first normal man I've met in years and*

he's only interested in his damn book. I probably scared him off by being so forward.

Her clock beeped once and instead of crawling into bed, she just

collapsed back onto the floor into her old blankets to sleep in front of

the TV.

She slept fitfully, dreaming of being chased by some strange creature. In her dream she ran screaming until ready to drop, but when she turned to face the beast and fight for her life, she only saw Michael standing there holding his hand out to her. She woke up screaming several times with his name on her tongue. Finally exhausted and miserable, she took a shower and fixed a cup of instant hot chocolate and sat curled in her nest on the floor watching some early morning advertisement about space bags.

Kayla watched the light in her window brighten with sun light and wondered what day of the week it was. She hadn't cared about days or even months for quite a while. The advertisement went off and the early morning news came on. It was Monday October 27th. It was her birthday. *Wow, I've lost a lot of time. I barely remember my birthday from last year.* There was a knock on her door. She set her mug of chocolate down on the coffee table and answered it. She was shocked to find a police officer standing outside her room.

"Can I help you, officer?" She asked him. The officer's name tag said Garrett and he looked like he was an old hat on the force. He had probably seen everything you could imagine and things you didn't want to imagine. He had salt and pepper hair with deep brown eyes that made him look somewhat sinister.

"Well there was a murder next door Miss . . . "He began.

"Kayla Sutherland"

"Miss Sutherland, your neighbor Mrs. Bernard in 2 C. I just wanted to see if you heard anything." He had a note book out and wrote down her name.

"You mean the lady who always has lipstick on her teeth? What in the world happened to her?" Kayla's heart thumped unhappily in her chest.

"Yeah she did have lipstick on her teeth when her sister found her earlier this morning. I can't go into too many details, but someone slit her throat in her shower. We assume they washed most of the evidence down the drain. So you didn't hear anything unusual?" He flipped through his notepad and started to jot down more notes as he spoke.

"I didn't hear anything unusual at all last night. I have a hard time sleeping sometimes without noise. I had the TV up a bit and slept with it running all night. Does she have any family that needs to be told? Can I do anything to help?" She twisted the end of her shirt in her hands. "Should anyone else in the building be worried? Will the killer come back?"

"We don't think so Miss, but keep your door locked just in case. We've already seen to contacting the rest of her family. Thank you for your help. If you think of anything don't hesitate to call the station. Oh, and Miss Sutherland, Mrs. Norris in 2 A told me of your profession. You may want to take extra precautions when you go out, and don't let me catch you turning tricks or I will be forced to bring you in." He nodded to her, turned and walked away.

Oh my God! A murder in my building, in the room right next to mine! I think I need to move somewhere safer, but I can't afford anywhere else. What the hell am I supposed to do? I wish Michael were here. What am I talking about, I barely know the man. He could even be the killer. There have been a few times he's looked at me like he was hungry.

She closed and locked her door behind her, and sat down with a thump on the edge of her bed. She didn't know what she was going to do. She knew she needed to set an appointment with the clinic down the way to have herself tested. *It would just be my luck to avoid the murderer and end up dying from some kind of crotch rot.*

It took her a little while to get ready and head to the clinic to set up the appointment. She had to do most things in person, because she just couldn't afford a phone. The lady at the front desk of the clinic said that they had an opening that she was able to squeeze Kayla into, but

she wouldn't have all of the results until the end of the week, It still left

Kayla feeling better about herself to at least have gotten the test done.

She hit the corner store again before making her way home deciding to

get herself a pack of Reese's pieces along with shampoo and things that

she didn't have to steal for a change. She checked her mail box out of

habit on the way by and was surprised to find an envelope addressed to

her inside.

Thinking it was either a letter from her Mother who had finally

tracked her down or a bill collector; she tucked it into her purse and

carried it upstairs with her. She put her things away and then sat in her

plastic chair in front of the coffee table to open the letter. There was no

return address on the front, just hers and on the back there were two

punctures about an inch or so apart in the flap that seals the envelope.

Thinking the marks must have happened in the post; she

opened the letter and began reading the neat hand writing.

Kayla,

I don't have long to write this letter to you. I'm going to be away for a good

bit longer than expected. Things have come up in my home town with my businesses that I absolutely must take care of. I am sorry that we never truly finished your

interview; I found our conversation very pleasing. I promise that you will see me

again, though I am unsure as to when. Enclosed you will find a check for the full

amount of what I normally pay a person for an in depth interview like the one you so

graciously gave me. Please forgive me for my rudeness. If I may be so bold as to make

a suggestion about what to do with the check, I would like to see you get a checking

account and move to a safer neighborhood. I know there is a law office near the

outskirts of town that is looking for someone just to file things for them. It will pay

decently well and I have already put in a good word for you, as I often do business

with that law firm when I am here in town. Thank you again for your hospitality

and your honesty.

Forever in your debt,

Michael.

Kayla let the note fall from her nerveless fingers as her heart

took a hit. What was she going to do if she never got to see him again?

He promised to see her again, but things did not always work out as

planned. What if he was lying to her to make her go away? She was only

stunned momentarily then her survival instinct took over. *Screw it; I go*

on, like I always do. Let's see this check. She reached into the envelope and pulled out two folded pieces of paper; one was the address for the law

office and the other was the check. She nearly fainted when she saw it;

he had written her a check for $5000 dollars. That was more money

than had been in her college fund when she had run away from home.

Inside the envelope was an extra $300 dollars. She was absolutely

dumbfounded that he would take the time to help her find a better job

on top of sending her so much money.

She took that and the remaining money out from under her

mattress and ran, literally, down to the corner store and bought several

large gym bags. When she got back to her room she began stuffing

things into them. She left the furniture and only took her clothing and

her few personal items. Once everything was packed she hailed a cab

and left everything she couldn't carry behind. There would be no need

for it if she were to get a good paying job at a reputable law firm.

She looked at the address for the law office, seeing as it was still

early in the day she should be able to make it to there, after renting a

hotel room well away from her current neighborhood and putting the

money into a new account. Thankfully she had purchased that nice

green dress just in case; she stopped at a gas station to change into it

and braided her hair so that it looked much more presentable. She got to the office just in time before they stopped seeing clients for the day.

She was sure that the lawyers probably stayed a while after to finish up,

but she didn't want to be a bother and was glad to make it on time.

The man she spoke with was a Mr. Kenneth Martin. He was

very polite and happy to meet her. He told her that he had spoken with

his acquaintance, sometimes client, Mr. Gage about her, and was ready

to hire her on the spot. He told her that the receptionist had been doing

both jobs, but that with the influx of new clients it was getting to be too

much for one person to handle. He was sure that the receptionist would

happily show her the job and he was glad to have her joining the team.

She filled out all of the paperwork right then, took the $200 sign on

bonus graciously and with a little surprise and left. She would start work

the very next day at eight am.

That sign on bonus was going to go straight to the big Wal-Mart

store with her so that she could buy more business like clothing. It

wasn't until she was back in the hotel room, her bags of belongings, new

and old, around her that she sat in silence and bemused wonderment at

all that had happened in less than twenty four hours. *I have a job! A real*

job! I have a checking account, and money in the bank, and new clothes! There must

really be a patron saint for street walkers. Not that I follow organized religion.

Michael left for home as soon as he could, ignoring the driving need to see her one more time. He took the scenic route back to his home, and he sought out Jenna as soon as he arrived. She was in the room reserved for her when she was visiting.

"I did warn you that someone was waiting for you there." Jenna, who sat across from him, was not very tall, but exuded such a presence that it more than made up for her small delicate stature. Her hair was long, past her waist, and curled in luxurious red waves. Her brown eyes always held a sparkle of mischief. She had a scattering of freckles across her nose and shoulders that told of Scottish heritage. He didn't know her full name, but a vampire's past and history was their own to keep. It didn't matter to him anyway; she was family like no other person had ever been.

"You did. She could be my partner as much as Roland is yours. I have never met anyone like her. Hopefully she doesn't slip back into drugs while I am gone. I did leave her with a large amount of money." Michael paced in front of the fire place in his home. The expensive furnishings, the marble of the fireplace, the exotic hardwood floors, they all seemed a bit cloying after spending so much time with Kayla in the slums.

"She will be fine, Michael. You worry so, my blood son. From what you have said, I do not believe she would have fallen to drugs of her own free will. She seems to have strength and spirit as you say." Jenna sipped her wine and wrapped her shawl around her shoulders tighter. She always seemed to be cold these days and only when she fed was she truly warm for any length of time. It was what a vampire had to deal with when the length of time they had been alive reached triple digits.

"Hearing you say that certainly eases my mind some. I was on my way back anyway, but you called me back, what have you been hearing?" He sat down finally coming to the point and trying without much success to put Kayla out of his mind for the moment. Mental flashes of her face, her eyes and other things kept intruding on his thoughts.

"You are distracted my son. Is she that much on your mind?" Jenna smiled at him in the glowing candle and fire light. She loved the smell of warm candles and seemed to crave the warmth of the fire, so when she was here it was kept burning no matter what the time of year was.

"She is the most astonishing distraction. I want so bad to rush back and bring her here. She is not what I came to discuss though. Please, I will try to focus, tell me what is going on."

Jenna sighed and seemed reluctant to speak at first. "You know that I try and keep as much peace between the factions in your house as possible, but there is only so much I can do with *certain* individuals." She tapped her red painted fingernail against the side of her wine glass and stared at the fire.

"Her again?" Michael asked without naming any names. "I should not have allowed things to turn out this way. She played my emotions and my loneliness against me. She was a mistake and one of my few regrets. I can't believe that I could end up being stuck with that woman when I only ignored one of your warnings that one time. What is she up to this time?" He stood and began pacing again. His mind latched on to one terrifying thought, that maybe she had found Kayla.

"She has been spreading lies and now I found out through a trusted source that she is speaking with Nicholai, visiting with him even. You know what will happen if he gets his claws into her. She is bad enough without his influence; with it she will be a danger we can't afford now. What would happen if either of them found out about your new friend?" There was a small frown on Jenna's face as she spoke.

Michael knew her well enough to know that she was very worried.

"That must never happen. Don't even think about it. I'll do some work trying to smooth out the lies and troubles that she has started, but I will not be here for more than two or three months. I need to cultivate things and this little problem with Eliza will probably have set me back to the beginning. Hopefully Kayla will still be interested when I return." He sighed as he flopped back down into the chair. He felt so unsettled these days, the only time he was calm, sort of, was when he was in her presence.

"Do not worry dear; your charms will keep her interested. She probably dreams about you still, and your sad eyes must surely haunt her. Lesser women have been charmed out of their shoes *and* clothing by you." Jenna chuckled as she rose to leave. "If I had not had Roland I would have been one of them; as it was I could not watch you wither away, so you became my blood son instead. Take care and use caution. I will have to leave for at least a week or so." He stood and hugged her as she turned to leave.

"Jenna, thank you. You are, as always a comforting presence that keeps me on the right path. I love you; you are more of a Mother to me than my own was."

With a startled feeling, Kayla looked back on the five months since she had gotten out of the slums and could barely recognize her life. She hadn't had a drink or drugs since that night so long ago when she had been so very sick. The thing she remembered the most from that time was Michael. Unfortunately he was no longer part of her life. He had promised she would see him again, but as the days rolled into weeks and then right on into months, she started giving up hope. She would never forget all the help he had given her and somehow she credited him with her being able to finally kick the drugs. Maybe he had just given her the extra strength and hope she had needed. Maybe he had given her the perfect distraction, to keep her from thinking about the drugs.

She was happy with her apartment and her discount store furniture. She had built a wardrobe of clothing that was much more to her actual taste, donating all of her hooker gear to goodwill. Somewhere in the back of her mind she still thought about Michael and where he may be and if he still thought about her, but she knew she was better off, with or without him present. His generous check had made it possible for her to finally get out of the slums and into something respectable. She no longer had to sell her body for scraps and she had even made a friend at the law firm. The receptionist was named Nikki and she and Kayla went to a nice bar and grill every Friday night for Karaoke. Nikki was pretty good, and professed amazement at Kayla's talent.

It was after work on a Wednesday, so she sat on her new comfy sofa and munched popcorn while a TV show about vampire myths spoke of the fact that it could very well have been an actual case of a vampire being slain that started all the myths, and that it may be a virus or some mutation. They had several scientists on the show, one of which was a very pretty dark skinned woman that was involved in researching any samples that they thought would prove the existence. Kayla rolled her eyes and turned the channel, Buffy was on, but she was only halfheartedly interested. Wednesday nights were the worst, it was still a good ways until Friday night and there was never anything good on the TV. Nikki had gone out with an ex-boyfriend just to get "some" and there was no one else she knew that she wanted to see or talk to.

Out of nowhere, she couldn't shake the feeling that she was being watched. She hadn't felt like this since she had moved out of the bad neighborhood. She got up and hit the mute button on the remote listening with her body held tense and her breathing kept very shallow. Nothing sounded out of the ordinary, but she still felt eyes on her.

A quick glance around the room showed that all the curtains that she had put up were closed tight and there was no way anyone could see through the heavy fabrics she had chosen. She switched off the lights in the room and stood in the dark and quiet, feeling very frightened. She got the panicked impression that she may have left one of the doors unlocked or a window open, and then she was off like a terrified deer checking that everything was locked tight. Once that was done she sat in the middle of her living room and shook with reaction to this unknown menace.

"I am being so way past silly." She said to herself as the feeling eased, getting up to turn some lights back on and check the time. "Good lord it's nearly midnight. I have to work in the morning." She rushed about getting things ready for in the morning and then climbed into bed feeling more tired than she was normally.

Outside her apartment just on the other side of the curtains on her bedroom windows, Michael stood. He had chased off a young uneducated vampire that had been watching Kayla with interest. With

Michael's age and strength the young one would not come back to this place to hunt, ever.

He knew that Kayla was undressed and lying in her bed, just falling asleep and he could not resist the chance to sneak in and hold her in his arms again. The window locks were simple things that his mind easily moved and once he was inside, he closed the window behind him and locked it. When he left, he would make sure that everything was locked up tight as it was now.

He looked down at her sleeping form and smiled at how much healthier she looked now that all of the drugs and alcohol were out of her system. Her true scent wafted off of her as she breathed and shifted in the blankets. It made the cravings in him reach an almost fever pitch and he actually held his breath long enough to make his body behave itself.

She was his angel of mercy to save him from the lonely years ahead, and he wanted everything to be perfect. He took off his shoes and his coat and slipped down on top of the covers next to her folding his arms around her and sending her into a deeper sleep. She turned towards him and nuzzled into his chest breathing deeply in her slumber. He nearly wept with how happy he was to be next to her again, and he did weep when she mumbled "I love you, Michael." in her sleep. His

sleeve was damp with tears that he wiped away so that he would not

leave traces in the bed.

Her warm breath against his cool chest through his shirt sent

pleasure racing through him. His heart was squeezed almost painfully

with affection. *My gods, I have never felt like this for anyone. What is it between*

us? There's a magnetic pull that draws me to her so forcefully? He tried to

muddle through the emotions he felt for this young woman, but in the

end he decided to enjoy what he had for now. He just hoped that it

would last. Before morning he left and went to a hotel nearby. He

would leave his little message for her the next day. He had a friend that

was not affected by the sun that could leave it at her door once she had

left for work.

Chapter 5

It was Thursday and almost quitting time. Kayla was in her normal place in the file room making sure that everything was in order and that each of the four lawyers at this firm had the files they needed. No matter how distracted she got or how she tried to occupy her mind she always ended up thinking about Michael. She thought she could still remember the way he had smelt and how strong his arms were. His face swam in her dreams each night as she slept. There were some nights that she woke screaming his name and could almost feel him in the room around her.

The last of the filing was finished and she went to let her boss know that it was time for her to clock out. Nikki gave her a ride home from work since they both lived in the same apartment complex. She was silent the whole way home, professing a headache, so Nikki just dropped her at her door and went down the block to her own apartment. She turned the key in the lock and when the door came open an envelope fell out of the crack. She turned it over in her hands a few times, but there was not even a name on the front of it.

Once inside, she dropped her purse and keys in the tray by the door and kicked her shoes off by the sofa. She was still shocked to come home each night to an apartment this nice, with furniture that while purchased from a discount store, was nicer than anything she had ever owned before. She tore the envelope open and pulled out a single folded piece of paper onto which was scrawled her name in a handwriting that she recognized at once. She almost dropped it as her hands shook while she unfolded it to read. She threw the envelope down and tore a corner of the letter off trying to unfold it too quickly.

Kayla,

I hope this letter reaches you and finds you doing well. I am still tied up with problems here in my home town or I would have been to see you sooner. I can't seem to get your smile out of my head. The less I tell you about what is going on here, the better. Not all of my . . . let me just say that not everyone I know is nice. I'm not even sure how to talk to you. I assume you are probably very angry with me for taking off the way I did. I have to end this letter, but be sure that you will see me again, hopefully soon.

Spellbound by thoughts of you,

Michael

"Spellbound." Kayla whispered after she finished reading the

letter. There were tears in her eyes as she threw it on her coffee table

and went to the bathroom for a shower. *How can he play with me like this?*

I thought he left because I was a hooker. She scrubbed her makeup off of her

face and took a brush violently to her hair. Normally when she took a

shower she made sure to clean up her things, but this time she was so

disturbed that she just left her clothes strewn across the bathroom floor

and counter. A hot shower did a lot to calm her nerves and make her

feel somewhat better, and by the time the delivery guy brought the pizza

to her door she was almost back to normal, almost. Too bad that almost

wasn't good enough and now she was even more focused on Michael.

She worried that she would never be able to sleep tonight.

She crammed a movie into her new DVD player and sat back

with her extra cheese, ham and pineapple pizza. She thought about

calling Nikki to come over, but she just felt like it would be better to be

alone. When the movie was over, she shut off everything and crammed

the rest of the pizza into her fridge. It didn't take her long to strip to her

standard sleeping attire, tank top and undies, and then climb into bed.

She turned over four times, beating her pillow into a more

comfortable shape, but sleep seemed to elude her for a while. She could not help but wonder how he had found her address, or why he had

decided to contact her now.

Michael waited outside her apartment until the sounds of her

breathing slowed, then slipped inside the window of her bedroom again.

He knew it was wrong to make her feel so confused, but he was trying

to set things up in a way to cause her the least pain. It did not seem to

be going as he had hoped. He wondered how she would feel to know

that he was turning into what he would call a stalker, where she was

concerned. It was borderline creepy the way he kept sneaking into her

home at night.

As with all the other forays into her home while she slept, since

he had left her, the sight of her half naked and sprawled across the bed

tightened his chest and his groin. He could only stare in stunned silence

for a moment. Then he sighed with a smile and slipped into bed next to

her to hold her warmth against his cool flesh. *Out of all the women in the

world I finally have found my true match. Who would have thought that she would

be such a diamond in the rough?* He took a deep breath, reveling in her

wonderful scent. He wrapped his arms around her, cradling her head

against his chest and feeling her heartbeat through her skin. How he longed more than anything to make love to her and make her want him as much as he wanted her. He couldn't even tell how she felt about him; her mind was a confused tangle to him even with his ability to read most people like a book. If she hadn't said she loved him in her dreams he would be clueless. She stirred a little in her sleep her hands twisting in his shirt pulling him closer. He dared a quick kiss to her forehead and she stopped fidgeting. He stayed with her wrapped in his arms until early in the morning before dawn and then took off to his hotel. He would return to her the next evening to watch her dream again if he could.

Kayla rubbed her sleepy eyes and sat up in bed, sure for one moment that there was someone in the room with her. "Michael?" she whispered and then shook her head at her own silliness. There was no way he could have broken into her apartment and then gotten out again without her knowing. That still didn't stop her from thinking she could smell him on her sheets and from feeling like he had been holding her last night. *It must have just been a very vivid dream. He's gone for good and that is that, no matter what that letter says.* Kayla dressed with half of her mind still thinking of Michael and his letter. She couldn't shake the feeling that he was nearby.

Work was tedious and the only thing that kept her going was that it was Friday and she would be going out with Nikki. She was sure that going to the bar and getting a chance to unwind would certainly lift her falling spirits and distract her for a while. As if thinking about her had summoned her, Nikki came into Kayla's file room her blonde curls bouncing.

"It's Friday! Almost time to head out. Are we still going to O'Manny's?" Nikki had one of those happy faces that you just couldn't think of as anything but adorable. She was girl next door gorgeous in Kayla's mind. A runner in high school, she had kept up with it, even dragging Kayla along with her some days. There was good muscle under her cute retro 50's office wear.

"If it's Friday then yes, of course we are. I just have this last stack of folders to put away and I need to drop the Hiott file on Mr. Kenneth's desk before I leave. Are we stopping by your place to change or just wearing what we have on?" Kayla slid more folders away as she spoke and then tucked a stray hair from her braid behind her ear.

"You look hot as always and I'm not looking too shabby if I do say so myself. We go as is and make sure those boys know we are strong independent women." Nikki popped Kayla lightly on her bottom as she

turned to leave.

"You know if you were a man that would be harassment." Kayla

chuckled.

"Really now, it's not like we don't get into more trouble than

that when you spend the night at my place." Nikki winked, her lovely

blue eyes sparkling with mischief.

"True. I'll meet you at your car. Thanks for the ride again. I

never did learn how to drive and I'm not sure I really want to with the

way most people drive these days." Kayla shrugged and continued to

put away files.

"No problem. I mean, you live in the same apartment complex I

do. It's not like I'm wasting gas driving out of my way. Hell, we even

work the same schedule. See you when you get out." Nikki waved as she

darted from the file room. Kayla had never had a friend like Nikki. Yes

they sometimes shared a bed and physical affections, but Nikki loved

her like no one else ever had. They were best friends and Kayla knew

that Nikki would always have her back.

With the last file slipped into its home next to the rest of the

new batch, Kayla pulled the Hiott file and signed it out. She made sure to note that it was being left on Mr. Kenneth's desk so that if anyone came looking for it she would not be held accountable.

Mr. Kenneth was still at his desk for once as she came in with the file. He turned his chair to face her as she came in, the heels of her tasteful gray pumps clicking on the flooring. She took a moment to realize just how attractive he was. He was young for a lawyer, barely 35. He had brownish hair with lighter highlights and golden hazel eyes. He looked like he had a good sense of humor and he certainly smiled often. She could see his surfing pictures along one wall of his office which was why he always seemed to be just a little tan. If Kayla wasn't mistaken, he was also just a little bit infatuated with her.

"Ah, the Hiott file. Thank you very much Kayla. You are doing a great job. I'm very glad that Mr. Gage recommended you for this job. Just leave that on my desk. I'll get started on it in the morning. Would you like to join me for dinner tonight? " He blurted it out as if he really hadn't meant to say it even though by the look in his eyes he really wanted her to say yes.

"I'm sorry sir, but I made a promise to go with Nikki tonight. I also don't think it's a good idea for us to go out, it may cause some jealousy." She smiled at him apologetically. If she hadn't been twisted in knots over Michael, she just might have taken him up on his offer.

"I could always have you fired and then ask you out." He chuckled, clearly attempting to make a joke.

"That would certainly not induce me to go out with you. I'm sorry sir; I just don't feel comfortable with us dating." Kayla planted her feet carefully and crossed her arms, but she knew she had won. The words *I don't feel comfortable* were a code phrase for impending sexual harassment suits nationwide.

"Well, you can't blame a man for trying. Good work on the file room though. It hasn't been that clean since before we started putting files in it." He turned his chair around and went back to work on his computer. She left as quickly as she could and sighed when the office door shut behind her.

"What took you so long, woman?" Nikki asked as Kayla slipped into the seat of her sporty red car. She buckled up and started the engine as Kayla put on her own seat belt.

"I was just turning down a date invitation from Mr. Kenneth." Kayla sighed and rolled her eyes. "Do I have *'ask me out'* stamped on my forehead?"

"Nope, it's on your ass in those cute little pencil skirts you wear." Nikki grinned as she backed out of the parking space and left the

parking lot. "I hope O'Manny's is rocking. I've been waiting on Friday

for too long. How about you?"

"You wouldn't believe how much I'm needing this. Promise

you'll watch my soda while I sing and if I have to potty?" Kayla asked,

even though she knew that Nikki would say yes.

"I always do. I know how you are about not wanting anyone

spiking your drink with anything. I may be way off, but it sounds like

you may have had troubles in the past with drink and maybe even drugs.

Not that I mind. I did it too for a while." Nikki threaded her way

through traffic like a professional driver. She was caution personified on

the roadways, but she could certainly handle the car well.

"I did, and I made a promise to myself that I would never go

back to drugs, no matter what. I don't want to drag down the mood. I

want to have a really good weekend, how about you?" Kayla cranked

the radio to their favorite rock station. They always played the best

music on this station.

"Hell yeah!" Nikki made it to the bar and grill by seven, which

considering the traffic between work and there was making good time.

"God I remember New Year's here with you. We had a blast. I got so many phone numbers I spent a week cleaning out my cell phone." Nikki

said as she pulled into the parking lot.

They found a parking place quickly and went inside looking

around. The night time party people had not yet arrived and the lunch

crowd was long gone. They got a booth away from the door, but close

to the restroom and the Karaoke stage. They got paid on Fridays so

they normally got dinner while the house speakers played, softer than

the Karaoke machine would later on, but louder than most other

restaurants.

Kayla always tried to sit facing the doorway, an old habit from

her time in the slums. She could tell by the quality of light, or lack

thereof, coming through the front windows that it was after sundown.

She was just about to start talking again when a familiar figure walked

into the bar and took a seat near the door. Nikki must have noticed the

look of utter shock on her face.

"What? What's wrong? You look like you just saw a ghost?"

Nikki grabbed her hand a look of concern on her face.

"I . . . I think I did. That guy in the booth by the door is the

man that helped me get the job at the office, Michael Gage. I haven't

seen him in months. I thought he was gone for good. Oh God scoot over, don't let him see me!" Nikki scooted a few inches to the left so that Kayla was hidden behind her. She put her head in her hands for a moment and then straightened up to peek around Nikki's shoulder.

"Why don't you want him to see you? I thought you said he was gorgeous and fascinating?" Nikki pulled out her compact so she could look at him in the reflection. "Wow! He most certainly is gorgeous! Go talk to him!"

"No! Are you crazy? I still have no idea why he just up and took off. He said it was business, but maybe it was me." Kayla scrunched down farther in the leather booth seat. She hoped he wouldn't see her, but then there was that part of her that wanted nothing more than for him to come over here, grab her and kiss her till her legs stopped working.

"P-shaw, any man that turns you down is probably just figuring out that he is gay. All the Adonis God like ones are gay. Go say hi, maybe you can talk about stylish shoes together." Nikki giggled. She had no clue how many mixed feelings just seeing Michael was bringing up for Kayla and there was no time to explain everything now.

"You are hopeless, you know that? I can't just go talk to him. I mean, what would I say? Where is he? Is he still sitting there?" Kayla peeked around Nikki's shoulder again only to see that the booth was empty. She quickly ducked back down again and felt like her heart was going to split her chest open with its frantic pounding.

"I can't see him in the mirror anymore. I think he got up." She swiveled the mirror around trying to pinpoint Michael in its reflection. Kayla was torn between staying where she was and running to hide in the ladies room.

"I have no clue if I should stay put or have you take me home. I can't talk to him, I just can't!" Kayla dumped her head into her hands as Nikki tried to find him without turning around to look.

"Why can't you talk to me? You did just fine the last time we spoke." Michael chuckled warmly as he slid into the booth seat next to Kayla. Just the touch of him against her arm sent shivers all through her and she felt like she was going to faint.

"I, um . . . well . . . hi, there." Nikki was stunned by his charm and his undeniable good looks. It's like she lost too much blood flow to her brain around attractive men.

"Hello, I'm Michael. I'm sure that Kayla has told you about me." He smiled at Nikki and she blushed as red as Kayla had ever seen her before. She suddenly lost all ability to speak.

"Michael, this is Nikki, a friend from work, Nikki this is Michael of course." Kayla sighed and turned more in her seat to face Michael. Now that the initial shock was over, she was starting to get that annoyed look on her face that Nikki recognized as the "We need to talk right now!" face.

"I think I'm going to go talk to that lonely man at the bar." Nikki said sensing the strange mood that had descended on the table. "Maybe he'll buy me a drink." She stood up and Michael took her seat so that he could look at Kayla. He smiled and felt his heart squeeze when she gave him a small smile in return.

"You look like you are doing well for yourself. I confess. I was worried that you might have slipped back into drugs and alcohol after I had to leave so abruptly." He folded his hands in front of him, elbows on the table. He looked like he was in the middle of some big board meeting instead of talking to her. It was kind of disarming.

"I never really wanted the oblivion that came with drugs. The first couple of times that I got them in my system; they were forced on me by a . . . client to get me hooked. If it wasn't for your gracious gifts then I probably would be hooked still. I never got to thank you, so thank you very much. What are you doing back? I was sure that you were leaving because I was being forward." Kayla blushed and hoped

the dim lighting covered it. She felt all the confusion of those times

when he had seemed interested and had not gone forward with it

building back up. She watched his face and tried to tell if he was

speaking the truth.

"I left for exactly the reason I stated. There was business that I

had to attend to. I'm very glad to see you doing so much better. You

even look healthier." He reached out to brush his fingers down the side

of her face and again she shivered at his touch. She felt all shattered

apart inside, lost in a rush of emotion that showed no signs of ebbing.

"I'm used to being blunt, so I will get straight to the point. I was

very attracted to you and I hope that I was not misreading your

attraction. Why did you not go forward with it?" Now she was feeling

angry. She felt that he had toyed with her and then given her a pity gift

to keep her quiet.

"I was . . . I guess the best word would be scared. There are

things about me that make it dangerous to get close to me. I know

people that do bad things. I did not want to put anyone in danger,

certainly not you. I am attracted, which is part of why I wanted to help

you out of a very bad situation." He sighed and waited for her to speak.

She sat there for a minute trying to calm the flutters of her heart. He had said "I am" attracted, not was, am. That meant that he was still interested in her.

Michael's head suddenly snapped up and his nostrils flared. "Shit, not here, not now." He spun in his seat and turned to look at the door. "Listen to me very carefully. I want you to slap me in the face, get up, grab your friend, and get the hell out of here. Here's a few hundred, grab a hotel. I'll find you. Just act like your pissed at me and never want to see me. Do it now!" He shoved the money across the table at her and she took it staring at him in bewilderment. "Remember those bad people, one is here. Hit me, *now!*" He hissed angrily and his eyes widened.

Kayla shocked that he looked so very angry and sinister did as she was told. She slapped him across the face with her hand as hard as she could and he didn't even flinch, he just took it. She stood and went right over to Nikki, tears welling up in her eyes from the pain that was now throbbing in her hand.

"Kayla, are you okay? What did he say to you?" Nikki asked seeing the angry fear on her friends face. "Don't tell me I'm going to have to start a fight with that man?"

"We're leaving please, please can we just go?" Kayla dragged

Nikki out of her chair. "Let's go." Nikki nodded as Kayla paid the

bartender behind the bar and then they got outside into the car. "I don't

even want to go home now. Let's go to your place."

"Okay. Now, what the hell did he say to you?" Nikki pulled the

car out of the lot and headed back towards her apartment.

"I can't talk about it. I won't, it hurts too much." Kayla cried

and Nikki held her hand carefully. She went silent as Nikki drove, but

then added. "Maybe we could stop by the ER. I think I broke my hand

on his face."

"I see you have been rejected my Prince." The sickly sweet voice

raised the hackles on the back of Michael's neck. He didn't even look up

from his hands when she stepped up to the table. He was trying

desperately to not choke her until her head popped off.

"Hello again, Eliza." He sighed deeply as the young woman slid

into the booth across from him. She would have been pretty if it had

not been for the slightly sour look that she wore. She had sleek blonde

hair cut into a stylish bob and piercing lavender blue eyes. Her figure

was perfect if you were in to the tiny waif like type.

"What? Not happy to see me? Don't seem so depressed, you

used to enjoy my company." She pouted, but there was nothing

adorable about it. Something about Eliza always seemed to come across

as sinister. "Why must you insist on following me? I've told you that

there is nothing between me and you now." Michael sat where he was.

He was

not going to leave until he knew for a fact that Eliza would leave him

alone. The last thing he wanted to do was lead her to Kayla.

"You do not belong with these Bleeders. They are below us. We

should rule from the top, not slink around the bottom, hiding what we

are and what we can do." Eliza flashed a feral grin with fangs behind it.

It made her seem even more of an alien creature to him. How could he

have possibly thought that this woman would have been his mate?

"Are you crazy? We cannot let the general populace know of us.

And don't call them Bleeders; that name only applies to those loons that

Nicholai lets hang around." Michael lowered his voice, anger touching

it, just to send her a warning. His power far exceeded her own and that

meant he could control her to some degree just by tone of voice, also

she had pledged loyalty to him.

"I'm sorry Michael. I should have held my tongue. It is an

appropriate name though. They bleed for us . . . well. Anyway, when are

you coming home?" Eliza shifted in her seat; Michael was projecting his

irritation at her and causing her quite a bit of discomfort.

"You never did learn when to curb your speech. Do you still

consider me your leader or have you gone over to Nicholai?" The

sudden

look of shock on Eliza's face told him all he needed to know. "Ah, so

you have spoken to him, but you remain, at least for now, loyal to me. I

guess I should be glad you are so obsessed with me."

"Michael, you must know that his words have merit. Just listen

to him." Eliza pleaded to him before a sharp look silenced her

completely.

"I will never find merit in his ideals. He thinks that a world run

by vampires is the only way. He has seen that there are humans that will

live with us peacefully. Every time he visits my holdings he partakes of

those humans willing to give us what we need in return for protection,

affection and for some, eventually turning them. There is no need to

rule with an iron fist. Now, I am done talking to you. I need to find a

"meal" and *you will return home*." As the Vampire leader to the area that

Eliza claimed as home turf, Michael was able to give her commands and have them followed regardless of what she truly wanted to do. When he

put power behind his words they hit her mind like a brick to the side of

the head. His next words did just that. "You will never follow me

again!" Michael stood and left Eliza sitting in the booth recovering with

her eyes closed and her hands pressed against her head.

Michael wanted to scream in frustration as he walked calmly

down the street away from the bar. He had been about to start his plans

to draw Kayla closer to him, and Eliza had probably ruined it with her

abrupt appearance. There was something about Kayla that called to him

like a lighthouse in a storm. There was an amazing strength in that

woman; there was also a raging fire of passion just beneath the surface

waiting to break through. He feared that everything would fall apart

now that Eliza had caused this delay.

He sniffed the air and could still smell her on him even though

they had barely touched. He thought he could still feel the warmth her

hand had left on his face when she had slapped him. He craved her

smile almost as much as he craved her blood. He wanted the taste of it

on his tongue as they made love. Nothing was going to stop him from

pursuing a relationship with her, not even a demented ex-girlfriend.

He had to stop his thoughts and turn them to Eliza's impending betrayal. *I knew when we broke things off that Nicholai would use her anger against me. For now she will stay in the coven. Maybe I should allow her back in my bed on a temporary basis.* As he thought that, it turned his stomach. *No, the only person I want next to me is Kayla. I probably ruined things for good this time though. She'll never trust me again. I can't go to her until I know that Eliza has left and will not return.*

Michael crossed the street and went looking for prey for tonight at least. Maybe he would go back to hunting criminals for a while. It had been fun to read the rumors of animal attacks the last time he had done that. He knew for a fact that most of those he had fed from had changed their lives and were now trying to go straight.

He turned his strides in that direction and headed towards Kayla's old stomping ground. He found a victim almost at once; there was a prostitute standing on the corner smelling of alcohol and drugs. In a doorway not far away her child, a little boy about five years old, cried, hugging his tattered teddy bear.

Michael walked up to her. "I require . . . services. What is the fee?" He whispered into her ear. She shivered as he put a touch of compulsion into the question.

"Fifty for an hour, forty for a blow. All night is two hundred and you pay for the hotel room if you want one." She smiled showing

that she had a terrible case of meth mouth, but he was not interested in

what lay behind her lips, only what lay insider her veins.

"Forty and a dark alley will be just fine." He handed her the bills

and walked her to the nearest alley way. She wouldn't have refused, even

if he hadn't been using his powers.

She started unbuttoning his pants while looking up at him and

he caught her eyes with that special fascination power all vampires have.

She stopped, her eyes glazing over and her arms going limp at her sides.

She looked like she was catatonic and in a way she was. She would stay

like this until he gave her a command. He pulled her to her feet gently

and then whispered his first command to her.

"You will give me your neck please." The woman swept her

bedraggled over bleached hair away from her neck and tilted her head to

the side so that he had ample room to bite. "Thank you. You will never

hook again. You will go get help for your drug problem. You do not

have any children." He sank his teeth into her neck and the first rush of

blood made him moan. It was rank with the drugs and booze, but it was

still living fresh blood. He had always fed from criminals, or from willing donors. He would never force an innocent to give him blood, no

matter how small the amount he needed was.

The woman moaned and when he let go of her after the tiny

mouthful, she sank blissfully to the pavement. She would be fine in a

few hours. Michael never took more than he needed, which was much

less than a person would give if they were donating blood. The

weakness came from his use of mental influence on his victims. He

walked away from her and picked up the now sleeping child. When he

knew he was away from the sight of humans he took off back towards

one of his safe havens nearby.

Chapter 6:

Nikki shook Kayla's shoulder gently. "Hey girl wake up its nearly noon. I let you sleep. You seemed like you needed the rest." Kayla startled up out of sleep almost at once. Nikki was a morning person and looked like she had been up since sunrise.

"Really, it's noon already? Good gravy I haven't slept like that in a very long time. I need to get home and shower. Thanks for letting me crash here. I didn't feel safe being alone after last night." Kayla stood, went to the bathroom to change out of Nikki's borrowed sleep shirt and back into her own clothing. She had crashed in Nikki's bed with her, and they had shared more than clothing in the past.

When she came back out, Nikki was standing there with a biscuit waiting for her. "You two seem to have a bit of a . . . past. I'll leave it at that; I hate getting into the middle of those kinds of things. Anyway, you know you can crash here anytime." She handed Kayla the biscuit and gave her a peck on the cheek. "Eat before you go."

"Thanks." Kayla mumbled as she stuffed a bite into her mouth. Nikki made awesome biscuits. After she had finished the food, she left, waving to Nikki as she closed the door behind her to walk down to her apartment. The sky was bright and the cool spring air cleared her head, even if it did nothing to cool the fire in her heart. It had been a shock to see Michael again, and then with him acting so strangely she had absolutely no clue what to think. She could feel all the old emotions creeping back up on her. She just wanted to hide in her bed and hug her pillows for a while to cry things out.

Her apartment door was the only one on her row that was painted red instead of white. The owner of the complex told her she was able to redecorate "Tastefully" and had not minded the red door. She saw the white note posted to the door almost instantly.

When she tore it down she noticed that it was in Michael's handwriting. Her hands shook as she unfolded the letter and began to read. The more she read the more her hands shook and then tears welled up in her eyes. She didn't even open her door before reading the letter all the way through.

Kayla,

It seems that I am always leaving you behind with notes of explanation. I am truly impressed with how well you have done for yourself. You would never believe how happy I am to see you overcome the troubles you had started with. There is so much I have to tell you and yet I am sure that now is not the time. Thank you very much for going along with the little ruse last night. I noticed someone coming in that would very much liked to have hurt me through those that I care deeply about. Yes, I care about you more than I think I realized. I would like you to meet me again sometime at the address listed. Please only come if you wish to. This is not a command, it is a request. Some of the things I must tell you, I will tell you soon. Other things must wait until I am sure that you are safe and that you trust me.

Thinking only of you, Kayla, my sweet,

Michael

"This is not a command . . ." What odd wording for him to have used. Kayla wondered what that was all about. At the bottom of the letter there was an address that was a few miles out of town. She was thinking about how he had said he cared about her when the phone rang.

"Hello?" She answered it on the second ring, her voice sounding only slightly rough from crying.

"Kayla? It's Michael. I wanted to apologize more for what happened last night." His voice sounded unsure; something that she was not used to hearing. "You are probably very angry with me."

"I am angry, but more than anything, I'm confused. We need to talk, can you come over? I'd give you the address, but you already seem to know where I am." She wanted to yell and scream and rant about how he had been treating her, but just hearing his voice made her heart flutter.

"Not right now, but I can this evening, if that is okay. I can bring Taco bell and a movie." He chuckled nervously. She couldn't think about the anger when his voice was busy making her feel all warm inside.

"I guess so. Did you mean what you said about caring about me?" She asked in a rush, not wanting to invite him over if he had only said that to keep her interested.

"I cannot imagine my life without you in it. I can't get you out of my head; you are all I think and dream about. It's been that way since I first met you. Kayla, you are very important to me. Will you be okay with me coming over tonight? I don't want to cause you any more stress." He sighed into the phone and she thought she could hear a catch in his voice as if he was about to cry.

"I . . . yes, I want to see you." She knew it was true the moment it left her lips, she couldn't think of anything but having him near her

again.

"I am glad to hear you say that. It will be too long until this

evening and I get to see you again. Good bye for now, Kayla, my

sweet."

"Goodbye Michael." She whispered with tears in her eyes. She

was shaking when she hung up the phone. She looked around the room

at her place and began a cleaning fit. She wanted him to see the

apartment and her at their best. She got out her vacuum, attacking the

carpets and then she scrubbed down the floors, walls and everything in

the kitchen and bathroom. It wasn't that she didn't already keep the

house really clean; she just kept imagining that there were extra spots

that only he would see and disapprove of. She made a quick run, literally

since she didn't drive, to the corner store to get some sodas and things.

When she got back she dashed into the shower just as the sky turned

glorious colors during sunset.

She was dressed and toweling her hair dry when the doorbell

rang, sending her heart thumping up into her throat. She threw the

towel into the hamper and ran barefoot to the door. She kept the house

really cold and dressed warm for comfort. She was wearing a thin gray sweater that left her shoulders and neck bare and a pair of comfortable

jeans. She thought she looked like she should be in a commercial for a

holiday in Aspen.

"Who is it?" She asked as she checked the peep hole and could

only see a red blotch as if something was covering the hole on the other

side. She knew it was him before he spoke, she thought she could

almost feel him through the door.

"It's Michael, may I come in?" She unchained the door and

opened it. The red blotch turned out to be a single red rose that he

handed to her as he cautiously leaned in to kiss her cheek. She knew he

could tell she was trembling, but he was kind enough not to mention it.

"Thank you." She was breathless as she led him into the house.

He walked around the back of her sofa to the living area while she put

the rose in a small vase on the kitchen table. He sat the DVD and the

food down on her coffee table. She walked into the living room and just

stood there not really knowing what to do.

"You do have a DVD player I hope. I'm afraid VHS is hard to

find these days." He smiled as he looked around. "This is a much nicer

place. I see you have made yourself a perfect home here. Oh, I hope

you still like tacos. I remembered that from before." He sat on the couch and winked at her, while her heart flapped around in her chest

like a wounded bird.

"Yeah, they're fine. What movie?" She put it into her newly

purchased DVD player without even looking at it and handed him the

remote. She could feel his eyes on her as she was doing that, so she

squatted down instead of bending over. If this had been any other man,

then maybe she would have teased him some, but this was a man she

wanted to stay with, not just some fling.

"I brought 'Vampire in Brooklyn'." There was something almost

ironic in his chuckle. "I have a thing for vampire movies. Sit, eat, we can

talk once we have finished eating." He picked up a taco of his own and

she thought he took a bite. She watched the movie while they ate. It was

something she had never seen before and she tried to concentrate on it

but found it difficult to do since her heart was still pounding. After a

while she caught him watching her, his taco forgotten in his hand. She

turned bright red and put the rest of her food down. She took a few

sips of the drink he had brought and tried to still her heart. She kept

seeing him watch her and there was still a complete taco in his hands; he

still hadn't eaten any.

"Are you even watching the movie?" She asked with a bit of

irritation, turning so that she could look straight at him. She couldn't

help the chill of pleasure that raced through her to see him sitting next

to her again after so long of him being gone.

"I'm afraid that having you this close to me after so long has

made me rather distracted." He sat the taco back down on the coffee

table and turned so that he could look more at her. She blushed so hotly

that she felt her face was a glowing ember.

"Would you . . . rather talk now instead?" She asked rather

proud that there was only a tiny quaver in her voice. It felt too warm in

here, even though she had turned the temperature down just before he

got here.

"We can." He pushed the stop button on the remote, the room

now settling into a golden glow from the only lamp she had on. There

was a smile on his face that would have stopped her heart if it hadn't

been in overdrive already.

"Well, talk. You know everything about me and I know next to

nothing about you." She let a little of her frustration slip into her voice

and saw him grimace in response.

"I have things I can't talk about yet. I know you are angry and confused. I really didn't want things to get this....... muddled." His hand

came out of nowhere and settled against her face, cradling her chin in

his palm. "I swear that you will know soon. My Gods, you are

breathtaking. I can't believe I found someone like you." He sighed

letting his hand slide from her chin and cheek down to her neck.

Kayla sat like stone on the couch, her mind and body at war.

She wanted this more than anything she had ever wanted, yet she was

still angry that he was not telling her everything. When his hand slipped

down to her neck a quiet moan escaped from her that she only thought

he couldn't hear.

He did hear the moan and felt her body twitch as she yearned to

fall into his arms. He smiled and leaned closer to kiss her gently on the

forehead. He felt her arms go around him instinctively and he left his

lips lingering on her warm skin for just a moment. He could feel the

barrier between her mind and her body slowly dissolving. She was

starting to crave his touch almost as much as he craved blood.

"Michael." Her voice whispering his name was like a rush of

intoxicating drugs in his system. He could hear the passion that she felt

rising in her. "Please." She said, unsure herself what she was asking for.

"Kayla, my sweet." He said into her hair as he pulled her into his lap and held her against his chest. He felt her heart thundering behind

her ribs and her hands clinging to him desperately. He was almost in

pain with his needs and had to forcibly remember that this was not just

some tryst, that this was the woman that he wanted to spend eternity

with.

His cool body was impossibly strong and firm against her and

under her legs she could feel his manhood through his pants, telling her

everything she needed to know about how he felt at this moment. She

raised her face to his neck and kissed right next to his ear. Greatly

daring she nipped at his earlobe and heard a moan escape his lips,

seemingly against his will. Her hands found his hair and she tried to pull

his lips to hers, but he held back, his eyes closed. He looked like he was

holding his breath and concentrating very hard. She changed tactics

reaching for the buttons on his shirt, but he brushed her hands away

gently, still without opening his eyes.

"We . . . can't do this . . . not yet. I don't know if it's safe. I . . .

have . . . enemies. I will *not* have you hurt." He was gasping as he spoke

and she could see the almost pained look on his face. She was worried

that she had hurt his feelings by pushing the issue and placed her hand

against his face. He leaned in as if he could pull her into his soul through one little touch. He looked like he just might cry, which

brought tears to her eyes.

"I'm sorry. I didn't mean to get carried away." She never took

her eyes off of his face. If everything fell apart, she wanted to always

remember his face and her feelings for him right now. She knew she

cared about him, wanted his closeness. She couldn't picture going on

without him. The time that he had been away meant almost nothing at

this point, save to remind her of how hard it was to not be near him.

"I should have expected this." He said quietly, "I can't seem to

control myself around you. You are winding me around your little

finger. I know it would be a mistake for us to take things too quickly. I

want to, gods of my fathers. I want to drag you away with me tonight

and never let you go. Then there are the *other* wants." A look of fierce

passion and hunger crossed his face, startling her. "I really should go

before we do things we would both regret." He kissed her tenderly on

the top of her head and just breathed in her scent for a long quiet

moment.

"I'm not angry with you anymore." She said with a nervous

laugh. "Promise me, that I will see you again." Her heart was in her

eyes as she spoke and he was astounded that she loved him already, even though she had only said it in her dreams.

"How about we still meet up next Saturday, at the address on the letter?" He slid her off of his lap with reluctance and stood, walking to the front door.

"That's a week!" She asked as she followed him, twisting the end of her sweater around her fingers. She hated to sound so pleading, she was a grown woman, and a man should not make her feel this tangled.

"Trust me, my sweet; I need that long to get my heart to slow down." He smiled at her and brushed his knuckles against her cheek. "You have an astonishing effect on me." He leaned in and pressed his lips to hers, quickly moving away so that things would not escalate. "I will be waiting for you." He turned and left. He had seen the thought that drifted across her mind with his powers. He would not have made it out of the door if she had begun taking off her clothing in front of him. He had a lot of control, but somethings could break down, even his amazing will power.

He heard her bump into the door and then slide down it to sit on the floor. He sensed her anticipation and frustration as if it was part of his own. He walked away from her door slowly, completely forgetting the DVD, not that it mattered. His heart hadn't been this alive since before he had made the change. He almost felt like whistling,

but he kept his mind firmly on searching for anyone hiding around her

place or watching him.

It was Friday again, and Kayla opted out of the normal trip to

the bar with Nikki, who had a date with Mr. Kenneth, of all people.

There was no way she was going to sit there with them dancing on the

floor and knowing that Mr. Kenneth was watching her. She just could

not put her friend through that. She assumed the only reason that he

had picked Nikki was to cause trouble because she had turned him

down.

Nikki dropped her off at her apartment and then went on to her

own to change for the date. Kayla saw the note posted on the door

immediately and rushed up the two steps to rip it down and open.

Michael's handwriting jumped out at her and she sighed, her heart

skipping a beat.

My sweet,

I wanted to make a change to the location for our date. Here is the new

address; it's a house I have just finished renovating for sale. I feel it is a safe place in which to meet you. I must admit that I do not want to go to a restaurant or the

movies and have to share you with the mindless masses. I want you all to myself, as

selfish as that seems. I have been impatient for tomorrow, like I have been waiting for

eternity to end. I picked up the phone many times intent on calling you, but it seemed

best to keep to the original plan. My dearest, my heart is in your hands. Please come

to see me tomorrow evening. I will introduce you to a very good friend of mine, but

then the evening will be for us alone.

Thinking only of you always,

Michael

Kayla read the new address, it wasn't close enough for her to

walk, and she would have to catch a taxi there. She unlocked her front

door with one hand while clutching the letter to her chest with the

other. Michael's words struck her heart with needles of fire. *I want you all*

to myself. She walked straight to her room. A smile curved her lips as she

lay the letter down on her pillow. She could smell him on the letter, his

scent making her shiver. She lay down, her face next to the letter with

her heart pounding in her throat. She kind of felt like a silly school girl

with how he made her feel, and she tried to pull herself back into the

realm of adult.

Oh Michael, if you only knew how much I care for you. She didn't even

realize when it had happened, but she had fallen for him, hard and

deeply. How could she not already trust him; he had *her* heart in his

hands as if he had stolen it from her chest himself. She cried both out

of exasperation and joy. Never before he had come into her life had she

really thought about falling in love, and now that she had fallen, she did

not know what to do about it.

Well no use lying here and crying. Kayla spent the rest of the evening

thinking about him and trying on outfit after outfit to find just the right

one to impress him. She knew that he wanted her, but she wanted to

make it impossible for him to say no this time.

By the time morning arrived she was so antsy that she had to go

out for a long run. She started running not long after moving to her

new place, feeling the need to stay healthy after getting clean from her

old life, not to mention the fact that Nikki dragged her along willing or

not. The exercise did her good and helped her to clear her head long

enough to get things done around her house. She re-cleaned her home,

not that it needed it and tried to finish watching the movie he had

brought over last time. She kept thinking back to that night and just

could not sit still.

He wanted her to arrive about thirty minutes after sundown,

which would be about seven tonight. Right now it was only three

o'clock and she thought she would never make it. She went back into

her room to go through her clothes one more time. She had set the

alarm on both her cell and her clock radio to go off in time for her to

take a shower and get dressed. It was a good thing that she did, because

one minute she was sitting up on the bed, and the next she was passed

out in the pile of clothes she was going through.

Kayla stood up and went to the living room phone to call a cab;

she told it to meet her outside at six. Once out of the shower she dried

her hair and brushed all the tangles out of it. She pulled out her favorite

dress, a slinky black thing with one shoulder completely bare and most

of the back revealed.

She left her hair long and down her back and decided against a

pair delicate heels and went instead with the black leather boots with the

small sturdy heel. Her hands shook as she went through her very small

box of jewelry. One of the first things she had purchased for herself

aside from clothing had been a small star pendant with a silver chain.

To her, the night and the stars were where dreams and hopes lived, and

she had many hopes and dreams about her and Michael. She still felt that there was some strange connection with him, that she could not

explain, as if they had known each other for a very long time.

She took one last look at herself in the mirror before she walked

out the door; thinking she looked pretty irresistible. She looked back at

her apartment, furnished with things from Goodwill and from friends

and people from work. It was neat, clean, and orderly but it said nothing

about the person she had become. Thankfully it was hers and hers

alone. She was proud of herself like she had never been before, and

with that thought she locked the door, slipped her key into her purse

and got into the taxi she had called earlier.

The taxi ride was quiet, and for once the cab did not smell

terrible. It was dark outside as the taxi pulled into a silent suburban

street. Most of the homes were set back from the street and the people

who owned them must have more money than she could even imagine.

They made several turns onto similar streets and then finally pulled up

to one of the more modest looking homes. There was a dark SUV in

the driveway and there was Michael leaning against it talking to another

gentleman.

The man looked to be in his late twenties; he had long sandy

blonde hair with a slightly scruffy look as if he hadn't shaved in a day or two. The thing that stood out the most about him was his size. He

stood at least six foot four and he was broad and muscled like an

athlete. Both he and Michael turned to look at the cab as it pulled up

the drive, but only Michael smiled when she got out. The other

gentleman looked neither happy nor angry; he just looked bored.

Michael pushed himself away from the SUV and walked over to

her where she stood clutching her purse in hands that almost shook

with nervous energy. She wanted to be alone with Michael, immediately.

All she could think of was his arms around her, his lips against hers, and

other things she was sure would happen if she could get him alone.

"You look lovely, Kayla. I'm so glad you came. I think I would

have kidnapped you, if had you turned me down." He stepped up next

to her and placed his cool hand into the small of her back to lead her

forward. Some part of her mind was bewildered that he could have

hands that cold in Savannah spring time weather. "Let me introduce

you to a very good friend of mine. This is Logan. Logan, this is Kayla. I

hope you two can be friends." Michael smiled warmly as if this man was

as close as a brother.

Logan shrugged. "I can be nice to just about anyone." He held

his hand out to shake hers and she accepted it lightly hoping he wouldn't crush her hand in his massive paw. He looked like he was

sniffing the air near her. "Michael has told me a lot about you. You

certainly smell *cleaner* than I expected someone with your past would."

He chuckled and showed that he had very white teeth.

"Don't mind Logan, he's a bit strange. Being in the Navy Seals

will do that to a person." Michael turned her again. "Let's go inside, I

have dinner set up for us. Logan I need to talk to you later about the

other house, so don't go making yourself too scarce."

"You know me bro, always hanging around like a dog waiting

for a bone." Both Logan and Michael laughed as if this was an old joke

between them.

The front door was painted red, just like her own door and

when they stepped through Kayla could see that the place was well

decorated, but had a slightly unused feel. This seemed like it may be a

rental that was furnished or a summer home. The place was palatial

compared to her tiny one bedroom apartment. She was starting to get

the impression that Michael must have more money than she would

ever make in her lifetime.

He was always taking care of business out of town, and with

what he said to Logan, he seemed to have more than one house. He steered her through the home and into what looked to be a combination

great room, sort of a family room and kitchen combo. The beautiful

stone fireplace at one end was lit and burning cheerfully along with

several candles around the room. She could smell the candles in soft

vanilla, one of her favorite scents.

"Wow this is very . . . romantic and unexpected." Kayla took a

deep breath; this was the type of setting someone set up for a lover. She

got all feverish and excited just thinking about it. Terror and

anticipation ran circles around in her head for a moment while she

blushed and tried to breathe.

"You don't like the setting? We can open a few beers and watch

a movie, but I was hoping you were in the mood to be romantic. I hope

I haven't overstepped any boundaries." He stopped and turned to look

at her, a tiny trace of lust and hunger in his eyes that was positively faint

worthy.

"There are not very many boundaries that a former prostitute

would have. I think I was just startled. I don't want you to move

forward any faster than is comfortable for you." Kayla took a while to

set her purse down and look around at the home; it was a way to cover her knocking knees and heart palpitations.

"Then things are going at just the right pace." His smile lit up his face and he went into the room with the fireplace, Kayla trailing in his wake. On the other side of an extremely nice leather sofa was a large coffee table laid out with a few platters of finger foods and a bottle of nice red wine. This much nice food must have cost him a fortune unless he could cook, and even then it would not have been cheap. Kayla sat across from him on an overstuffed cushion on the floor. Thankfully she was flexible enough to fold herself lady like on the floor, even in a dress. Michael chuckled and shook his head. "I have yet to purchase a dining table I like for this place. I apologize; we can sit at the bar stools at the kitchen island if you would prefer. I didn't think about you coming in a dress." His eyes said loud and clear that he did not mind her attire one tiny little bit.

"No this is fine. Trust me; I have been much more exposed and much more uncomfortable before." Kayla picked up a glass and looked at Michael, "You do know that I have given up all drugs and alcohol right?" She quirked an eyebrow at him and smiled, hoping she was being flirtatious and charming.

"No I didn't. I assumed you were clean, but I didn't know you were not drinking alcohol at all. Would you prefer juice or water? I may

even have a soda or two in the fridge." He made as if to stand up, but

she put her hand on his and shook her head gently.

"No, I think, just this once a single glass won't hurt. So you are

in real estate?" She asked as he took his hand back to pour her a glass.

He offered her a small plate to put her food on and a napkin.

"Yes, among other things. Logan and I went in together on a

business putting security systems in homes and offices. He is putting his

protective nature to very good use for me. We've made a good deal of

money buying homes, fixing them up, installing security and then

renting or selling them. I have houses all over the eastern seaboard. I

want to expand westward, but the opportunities have not presented

themselves yet. Logan and I go way back; when he came out of the

Seals he was looking for a sparring partner and ran into me at a local

martial arts dojo." Michael took small sips of wine and a few small bites

of his own food, but he didn't seem particularly interested in eating,

Kayla hoped that he was more interested in her.

"You actually fight with that beast on purpose?" Her eyebrows

tried to infiltrate her hairline. "You are either very good, very brave,

very crazy or a bit of all three." Kayla shook her head in disbelief and

Michael tipped his head back and laughed out loud. It was good to hear him let loose and laugh. She wanted to hear him do that much more often, and she was very glad to see that the sad, almost haunted look had almost left his eyes completely.

"I think a bit of all three, and I know Logan would agree. I've been learning martial arts since I was old enough to walk. My father was good friends with this little old Japanese man that trained me. Let me pass on the advice he gave me when I started lessons. He said *'Son, if you are in a bar and a little old Asian man asks you politely to move out of his way, do it.'* He told me he had never been that bruised, in body and ego." Michael smiled as Kayla chuckled. She was so glad that he seemed to finally be opening up to her and telling her about himself. It seemed that the last time they had been together she had done all the talking.

"I have seen lots of movies about martial arts and it seems to me the best fighters are always little old men that flip you around without even breaking a sweat. I would not doubt your father's wisdom in the least." She was silent for a while with some half eaten tidbit in her hands. "Gods, it seems like just a few days ago we were back in my old apartment. I feel like I've known you my whole life, like I could tell you anything and you wouldn't flinch. Were you ever in the military?" She asked, getting the impression that he had seen a lot of things that would

turn most peoples' hair white.

"No, I respect the men and women of the military, but I do not

have the proper mind set for that. I am a shoot first and ask questions

later kind of man. It's the same reason I wasn't a cop like my father and

my uncle. I was an only child and I think not following in the family

business disappointed my father a great deal. He never said anything to

me while he was still alive, but I felt it." Michael sighed and sipped his

wine. While she finished a mini cheesecake with strawberry that made

her eyes close as she sighed in pleasure.

"You're not that much older than me. Your father should still be

alive; what happened? Was he hurt in the line of duty?" Kayla hoped

she didn't hit a nerve as Michael flinched. There was nothing she

wanted more than to keep him happy; it would make getting what she

wanted that much easier.

"You could say that. I'm twenty eight by the way, only 7 years

older than you. Dad was an old school cop, coffee and donuts were his

drugs of choice. I swear if he could have had and IV bag of black coffee

he would have. He died young, massive heart attack. That was when he was in his early forties, goodness I was barely twenty at the time. I never

really knew my Mother, from what Dad said she wasn't

parent material. She took off after I was born. She didn't even stick

around to name me. Dad and Uncle John split it, Dad named me

Michael after their father and Uncle John gave me the middle name

Aaron, since their mother's name was Erin. They did switch shifts so

that someone was always with me until I was able to care for myself.

Uncle John was the one that talked Dad into putting me into Martial

arts. He figured it would give me an edge when I joined the force, which

I didn't." Michael sighed again. "I was working two jobs when Dad

passed. I was giving martial arts lessons to young children during the

day, and working at an all night dinner as a cook. I'll tell you something

Logan doesn't know, I make a mean ham and cheese omelet." Kayla

giggled trying to picture him as a line cook with an apron and

everything; she failed miserably. She nodded to him when her giggles

were contained and he went on.

"When Dad passed I got his money from being in the force and

his life insurance. I took that money and bought two of my first

properties. I fixed them up while still working as an instructor. When I

finished, I sold one, lived in the other, and bought two more places with the profit from the one I sold. I've been doing that ever since. I took a long vacation to Europe right before I turned twenty eight, I met some very fascinating people there, and one of these days I will go back and visit Europe. It's wonderful over there in the fall. So now you know almost as much about me as I know about you." He smiled and sipped his wine.

Kayla had listened to Michael with interest and had finished her glass of wine, only now realizing that she had also been munching her way through the food. "Well I certainly have made a pig of myself." She dabbed at her mouth with the napkin and brushed crumbs off of her, thankfully, washable dress.

"Of course you haven't. I do hope you enjoyed the food though." He stood and began clearing the platters away. "I have more desserts and wine if you would like more." He put things away in the kitchen and then turned back to her.

"No thanks. I couldn't eat another bite. You mentioned a movie earlier, but I don't see a TV." Kayla stood as Michael was still in the kitchen, but her legs had fallen asleep and she stumbled almost falling backwards into the fireplace. She didn't know how he had done it, but somehow Michael was there holding her steady while she got her feet back under her. She couldn't understand how he had gotten around or over the kitchen island and the sofa to her side in time to keep her from falling. He held her very close, almost painfully crushing her against him for a moment before helping her to sit down on the couch.

"Are you okay? You didn't hurt yourself did you?" He sat down next to her, still not taking his arm from around her, which was really rather nice. She took stock of any non-existent injuries and used that time to cover her blushes.

"I'm fine, just clumsy. My legs fell asleep and I tried to stand up anyway." She blushed even redder and she really couldn't say if it was embarrassment or if it was just him being so close that made her all flustered.

"I'm glad you aren't hurt. I do know first aid; mouth to mouth as a matter of fact." He must have kicked the charm into overdrive because with him looking at her and smiling, she felt like she was unable to breathe. "As for the TV it's in the cabinet to the left of the fireplace. What kind of movie would you like?" He turned to the table beside the couch and pressed some buttons on a remote. The cabinet opened silently and the TV turned on. He pushed more buttons bringing up the DVD player. The cool fingers of his other hand were tracing patterns on her skin and she shivered in delight.

"Uh . . . I . . . anything really. I got into movies as a way of

escaping. I also write terrible poetry and some decent stories. I never

did get around to getting anything published though. Do you have any

martial arts flicks? Those really are my favorites." The movie started and

Kayla didn't know whether to lean against him or sit ramrod straight

and hope he gave her an indication of what was going to happen next.

The movie was one of Jackie Chan's and she had only seen it

once, but really liked it. She wouldn't mind watching it again, if she

could just get the thought of his hands on her skin out of her head long

enough to be able to breathe and focus. He must have noticed her

shivers. His next statement was said with a chuckle and his hand

stopped tracing and lay against her spine, still for the moment.

"There is a blanket behind you if you're cold and please get

comfortable, kick your shoes off and tuck your feet up. There is no

sense in you being beautiful if it's not also comfortable." He kicked his

own shoes off and then pulled her body against his. His skin still felt

cool to the touch, but she shrugged it off. She had known some of her

friends from school that were always chilly. Some people just ran cooler

than others. She snuggled happily into his shoulder and leaned her head against him anyways; for once in her life completely content. "This is how I like my evenings to be spent." He said out of the blue, giving her shoulders a gentle squeeze.

"What, charming some gullible young woman and then disappearing for weeks?" She wrinkled her nose at him, trying to be cute.

"Not just any young woman; I hope I'm charming you. I only disappear due to work, and I always come back for the things I want." He leaned forward and kissed the end of her nose, sending goose bumps down her back. His lips gently brushed the top of her hair, her eyelids and her cheeks, while she sat almost breathless in his arms, her heart pounding a mile a minute. She was sure he could hear it thundering in her chest. "Your blushing again Kayla." He smiled for just a moment at the startled look on her face and then he covered her mouth with his own.

The embrace lasted only seconds but to Kayla it was a lifetime. She knew then that it was more than charm and infatuation that drew her to Michael. She knew that this man, among all the many that she had known, been with, spoken to or even cared about, was her true match, her partner. She would walk through fire and hell for this man if only he asked it of her.

They broke the kiss off and sat watching the film for a while. She took his hand in hers boldly and kissed the back of it. He turned to her and planted another longer passionate kiss on her lips that sent fire down into her groin and her heart up into her throat. When he pulled away he grinned at her mischievously.

She was staring at Michael and he was smiling back at her one instant and the next he threw his head up as if he was a startled deer in the woods hearing the hunter approaching. He swore colorfully and stood up quickly disentangling himself from her arms. She hadn't even realized that she had been holding on to him.

"Bloody great, you have got to be kidding me." Kayla swore colorfully like a well-educated sailor for a moment and then continued. "What this time? I knew it was too good to be true. Are you married or something?" Kayla stood up yanking her boots back on and almost fell in the process. He tried to reach out to steady her, but in her anger she pulled away. She immediately hated herself for it as she saw the hurt look that spread across his face.

"No, I'm not married, never have been. Kayla, there are things I have to tell you about me that may frighten you away. I can't explain now. I need you to be very quiet and listen carefully. I told you about

my enemies, that is why I acted the way I did in the bar the other night.

I think they may be here. I have a really good feel for things like this. If

they found you, they would either kill you out of hand or use your pain

to torture me. I need you to get out of here; I have to know you are

safe. Take the SUV. I couldn't live with myself if they hurt you. Do not

go home. Here take this money." He stuffed money into her purse and

handed it to her. "I'll send Logan with you and he'll do me the favor of

protecting you." Michael held her face in his hands for just a moment

and planted a kiss on her lips that was passionate to the point of

possessiveness. "I . . . I love you." He said when he broke off the kiss.

That spun her head around and she was dizzy with the

emotions. She could hardly even make sense of things as Michael

helped her out of the front door and into the passenger seat of the

SUV. She turned just in time to see as Logan came running up the drive

way from out of nowhere.

"Michael, they've located you." Logan said as he snatched the

keys from Michael and climbed into the driver seat. "But I see that you

know that already. I'll take her someplace I know is safe and I'll stay

with her until you come for her. You know you can trust me." He slammed the car door, started the engine and then pealed out of the

driveway.

Chapter 7:

"Thank goodness tomorrow is Sunday." Logan spoke up after he had been driving for a while. "We will not have to make excuses to your work as to why you aren't there." He had given Michael a 'thumbs up' as they drove away. Kayla could only cling to the door and stare in shock.

If she thought Nikki was a good driver, she was mistaken. Logan drove like a getaway driver or a formula one racer, she wasn't sure which. For a while the only sounds were the tires on the roadways and the radio playing some random rock station. When Logan did speak up again she jumped, and squeaked, completely startled.

"I didn't mean to startle you. So did he tell you anything?" Logan sounded suspicious and that rattled her nerves even more.

"Nothing that would explain being semi-kidnapped by his sparring partner." She snapped back at him. Being scared often put her in nasty temper. She didn't want to take it out on Michael's friend, but she almost couldn't help herself.

"You seem to be taking this well, or else you are in shock." He turned the radio off so that it was quieter in the car. He kept glancing at

her out of the corner of his eyes, which in a way made her even more

annoyed.

"Probably shock. That is the second time that man has literally

shuffled me out of his presence without much, if any explanation.

Either he is a dangerous man or a man with dangerous enemies. I don't

know which, but I intend to find out." Kayla leaned her head back into

the seat and closed her eyes as her stomach did terrible flops inside her,

making her feel slightly ill. She wasn't sure how to feel at this point. He

said he loved her, but yet something had made him send her away again.

She wanted to believe he was protecting her, and she was very worried

that whoever he was protecting her from would hurt him.

"It's a bit of both actually. I don't know if he told you, but he

taught me everything I know about true martial arts. Not just the

sparing, but the quickest way to take a person out without a sound.

Stuff the Seals don't even know. That man could kill someone with a

paper cup, I swear." Logan laughed, he had one of those very manly

voices and it rumbled her chest when he chuckled. Kayla still had her

eyes closed and she could feel the tension in her neck cranking up to a

migraine inducing status.

"Well, that's kind of scary. I could tell that there was more

strength in his arms than he looks like he should have and damn if he

isn't quick. I almost fell and he was across the room to catch me before

I could blink." She felt like she was duct taping herself together just to

keep from crying, screaming or punching things. It was one of the

reasons she was still talking and not trying to dig the headache medicine

out of her purse, not that she had anything to take it with at the

moment.

"Perceptive." Logan left that one word comment hanging in the

air like a cloud. There was silence in the vehicle for some time while she

sat and alternated views out the window with views of the back of her

eyelids. There were only a few headlights passing them now as they

turned onto more rural stretches of road and she would shut her eyes as

they passed to save her now pounding head.

"I can certainly see why he has fallen for you. When I first saw

you, I thought, *'great, another wilting flower'*. I've dated a few like that and

so has Michael. They fall apart at the first sign of trouble. You on the

other hand have been through the wringer from what Michael has told

me, and you handle stress well it seems." Logan turned the car down a

very narrow two lane road driving farther away from Savannah. She was wound pretty tight right now and she had jumped again when he started

speaking.

"I *have* been through a lot. I don't know what he has told you

about me. Having him rushing me out of a house and sent packing to

escape from some nameless enemy, doesn't seem quite as bad as some

things I have seen and dealt with." She opened her purse and folded the

money he had stuffed into it neatly and stuck it into her wallet. "The

thing I don't understand is why in the world he always shoves money at

me when he has to leave. Does he really think that will fix everything?"

Exasperation made her sigh and roll her eyes. She really could not

fathom why he always gave her money. If he was going to send her

packing with Logan as a guardian, why in the world would he have

needed to give her money at all?

"I think it's because he feels that he is bringing chaos into your

life and that having money to take care of the everyday needs will help

with the feeling that things are out of control. That is the way it was

with me when he and I met." He coughed and seemed to be thinking

things through. "I don't know what he has told you about me and I'm

pretty sure I know what I am not allowed to tell you yet. Would you like

to know a little about me, what I can tell you that is?" He glanced over at her, and he really could see why Michael wanted her, she was

gorgeous. He would have snatched her up in a heartbeat if she hadn't

been with Michael.

"Yeah, I guess so. Maybe knowing more about you will help me

know more about him. He was just starting to tell me about his family

when this happened." She shook her head, things were definitely not

working out the way she had planned them. This evening had turned

from a romantic meal that should have led to other romantic acts, to

some kind of action thriller kidnap movie. She was not pleased with that

outcome, not at all.

"Okay, well, I was injured in the last mission I went on. I

thought I would never function normally again, really I should be more

thankful that I didn't die. Too many things got broken or dislocated. A

lot of soft tissues were torn and had to take a very long time to heal.

When I got back to some semblance of a normal life and started trying

to get back to the fitness level, I had been in when I was in the Seals. I

walked into a late night martial arts studio because a friend

recommended it for me to get back my flexibility. I saw Michael in there

doing a kata. He moved like lightning on speed. I've never seen anyone

that quick before. We started talking, then training and then hanging out. Now we watch each other's backs and he does tend to throw money away like TP being flushed. Anyway now I'm stuck being a baby sitter." He patted her head like she was a small child.

"I'm hardly a baby." She said chuckling, even though her mind was still in turmoil. He seemed so much less mysterious than Michael and much more normal.

"Well let's call it *Babe* sitting. I will tell you this much. Michael has an extraordinary taste when it comes to women." He waggled his eyebrows at her in a lewd fashion and she just rolled her eyes.

"Where are we going?" She asked watching the road; the trees and very few homes fly by. Her headache eased slightly as Logan talked and she started to relax some.

"Michael has a farm out this way. Pretty much, just him and myself know about it. He has two family members as caretakers. He loves animals; he has horses, a few cows, some goats, pigs, and even a few nasty, annoying, chickens. Guh, I hate those clucking nuisances. I'm not that fond of the horses either; actually they hate me. I never go near the barn, but feel free to go say hi to them all you want. I'm sure Michael won't mind; just don't ask me to help you saddle one. I've been bitten, kicked at, had my foot almost stomped flat and been bucked off.

That was just from trying to ride one of the foul things, *once*." He laughed and shook his head taking a turn to the left onto a different road. "Now cows. . . I like cows. Calm placid and only spook for a very good reason." Logan went silent for a moment and rolled down the window on his side. He looked like he was listening to something very intently. He even leaned his head closer to the window. It was so strange and out of place for someone driving a car in back woods Georgia, if she hadn't been freaked out just a little, she would have laughed. She could also see that it looked like his nostrils flared slightly, like he was trying to catch a scent.

What in the hell is going on with these two? She thought to herself. *I'm already emotionally wrapped up in Michael and yet I can't help but think he might be a danger to me. And now I'm being semi-willingly driven off into the middle of who the hell knows with a friend of his that I just met tonight. Where in the world is my survival instinct now, when I need it? What was I thinking?* She watched him as he turned his head slightly while still watching the road and sniffed at the air again. Something very strange was going on with this man.

"Is your Spidey sense tingling?" She asked half-jokingly but went silent when his head snapped around to look at her in shock. "What?

You really do have a Spidey sense like Spiderman?" She asked when he

had turned to look back at the road and shook his head.

"No. I was just startled. How much did Michael tell you about

himself and about me?" He looked more than startled, he looked like he

could not trust her and was worried that she knew too much about him.

That was a frightening thing for her to realize, since she knew this man

was probably dangerous to enemies. She did not want him putting her

in that category.

"Not much. You heard what he told me about the Seals. He also

told me that you two spar sometimes. We talked mostly about his

family, his father, and uncle. Look, I'm sorry about the comment. I

didn't mean to offend you." She looked out the passenger window at

the dirt road that Logan was now turning onto.

"I'm not offended. You . . . are much more perceptive than I

would have given you credit for." Again silence descended on the

vehicle as it bounced down the dirt road. There was not much to be

seen through the dark but the trees on either side as the headlights

illuminated them. She wished that Michael had been able to come with

them. She was worried about him and scared that he would be hurt by

his enemies. He had only just told her he loved her this evening and she very much wanted to find out where this relationship, if you could call it

that, was going. She wanted to tell Logan to turn the car around and go

back to Michael and help protect him. She wanted him to leave her

somewhere safe and then make sure that the man she was in love with

was also safe.

Logan cursed and tapped the brakes, scaring the life out of

Kayla as the tires slid on the soft sand and clay dirt road. She nearly

jumped out of her skin when a few deer darted across the track in front

of them. Once they had passed Logan kept driving like nothing had

happened, but she was staring at him like he was some kind of freak. He

had tapped the brakes before the animals had even broken out of the

line of trees. There was no way he could have seen them and she

highly doubted he could have heard them over the sound of the engine

and the tires rumbling down the road.

Things were starting to get twisted up in her head and she was

not sure she liked the direction her mind was racing in. First there was

the way Michael had acted like he had smelled something awful at the

bar before making her leave, then he covers the space between his

kitchen and where she had been standing near the fireplace in half a

heartbeat; and she could have sworn that it was something he had heard that made him force her to leave this evening. Not counting all those times that she had seen that hungry look in his eyes when he was watching her.

She took a long look at Logan out of the corner of her eye. He had told her, she smelled *clean*; putting the emphasis on the word as if he were referring to someone who was not on drugs versus one who was. There was very little chance that he could smell the difference in the chemical make up between a druggy and someone clean, so why make such a comment. There was also the fact that Michael had not called him on the phone to come and get her, he had just appeared out of nowhere as if he knew that he was needed. Maybe he had sensed the same thing that Michael had. He had acted a while back as if he had been listening to and sniffing for something outside the window, then he had that strange reaction to what she had said something about Spidey senses. Now there was this odd incident where he seemed to know there were deer about to jump in front of the car.

She turned her head to look at him fully. Were he and Michael some kind of super humans or were they something much darker, much more sinister. She stared at him so long trying to figure things out that she started getting the headache back; the bouncing of the car on the road certainly was not helping. "I'm not feeling well. I'm going to lay

back, please wake me when we get there." Kayla tilted the seat back and

curled up on her left side so that she could still watch Logan covertly.

Whenever she would close her eyes to keep him from seeing her staring

she could feel his eyes on her and she wondered what he thought of

her. She tried to keep her eyes barely open, but she was fighting

emotional shock, and finally fell asleep despite her best efforts.

She had a short dream that Michael and Logan were fighting and

they were throwing houses at each other. It was a very odd dream and

some things about it lingered in her mind after she woke to the

sound of Logan talking. It sounded like a one sided conversation, so he

was probably on the phone. She kept her eyes closed and tried to keep

her breathing still so he would not know she was awake.

"I'm almost there. What did they say or do?" There was a

pause." I told you they couldn't be trusted to keep to the pact. I warned

you not to trust those Dogs." He paused again." Yes, well, it is

unfortunate that the hunting parties have already gotten her scent.

Michael I have to go, I think she's waking up." There were a couple of

clicks and then Logan went silent again. Kayla made a pretense of

shifting in the seat and sighing as if she truly were just waking up.

"Are we there yet? How far away are we going?" She rubbed her eyes carefully due to her makeup. She felt like a dish rag that was all rung out. Too much shifting emotions and she was awake way past her normal bedtime.

"We should be there in about five or ten minutes. I'm pretty sure Michael has all the things you would need for a shower if you would like. Are you hungry?" Logan was trying to be casual but she could almost feel the tension vibrating in him. She fumbled around on the side of the seat to try to sit it back up.

"I could probably eat a little. I thought I heard voices in my sleep. Is everything alright?" The lever on the seat chose that moment to click into place and pinch down hard on her finger. She yelped and pulled her finger out, but the damage was done. She had a small nick and it was bleeding.

"There are band aids in the glove box for that cut." He wasn't even looking at her finger; now she was getting very curious.

"How did you know I was cut? You certainly can't see anything in here its pitch black." She sucked her finger while digging for the band aids. She found them at the bottom of course and began putting one on the cut.

"With as loud as you yelled, you had to have cut something,

besides I can smell the blood." He tapped his nose. "It's a strange gift,

sometimes a curse, but it comes in handy having a very sensitive nose."

He made another turn onto an even smaller dirt road, this one almost

completely encased in trees.

"Oh." She replied as she struggled to get the band aid on her cut

by the light of the glove box. "Well, if you talk to Michael, tell him I'm

worried about him, and that we need to have a nice long conversation

about . . . well, about some stuff." She folded her arms across her chest

and rubbed them to warm them. Somehow in the flight from Michael's

home she had forgotten her jacket and was now rather chilly. "What

time is it anyway?" She spoke up after a few minutes of quiet.

"It's about two in the morning. I did speak with Michael on the

phone while you slept. He said to tell you he is fine and he will come get

you as soon as possible. Oh, and he called your boss and told him that

you had a family emergency and needed to take the week off." Logan

slowed the car to a crawl and stopped in front of a red gate. He tapped

a button on the dash and the gate slid open.

"He does realize that I have bills that need to be paid, right? I need the money from that job." She was about to demand the phone

and call her boss and tell him she would be there anyway, but a

stubborn look from Logan made her clamp her mouth down on that

request.

"Michael has made sure that your bills will be covered. It's paid

time off." The SUV pulled through the gate and it closed behind them.

There was a long winding driveway, where neither of them said

anything and then a field opened up in front of them and she saw what

looked

like a giant log cabin with several buildings behind it and a barn off to

one side.

"Wow that is some farm." Kayla forgot all about being out of

work for a moment in the wonder of this place. She had never been to a

farm growing up. Hell she had never had a dog, or been to a petting zoo

either. If it wasn't for Nikki having a very sweet dog, she would

probably still be a little leery of them.

"Now you won't be alone aside from me. There is an older

couple that live here doing rescue work with the animals. That would be

Marge and Hank. They're the sweetest people I've ever met; makes my

teeth hurt every time I see them." He chuckled. "I called ahead; they know we're coming in. You know, Marge may have some clothes you

can wear. You're not much different in size. You would think that a lady

of forty would have let herself go by now, but Marge is still fit and trim.

Hauling hay for those damn horses will do that to you." He pulled the

SUV around to a garage and pulled it inside. There were motion lights

that had come on and she could see two people standing in the door

leading from the garage into the home.

Kayla stepped out of the car as soon as it was completely

stopped and walked around it towards the door. "Hi, I'm Kayla, I'm

very sorry about all this. I hate to wake you guys in the middle of the

night, but I'm just following... well I guess they aren't exactly orders."

She held out her hand to both of them which they shook and smiled at

her like she was their own child. Logan had been right the lady, Marge

was still very healthy and trim for her age. Her hair had one long gray

streak in the soft brown and there were smile lines around her eyes and

mouth. The man looked to be a touch older with a head full of salt and

pepper hair. You could see the muscles under his shirt sleeves, probably

from doing farm work every day. Both of them seemed to be the

epitome of happy country folk.

"It's alright dear. We understand." The lady said." I doubt *you* understand much of what is going on. Well, come in and I'll get you something to eat, then you can shower and get some real sleep. Logan said you dozed in the car, but really that's not good enough sleep for your body to recover from stress like this. I don't think anyone told you, but I'm related to Michael through his Uncle John. Hank and I are big time animal lovers, so Michael helped us set up this rehabilitation and rescue center." Marge chattered on about the types of animals that they rescue and how lovely it was to meet one of Michael's friends. "We see Logan and Michael whenever they can make it, and of the two only Michael can handle the horses. They hate Logan, bless the poor boy, or he would help."

The main living area was huge and opened up to the second story. There was a walkway on the second level that probably led to bedrooms and things. This area was the living room, kitchen and dining room all in one. When they got to the kitchen she took a seat at the counter on a well-padded stool. Marge was puttering around in the fridge and Hank had disappeared back up the stairs to her left possibly to get back to sleep.

"Thank you very much for your hospitality. Are you Michael's cousin?" Kayla leaned on her elbow with her chin in her palm, hoping that finally she would get some answers about Michael.

"Well, yeah something like that. His Uncle was older than his father but he still outlived Michael's Dad, though not by much." She went oddly silent. "Well, let's see, what would you like to eat? I have some sandwich fixings." She opened the fridge and started pulling things out.

"A sandwich would be fine. Then I really will need to get some sleep." Marge set all the sandwich items down on the counter in front of Kayla.

"I need to get back to bed myself. Just put things away when you are done. Logan will show you the bedroom to use." She nodded to Logan who had entered the house without her hearing him. He looked, different somehow, she couldn't quite put a finger on what it was, but it was something slightly dangerous feeling.

"Michael called again. He had to make a trip out of town and will be here tomorrow night. Well, since it is after midnight, I guess that would be tonight. He's fine before you ask. He said that you were not to worry and to get some rest. There is a lot that he has to talk to you about when he sees you again." Logan flopped on a nearby couch. "Finish your sandwich." Sitting quietly in that warm cozy kitchen she did as she was told and then cleaned up after herself. She was really drowsy and knew that if she didn't get some true sleep soon, she would pass out on her feet.

"Where am I sleeping tonight?" She asked turning to look at Logan after she put things away. Logan stood up and pointed towards the stairs. He followed her up them and she was aware that his eyes were on her hips and bum in front of him. She was startled by how much of his mood she could really feel. It was like he was radiating his emotions. He was ramped up from the thought of danger and now all of that energy was turning to sexual frustration. She was not egotistical, but she knew now that she was healthy she was a tempting target for male attentions. She was so exhausted and twisted up in her thoughts that she missed the top step completely and fell un-ceremoniously back into Logan's arms. She yelped in fear but he caught her and held her safe for a moment.

His eyes narrowed as he looked at her in his arms and he leaned forward to, there was no other word for it, sniff her. "Yes, Michael does have wonderful *taste* in female flesh." He turned her loose, setting her back on her feet but leaving her feeling totally bewildered by the odd inflection he had used on the word taste. "Yours will be the third room on the left down the hall to the right. It has its own bathroom." He

patted her bottom gently in the right direction and she squeaked. "Now

don't get lost. I have the room right next door to yours if you need . . .

anything." He spun and descended the stairs and she could see when he

looked over his shoulder that he had the left corner of his mouth turned

up in an almost sinister smile. It made her shiver down to her toes and

she quickly went to her room.

　　With the door safely shut behind her and the knowledge that

she was a light sleeper and would wake if anyone opened the door, she

felt better. She tumbled her troubles around in her mind for a time

while sitting on the edge of the bed with her knees tucked up to her

chin. She felt like she was swirling in the middle of a hurricane of

emotion. She knew she loved Michael, there was no denying that, but

she also knew that she would never put up with him keeping things

from her the way he had been. *He had better come clean and soon or I'm*

walking. That thought had plenty of anger behind it. She knew she

deserved better than to be dragged along with something that seemed

dangerous without knowing everything possible to help her protect

herself.

　　She decided to at least get ready for bed and maybe get some sleep. Exhaustion was quickly catching up with her and she didn't need

to fall out and break her nose on the floor.

There was already a stack of things on the corner of the bed.

She found a set of soft pajama bottoms and a t-shirt, a towel, a pair of

socks and a robe. She really wasn't in need of a shower so she just

stripped out of her dress, kicked her boots off and brushed out her hair

with the brush she found in the bathroom. She made sure to wipe all of

her make up off so that she wouldn't have raccoon eyes in the morning.

Then she slipped into the pajamas and threw the robe and towel over

the edge of a chair that was in the room. She tucked herself into bed

and was quickly asleep.

Chapter 8:

"How is she?" Michael asked of Logan for the third time in as many hours. It was predawn and after a night of arguing, running and throwing his vampire political weight around, he was strung as tight as a bridge supported by wire and he hoped he had the strength not to snap.

"She's asleep upstairs still. I can hear her breathing. You do know that if you don't tell her, you will have to wipe her mind. Like you did with that last one you tried to bring into your life." Logan replied, he was pacing the living room floor as he usually did in stressed situations. His mind kept playing images of Kayla through his head, especially the way she looked when she tumbled into his arms on the stairs. He had to keep shaking his head to clear it and telling himself that she was not available on any level. He took himself out on to the large front porch to feel the slightly cool spring air on his face; maybe it would clear his head.

"I am surprised she went along with you. I know I need to tell her and Martinique was a mistake that I will never make again, much like Eliza. Beauty and intelligence do not go hand in hand. Besides

Kayla is a totally different person." Michael sighed across the phone

line; his heart was thumping with the memories of her lips on his and

his hands in her hair. He was so close to getting what he wanted and yet

at this moment the whole of it was balanced on the edge of a knife. His

nerves were rubbed raw with stress and an overabundance of emotion.

"I know. She is a very strong woman. I was impressed with how

calm she seemed, at least this one has some substance. Just to let you

know, I can tell she is getting suspicious of several things. I think she

may be smarter than you give her credit for. I can see it in her face that

she is starting to wonder if the fact that I am a former Seal and you a

martial arts teacher covers all the "incidents" that she has seen." Now it

was Logan's turn to sigh, and Michael thought that he knew why. "I

almost hate you for making me come with her. Not only is she a total

babe and smells incredible, but she is smart, observant and strong. If

there was ever a mortal woman to turn my head, it's this one." Michael

started to speak, but Logan interrupted him. "Don't worry though; I can

see her heart in her eyes every time she mentions your name. She is

smitten." Logan punched one of the giant wooden support beams on

the porch in frustration, leaving knuckle prints. He couldn't help

thinking how Nicholai had taken the only woman he had loved from him.

"I can't imagine not having her with me, and Logan, I want her as a true partner." Michael mumbled something to someone on the other end of the line. Logan went quiet for just a moment to let Michael speak to the other person.

"You mean to turn her don't you?" Logan asked once Michael had finished talking. He was sure that he knew the answer before he had even finished the question. If Michael wanted her as a partner there was no way that he would leave her human and in danger for any length of time.

"As soon as I can safely turn her, then yes, I fully intend to do so. I want her to know what we are and know what she is setting herself up for. I want to tell her everything. I want the choice to be hers and if she turns me down, then you should feel free to plead *your* case to her." Michael was pretty sure that Logan would say no, but a touch of jealousy flashed through him as Logan took longer to answer than he would have liked.

"No, no, I don't think so. I will never turn a woman. Female wolves are few and far between and rarely are they sane enough to carry on a normal existence. Lily was one of the very few and now that she is gone I'm pretty sure I would never be able to replace her."

They talked a little while longer about other things, and then Michael asked Logan about Kayla's father. "Yeah I knew him, knew him very well, since he was the one that turned me. We got sent out on a mission together and I was there to keep him safe while he picked off targets. He was safe all right, but I got captured and tortured. I thought for sure that I had told you all this before."

"Yeah you told me the story, but I never knew it was her father. Great good gods, how do we tell her about that?" Michael was stunned. For once in his life he had no plan for this sort of circumstance. "I think we should wait on that. There is enough to worry about at this point. Tell me more about her father though." Michael continued.

"He was a great man, the most amazing sniper I've ever seen. He not only saved me from my captors, but he saved my life when it was clear that I was not going to make it without some help. Still he gave me a choice, not many would have. Hold on a sec." Logan went silent for a moment, listening to the sounds of the house around him. "I think she's having a nightmare, her breathing just increased. Then again she could be playing with herself." Logan laughed a malicious kind of chuckle. He only had one thing on his mind most days and that was pretty women.

"You, sir, are a pervert. I have to go now. I'm laying a false trail and I want to make sure they follow me. I got a map from a gas station just a second ago, I've got my sun suit, and I'm going to hike the Appalachian Trail. I'll be there probably by 9:00 or 10:00 pm. Don't let her out of your sight. Scratch that; don't let her go off alone. You do not need to follow her to bed or to the shower. I know your dirty mind." Again Michael laughed, reassured that Kayla was safe and well taken care of in his absence.

"Michael, you take care of yourself. I still don't trust those suits, they haven't been tested enough. I won't let anything happen to her. I can tell how much you care about her. You feel towards her the way I felt about Lily. I'll see you later." Logan waited until he heard the phone click on the other end and he hung up. He turned around and came back inside the house from the front porch. The volume of her breathing from inside the house was a good bit louder to him. He wanted to go up to her room and watch her in her sleep. He knew he shouldn't, she was Michael's girl and he owed him so much. He just couldn't keep her out of his mind, so he did what he wanted to do and crept up the stairs and into her room.

She never heard him with as silently as he could walk. He smiled

to see that she was asleep and sprawled across the bed with blankets and

pillows strewn in every direction. Her dark hair was flared out across the

bed around her, and her face was scrunched as she thrashed in a

nightmare. Honestly he was usually much more into blondes, but for a

women like her, he would have made an exception. In all good

conscience he could not sit and let her dream something bad when he

could shake her awake.

"Kayla." He shook her shoulder as gently as he could with his

large hand. "You're talking in your sleep."

She screamed and about fell out of the bed trying to get away

from him. He held his hands out palms showing towards her. He

wanted to laugh at the idea that she would try and attack him, but bit his

tongue instead. He didn't want to hurt her feelings.

"It's okay. I'm just waking you up because you seemed to be

having a bad dream." He smiled noticing that she had grabbed the table

lamp next to her as if to use it as a bat on him. "I'm not going to hurt

you, and that is definitely not going to hurt me." He sat down in the

chair in her room. He watched her slow her rapid breathing and then sit

the lamp back down. He was impressed all over again.

"You're probably right, but better armed, even uselessly than to

go down without a fight." She ran her hand through her tangled hair.

"I'm sorry I was making noises in my sleep. Did I keep you from

sleeping?" She looked confused still, but she was waking up quickly. She

sat back down on the bed pulling her legs up to sit cross legged.

"No. I was coming up to the bathroom and heard you. It's

starting to get light outside, did you want breakfast? I know Marge is up

cooking already and Hank is out with the horses if you want to walk out

to see them." He stood up, like he was going to leave and then stopped,

looking at her again. "Are you going to be okay? Would you like to talk

about the nightmare?" Kayla noticed as he spoke that he looked nothing

like the nearly sinister creature that he had been last night after he

caught her. He looked friendly, approachable, and totally hunky, Nikki

would faint.

"It's just silly, just my mind trying to catch up with the stress.

I've had dreams like this before warning me about stuff. It's not like

premonitions or anything. I was being told in the dream that you and

Michael were dangerous. I walked in on you and him sparring and you

were throwing houses at each other and I was getting pelted by the

falling pieces. When I tried to run away you both followed me by the smell of my blood on the ground. It was silly really; nothing like that could ever happen." She chuckled but saw his eyes widen at the mention of the word blood. He recovered quickly, smiling.

"No, I mean I'm pretty strong, but a house . . . maybe a camper or a tow behind trailer, but never a house." He laughed it off, but she could see that something was still bothering him.

"I think I should get up now, I'll be down in a little while. If you don't mind I need to get dressed." She stood up and tugged on the robe. She walked around the bed towards the bathroom, before she noticed that he hadn't left yet.

"I don't mind at all, go right ahead. Pretend I'm not even here." She gave him a look that said 'get out'. "Oh, you want me to leave. I'll see you downstairs then. Marge left you some clothes in the closet. It will be dawn soon, so Hank and Marge will be up doing farm work." He smiled at her charmingly, and then left her alone to change.

She did indeed find a few items of clothing in the closet. There were a few pairs of jeans and some t-shirts. She also found a few pairs of shoes, mostly work boots and tennis shoes in a half size larger than she wore. She stripped and tugged on the first pair of jeans she laid her hands on. They were a bit baggy but very comfortable. A blue t-shirt came next. She put on a pair of clean socks and then found one pair of

what looked like hiking boots that fit, even though they were not her

exact size. Once she was dressed she made a quick stop by the

bathroom to brush her hair and pull it into a pony tail with the hair

band she always kept in her purse. She glanced at herself in the mirror

and even with lack of sleep and extra stress she still didn't look like most

women would have. She had none of the dark circles, none of the

haggard expression, and if her skin wasn't quite as bright as normal, no

one was going to notice that.

She came down the steps and Logan was in the kitchen

devouring a plateful of food. He nodded to the kitchen island that had

become a breakfast bar. There were pancakes, eggs, bacon, grits,

sausage, toast, biscuits, fresh fruit, and waffles. Beside the vast spread

were plates, forks, knives, milk, orange juice, cups and napkins.

"Wow, uh . . . does she always cook like this?" Kayla grabbed a

plate and chose some of her favorite breakfast foods and turned to sit

down next to Logan who was sitting at the section of the massive

island set aside as an eating nook.

"Yep, good stuff too. Marge thinks I only come here for the

food, but she's a nice old gal and well, I kind of think of her as a Mom.

So Michael said your father was in the military, what branch?" He had

actually stopped stuffing his face temporarily to talk.

"He was a Marine sniper from what I can remember. Mom used

to tease him and call him Gunnery Sergeant Dad. He died when I was

really little. As far as Mom knew, he was doing things no one should

know about; they never even told her how he died. She used to cry

about it when she would get drunk. There was no body to bury, but he

has a headstone and grave never-the-less. The last thing I remember of

him was him singing to me over the phone. Mom said he had told her

that he would take us to a rain forest someday. I don't remember a lot

about him, except as a warm safe presence and him smelling like some

kind of oil and old spice. Mom and I loved him so much. I think his

death unhinged her. She was never the same after him. Only decent

man my mom married." She took a deep sigh and she took a few bites

of her breakfast.

"What was his name? The Seals used to work with the Marine

snipers on a regular basis. Maybe one of my commanders knew him.

They used to tell us stories about some of the older snipers; some of

those men where scary good. I heard about one sniper that took out

another through the scope of a rifle. That would be cool as hell." He took a bite of toast and washed it down with juice.

"Daryl Sutherland. He died in the line of duty is all I know. I think it was in 94." Kayla ate quietly while Logan tapped his chin in thought.

"I think I have heard that name. 94 was a very touchy year. W . . . the military was doing a lot of things they were not supposed to talk about. If I remember one of my commanders was in on something in a jungle in Suriname where they were routing out rebels. He mentioned a sniper named Daryl who may have been your father. He was supposedly responsible for 17 confirmed kills in 5 days. My commander said it was like where he looked, the bullet hit. Made quite an impression I think. I don't know what happened to him though, Commander Dickson never said." Logan sighed. "I wish I could tell you more, but well . . . Anyway, Michael should be here by nine or ten tonight. Want to go help with the horses? I'll be helping Marge feed the cows once we finish clean up." Logan stuffed his last three pieces of bacon in his mouth at once and stood to put his dishes in the dish washer.

Kayla handed him hers as she took a last piece of toast for herself. "I think I would like that. I always wanted to ride a horse. " She stood up and helped put away the breakfast, while Marge bustled around, finding plastic containers for the piles of extras. Kayla guessed

they would be making lunch out of whatever was leftover, not that she

would mind. All of the food here so far had been very tasty; it wasn't

often she got home cooked foods.

That was when the phone in Logan's pocket rang. He picked it

up and Kayla, rude or not, listened intently. If there was anything to

learn about Michael she wanted to find out immediately.

"Yeah, what happened? You didn't? You know that will cause

problems. Well if it couldn't be helped. What did you do with the um . .

. leftovers? Yeah, it smells awful when you do that. I have a bug in my

ear so I can't say. I'll tell her. Be safe." Logan turned to Kayla. "Yes that

was Michael. He had a bit of a setback. He is fine and he will still be

here tonight. You can stop listening in to our conversations. It's rude

and there are things you should just not know yet." He turned away and

walked out the back door heading for the field where the cows were,

not giving her a chance to reply.

Not knowing what else to do she went out to the barn to help

Hank with the horses, but he had already done everything that was

needed at this time of the day, so he helped her saddle a pretty gray

horse that he told her was an American saddle bred. The horse was named Beau and he nibbled at Kayla's hair playfully as she scratched

behind his ears. Hank showed her how to mount and "steer" and then

he told her where a few trails that they had cut for riding started and

made her promise to keep to them no matter what. It didn't seem like

that much of an odd request because she didn't know the area and did

not want to get lost.

Kayla found the trails no problem and was in love with the

gentle temperament of Beau as he made his way smoothly down the

trail. It was a path cut through the trees and wide enough for two

people to ride side by side with room to spare. She could hear birds

above her and the warmth of the horse beneath her made her feel safe

and secure. She found that she was naturally good at riding and Beau

responded to her like he was an extension of her own self. She was so

comfortable that she had plenty of thinking time and she set about

trying to put things together.

Okay, so Michael is into real estate, security systems, writing documentaries,

and obviously something that may or may not be legal; considering the whole enemies

thing. Both he and Logan seem human, but clearly have certain abilities that make

them seem to be more than your average normal human. I feel like sometimes when I

talk to them that they are hiding something from me, and even Marge seemed that way a little bit. What in the world are all these people hiding from me? They seem so

nice and Michael said he loved me.

That thought made her heart scream and race. She actually had

to set about trying to still her heart and calm her breathing for a

moment.

Then there is Logan who certainly would not have turned down an

invitation to my room last night, even though he is Michael's friend. Maybe he was

testing me to see if I was trustworthy enough for Michael; like I would ever do

anything to hurt him or chance losing the one man I have ever fallen in love with.

She heaved a deep dramatic sigh and giggled as Beau swiveled

his ears back and snorted at her. She chuckled and scratched him

behind his ears which made him sigh, and even stop mid step to enjoy

it.

That was when she heard a deep growling sound and her head

shot up to stare at the woods around her. Beau also heard it and she

could feel him shivering under her as he started stamping. He looked

left and right, his eyes wide and frightened. She wondered if these

woods had wolves in them. She couldn't see anything, but she knew she

felt eyes on her and she did not want to stick around in the woods by

herself and find out if there were indeed wolves. She turned Beau around and let him set his own speed back towards the safety of the

barn.

He decided that he wanted out of there rather quickly and he

was nearly galloping by the time that they broke out from the trail and

were in the open fields around the house and other buildings. She just

clung on for dear life. First time on a horse and she was terrified that it

may be her last if she couldn't manage to stay on him. He slowed a little

as she pulled lightly on the reins, but he was still twitching when she got

him to the barn and dismounted.

"I didn't expect you back quite so quickly, what happened?"

Hank asked as he put his hand against Beau to try and steady him.

"I don't know. I thought I heard growling in the woods and

then Beau seemed scared so I turned him around and let him get out of

there at his own pace. He was almost running, so he must have smelled

something he didn't like. Is he okay?" She walked around to where

Hank was holding Beau's halter. She scratched his chin and he did seem

to be calming down some.

"He should be fine. He really likes you though, see." Hank told

her and she noticed that he was leaning on her as she scratched him and

his eyes were even starting to close.

"Are there wolves in these woods? I would not have expected them so close to the house." She asked as they led Beau back to his stall and started taking off his tack and brushing him down.

"Um . . . wolves . . . well not according to the wildlife rangers." Now Hank seemed like *he* was evading something. She finished helping without saying anything else and went back into the house.

She found Logan had just come in from the back door and he looked decidedly wind-blown and his clothing had pine needles stuck in some places. He didn't even look at her; he just ran up the stairs, went into his room and shut the door behind himself.

I'm getting pretty sick of all this evasion and not telling me things that I feel I need to know. She went upstairs and went to his door and pounded on it.

"Get out here. I need to talk to you." She was angry and demanding, but she was completely flustered when he came to the door in just his jeans, his bare chest making her heart flutter regardless of how she felt about Michael. You just could not look at a wonderful piece of man flesh like that and not get a little bit weak in the knees. He was all muscle and tanned skin and she was positive that if Nikki ever saw him she would pass out from lack of breathing.

"Just what would you like to talk about?" He smiled that same sinister grin from when he had caught her. He must have realized that she was staring in shock.

"I . . . uh . . . have questions. Things around here are odd and I do not like the way I feel like there are things people are avoiding telling me. Just what is it that you guys are not telling me?" She had started off stumbling but quickly her anger ran over her body's reaction to the perfection of his muscles.

"I can't tell you everything. I knew you were smarter than Michael was giving you credit for. Not that he thought you were stupid, but he often allows his affections to blind him to other things. Come on in and have a seat. I'll tell you what I can and he will tell you the rest tonight, I promise. If he won't, I will. You need to know or you will probably take off and never want to see him again. That would break his heart, and maybe even his spirit. I will not see that happen to a friend." He stepped out of the door and let her take the comfy chair in the corner of his room. "Ask away." He said as he tugged on a t-shirt, making it easier for her to concentrate.

"You and Michael aren't quite human are you?" She blurted out and was only slightly surprised to see his eyes widen.

"You are very perceptive, as I said before, and no, not quite.

Let's just say it's a genetics thing." He shook his head with a smile on

his face. "He's never going to believe just how much you have guessed

at."

"Was that a Military thing?" She asked him her brow wrinkled

with the first signs of a head ache approaching. She knew if she didn't

take something to fix it soon, it would turn into one of her raging

migraines. Tension and stress did that to her.

"For me, it was kind of a military thing. Michael was different."

He ran a hand back through his shaggy blonde hair and scratched at the

stubble on his chin, waiting for her to ask more questions.

"Is that why the enemies and the running off and sending me

into hiding?" Kayla folded her arms across her chest. "I seriously doubt

the real estate business is quite that cut throat." There was aggravation

written in every line of her face and body, she was tapping her foot

even.

"It most definitely is. I'm impressed, and I do not impress

easily." He leaned back on the bed his t-shirt stretching nicely across his

chest and distracting her again.

"Marge and Hank know about this too, because they have been

evasive with some of the things they have answered or said." She stated

what she believed to be a fact.

"Yes, they know." He chuckled. "No wonder he is in love with

you. I know he has never met anyone like you. Neither have I for that

matter." His look said without a doubt that if she was single at this

moment, he would not hesitate to elevate that status to taken.

"Was that you out in the woods when I was riding?" She asked

getting the impression that his animosity with horses could have

accounted for the growling and she just knew, somehow, that Michael

would have told him to watch her. She watched as his eyes flew open

wide and he sat forward in shock.

"How did you come to that conclusion?" He was startled,

worried even. "What did you see, or hear?" Now he was the one

completely agitated and he stood up looming over her, and frankly even

as tough as she was, she was pretty frightened at that point.

"I didn't see anything. I heard what sounded like a growling

noise. It could have been a wolf or just a really good imitation. You

came into the house with pine needles on you, and I know that there are

none of those in the cow pasture, but plenty in the woods around here.

I assumed Michael wanted me watched." Now she smiled as she

watched his eyes widen even more.

"I'm done answering questions. The rest will have to wait until Michael is here." He stood and pointed towards his door. When she didn't move he opened it for her and stood waiting.

"Answer me, was it you in the woods?" She asked as she stood and traded him glare for glare. She refused to let him back her down on this. She felt she had a right to know. If it was him that had scared the horse, he could have gotten her killed. He knew she had never ridden before, and the horse could have easily thrown her. "Tell me or I walk out of here right now!"

"Yes, I was in the woods. Now out!" He slammed the door behind her as she left nearly tearing it off the hinges. She heard a ferocious growl from his room as she walked away.

She didn't want to make an enemy of Michael's friend but there was no way she was going forward with a relationship when she had so many questions and so very few answers. Now she just needed to get Michael to give her answers for all the crazy things she had running through her head.

She went back to her room and dug through the bathroom cabinets coming up with some Tylenol for her head. She took two with a handful of water out of the sink and then collapsed onto the bed

hoping she could sleep off the headache. *What am I thinking? What in the*

world am I still doing here? I should get up and leave right now. There is nothing

stopping me. Well except for the fact that I have absolutely no clue where the hell I

am or how to get home from here.

Chapter 9:

When she finally did collapse into sleep, her dreams were frightening and she tossed and turned like she was having a fit. In the dream she was being chased by a pack of dogs that were barking and nipping at her heals as she ran through the woods. She couldn't run fast enough and the pack of Dobermans and mastiffs soon had her cornered up against a river bank that she couldn't climb. She woke screaming and flailed her way out of the covers, and straight into the cool embrace of Michael.

"Was that a nightmare, my sweet?" He asked holding her as she trembled and cried in his arms. She hadn't had dreams this bad since she had moved away from the slums. She hated to cry in front of him, it made her feel weak and pathetic, like she was begging for sympathy. She just couldn't help herself at this point. All she could do was nod her head in answer to his question.

He gently picked her up and sat on the bed with her cradled in his lap almost like a child. He kissed her on the forehead and rocked her until her fears were soothed and she stopped shaking and dried her tears.

"I'm sorry." She hiccupped. "I normally don't have dreams that bad." She stayed curled up in his arms and nuzzled into his neck and shoulder. He felt like he had been sitting in front of an AC; his skin was chill and it felt great against her face, that fear and the nightmare made her feverish. She wanted to be angry with him, but right now she desperately needed his strength and closeness to chase her fears away.

"It's okay; you've been through the wringer as some people would say. I have you now and you're safe. Would you like to go back to sleep, or would you like to talk now? Logan has told me just how much you have guessed at." He ran his hands through her hair gently, holding her like he never wanted to let her go.

Kayla loved the way he seemed to smell like fresh pine forest at this moment. It was a change from his normal cologne or whatever he used to smell so damn tempting. She needed and wanted to talk to him, but was distracted by his bare neck so close to her lips. Daringly, she kissed the curve of his neck, just below his ear and felt him shiver slightly and chuckle.

"You keep that up and we'll end up in bed together, but not sleeping. I know how confused you must be. I think we should talk;

even if my body disagrees with me." He scooted her off of his lap, but

kept hold of her hand. He sat there like that for a very long time, just

looking at her. He seemed unsure of how to proceed and she didn't

want to rush him. She needed answers, but not at the cost of possibly

losing him. Now that he was sitting in front of her, she knew there

would be no way she could leave him. Nothing was going to prevent

her heart from longing for this man. They were connected and she

knew it down deep in her bones.

"Please," He began, "No matter what I tell you, no matter what

you find out, believe that I love you and that I would never hurt you for

any reason. I will always protect you, even if you reject me after what I

tell you." He looked like every word was pulled out of him by claws and

it pained him to even speak the thought that she may leave him.

"Reject you? Michael, I love you." There, she had gotten it out

and now he knew that she felt the same about him as he did her. "I

can't imagine not having you with me. I think I loved you from almost

the moment I met you. I don't care if you are into the mafia or a hired

hit man or some sort of genetically whacked out experiment." She put

her hand against the side of his face, her heart and honesty in her eyes.

"I am amazed to hear you say that. It will make this much

easier." He took a long pause, long enough that she almost spoke. Then

he began again. "Surprisingly, the genetic experiment is not too far from

the truth. What I am *is* genetically different from humans; it's a part of a

species thing, part virus or disease and mostly too far over my head

scientifically to explain well." He grinned ruefully, taking deep breaths,

trying to keep himself calm.

"Disease? It's not contagious is it?" She gave him an odd look

that he couldn't interpret right off the bat, and that made him very

nervous.

"Not without very specific conditions. We can do just about

anything and you won't catch it. I have to do two very important things

together in a very short period of time in order for you to *catch* it." He

sighed. "Logan has a very different type of condition. It is much easier

for what he has to pass on, but it takes a lot of exposure for it to pass."

Michael went silent and he looked like he was building up his courage.

"Have you . . . well I guess . . . Oh hell, I'm just going to be as blunt as

possible. I am what most people would call a vampire." He looked

down at his hand holding hers and expected her to pull away in terror.

Instead she shook her head and started laughing. He snapped his head

up to look at her his eyebrows scrunched in confusion. That just set the laughter into overdrive. She had to take some time to get herself enough oxygen to breathe. Her ribs hurt by the time she was done.

Once she stopped howling and gasping for breath she spoke. "That would explain a lot. Like one of the first times I saw you I could have sworn I saw fangs behind your lips. It also explains your enemies; others of your kind probably would not like you fraternizing with the food. It explains why you would never stay at my place if it was close to morning, and why you kept pushing me away. Not that I am sure I completely believe you . . . yet." She waited to hear his reply, she wasn't sure if she truly believed what he was telling her or not, but she was sure that he was being serious.

"I would prove it, but I'm afraid that really would scare you away." Michael stood and began pacing, agitation written in every line of his body. He went to the window peeked out the curtain, then walked to the door to peek out into the hall. Then he turned around and walked back to the bed where she was sitting, not yet returning to his seat.

"Well if you are a vampire then Logan has to be a werewolf." She started to laugh again, but then stopped at the look of utter shock on Michael's face. "What? You have got to be kidding me. Are you telling me he really is?" She sat on the bed completely stunned.

"Logan is right; you really are way too perceptive. Yes, he is a werewolf. You know, I never meant to fall in love with you. It's normally not a good idea and we don't like to broadcast what we are to the rest of the world. Marge and Hank know and back at my actual home there are some assistants and very close friends that are human and know." Kayla sat in silence thinking she should call someone to come pick Michael up for the loony bin. "I have to make you believe me. We can't go on without you knowing the complete truth. I will *NEVER* hurt you. Do you trust me?" He asked coming to sit next to her and feeling very relieved when she did not pull away but put her hand on his leg trying to comfort *him*.

"I trust you. I think you are one short step from a round rubber room, but Gods forgive me, I trust you." She watched him closely and saw his eyes take on that decidedly hungry look that he had worn sometimes when she had been close to him. It was a very intense look that she found equal parts sexy and creepy. The creepy factor actually made it just that much sexier.

"You can't even guess how hard it has been to keep my nature hidden with as wonderful as you smell. I have wanted to do this for a very long time. I will not hurt you, and from what I have been told it is very pleasurable to the humans that allow me to." He smiled and now she really did see the fangs in his mouth and watched in fascination as they elongated slightly. "I will not force you with my abilities, so I would like to ask you if you will allow me a small taste." He looked so very sexy and Kayla's heart was pounding so loudly that she knew he could hear it. He let the Hunger slip loose just enough for her to see it behind his eyes and he watched her closely for too much fear. Her heart was thumping and her eyes were wide, but he could smell the faint trace of arousal from her, so he didn't even consider stopping at this point.

She had never realized that she would get excited about the idea of being bitten, even in a normal sense, but the warmth spreading to certain body parts, told her she was most definitely aroused. "Will I be weak afterward?" She asked quietly, as she leaned closer to him showing him her neck as an invitation. He had to clamp his muscles tight to not throw her down to the bed and take what he wanted right then and there. The willing offer from a human was always powerful, but from her it was damn near a command that he do as he pleased. His will power was tested to the utmost at that point.

"Not at all. I will barely take even a tablespoon of blood." He ran his lips across her neck and moaning softly, he pulled her body

down on top of him as he lay back on the bed. She could feel her body

pressed against the full length of him and *he* was most assuredly excited.

"Quiet now. I want you to enjoy this." He kissed her neck and it was

her turn to moan as he ran his fangs gently across the skin. Shivers and

chills ran up and down her spine and she tilted her head farther to give

him more access. He did not need further invitation and he gently slid

his teeth into the skin of her neck.

The explosion of pleasure sent her reeling and she pressed

herself harder against him digging her fingernails into his arms. She

rocked with him as he sighed and moaned beneath her.

Michael could have wept with joy as he sank his teeth into her

and the first taste of her blood entered his mouth. Her smell was

delectable, but her taste nearly blew his mind. He had never had blood

like this. The flavor was richer and more amazing than the best wine he

had ever tasted. Somewhere between bliss, Hunger, desire and passion

he had the odd thought that maybe he should stop drinking from

criminals if the average clean human tasted this much better. He drank

very little and very slowly to make the pleasure for himself and the

pleasure he could tell she was having last longer. He could smell the arousal on her as she ground herself against him nearly panting. He

knew the precise moment to stop and when he did he bit his lip to let

just a tiny drop of his blood seep onto the punctures on her neck. They

would heal with the help of his blood, in minutes.

Kayla felt him pull his fangs free and then it felt like he licked

her neck. She was so turned on at this point that she was almost

frenzied. She clung to him desperately kissing any part of his skin that

she could reach, noticing oddly that he was now much warmer than he

had been just moments ago. When he turned her face to his she planted

her lips on his and tried to make him feel her passion, but he gently

pushed her away.

"Easy. I want that as much as you do, but there is more

discussion we need to have." He tried to pull back from her more, but

she determinedly held on with all her strength.

"I think talk can wait. I'm not going anywhere and for what I

just did for you, I should think you would owe me *something*." She

reached down to stroke him through his pants. "And you are obviously

willing. You may have wanted what you took for a very long time, but I

have wanted this for just as long." There was a noise from the room

next door that sounded like either a cough or a snort of laughter.

"Go take a walk Logan, a long one, and stop being a perv."

Michael said out loud. The sound of a door opening and closing was

followed by the sound of laughter and steps descending the stairs. Kayla

was shocked that he had been able to hear everything through the walls.

"I suppose that now that we are alone without listeners, maybe we

should just continue on before *you* bite *me*." Then he kissed her back

with as much passion as she had shown him.

They built the fire up in each other, their bodies meeting like

two parts of a whole; electricity touching every nerve ending. They

moved as one, each finding exactly the right moves and touches to drive

the other mad with need. And when the end came, it was like fireworks

exploding in Kayla's body; so powerful it made her scream. Her nails

dug into Michael's back and she was sure that she had drawn blood.

"I . . . wow . . . uh . . . breathing." Kayla lay on her side clothing

thrown all about the room and Michael lay just as naked facing her, his

hand gently brushing her face, neck and shoulders. He smiled at her.

She was sweating slightly and breathing heavily. "That was . . . certainly .

. . energetic."

"Did I meet expectations?" He asked grinning at her.

"Met and exceeded beyond my wildest dream. Was I, did I meet expectations?" She had never felt unsure of her bedroom abilities

before, but being a hooker did not make one a good lover, it just made

you familiar with sex.

"Oh my sweet, no one could have been better. I am blown away

by you." He kissed her on the end of the nose and hugged her for a

moment, while she blushed.

"Did I hurt your back?" She asked kissing his hand as he

brushed her lips with the backs of his knuckles.

"My back, why what do you think happened to it?" He rolled so

that she could see there was not even a mark on his back.

"I had my nails digging into your back. I thought you would be

bleeding." She ran her hands over his back and didn't even feel any

indents.

"You don't have enough strength to cut me with your nails. It

would have to be something much sharper with a lot more force. Our

skin is very resilient." He pulled her against him holding her tight and

his mind was whirling with unpleasant thoughts. "Why are you not

scared of me?" His voiced turned sad. "I thought you would be

repulsed or at the least too freaked out to stay around me."

"Michael, I have seen the worst that men and women can do to each other on the streets and I have had some of it done to me. You

have done nothing but make me feel safe, helped me get away from all

of that and made me happier than I have ever been in my life. You may

not be Human, but you are certainly more humane than many of the

people I have met and known. Hell, my own Mother allowed me to be

abused by her husbands and did nothing to stop it. I don't care what

you are, who you are, or what you do for a living. I only care that you

treat me the way you do and love me." She kissed him playfully on the

cheek and then gave him a very loving kiss on the mouth.

"Amazing; you are unbelievably amazing. I cannot even begin to

understand how I have become so very lucky." He hugged her to him

just reveling in how nice it was to have her next to him, knowing what

he was and still loving him.

"You're lucky? Sheesh, how do you think I feel? I was a drugged

up alcoholic hooker living by the skin of my teeth until you. Now, I get

you throwing money at me every time I turn around." They both

laughed and then went silent to snuggle. Kayla fell asleep and for the

first time in a long while didn't have any dreams at all.

Several hours later she woke to the sound of voices outside of the room and recognized Michael and Logan. She lay as quietly as possible; wanting to hear what had to be said. She prayed that Michael would no longer keep secrets from her at this point, but she still didn't know everything and she realized that.

"How soon will you turn her?" Logan was asking.

"Not yet. Things are too unstable and I want her to know more than she does. She has to make an informed decision. I will not make any choices for her; I love her way too much. I would like to get her farther away from Savannah, but I'm not sure if that is a good idea either." She could hear Michael sigh.

"I can't believe she accepted things so easily. You told her about me?" Logan asked.

"Yes. She believes me about myself I think, but there is still doubt about you. I know she recognizes that you are not normal. Heaven help me, I think you're going to have to show her for her to believe." Logan chuckled at Michael's statement.

"I love changing in front of people for the first time. It's so nice to watch that much shock on their faces. She doesn't have a twin by chance does she; I kind of want one of my own now. The only woman I have ever met that was that strong was Lily, damn Nicholai." There was the sound of someone patting someone on the back.

"I still can't believe my luck. I think she's awake now. Check the perimeter I'll be down shortly." Michael said his hand rattling the handle.

"Take your time, with a woman like that, I certainly would." Logan laughed and she heard him take the stairs down.

Kayla was sitting up in bed with the sheet wrapped around her when Michael came in. He smiled and bent down to kiss her softly on the lips. This time she didn't get the impression that he was trying to seduce her and she was too tired to want to have another go so soon after such enthusiastic lovemaking.

"Check the perimeter?" she asked. "Your enemies must be very nasty. What did Logan mean by turning?" She asked through a yawn as she stood from the bed to go get cleaned up and dressed. She didn't cover up, just let the sheet slip from her body as she stood. She had never really been insecure about her body and after years as a hooker not much made her shy. She could feel Michael watching her as she walked across the room to the bathroom to brush her hair out of its tangles.

"They are very bad and very determined to hurt me by any

means. By turning, Logan means turning you into what I am." He answered sounding almost worried about her reaction. He continued watching her, no longer looking hungry, just as if he wanted to hold her again. She started to tug her clothing back on, but had to stand on the bed to retrieve her panties from the ceiling fan blade where they had been flung. She was dressed and getting shoes back on by the time she had decided what she wanted to say.

"I think I really would need to know a lot more than I do before I make a decision like that. For now I am happy to be with you and to love you. Now that there will be no more secrets . . ." She paused. "There won't be any more will there?" She raised an eyebrow at him in inquiry.

"No, there will be no more secrets. Ask me anything and I will give you the honest truth, no matter how much it hurts." His voice sounded like he had gone through a lot of painful things.

"Well, first, I want to ask a silly obvious question. Are you really only 28 years old? I've seen movies about vampires and I have read a few books, how accurate are they?" She sat down right in his lap putting her arms around his neck and leaning her head on his shoulder. He sighed and hugged her close; still amazed that she wasn't running from him in terror.

"I was born in 1940 and I was turned in 1968. I will not age, like most of the stories and myths say. In fact I'm old enough that Marge is my Uncle's granddaughter. Werewolves do not age either. I *can* go out in the sun for a very short time, though only with lots of clothing, sunscreen and having fed immediately beforehand, but that is because of the strength I got from the one that made me. Younger, weaker, vampires would burn and blister, most to the point of having their skin fall off, some even die. It is very difficult for us to stay awake after the sun rises though. As we age we get stronger, and the stronger the vampire that turns us the stronger we are.

There are some things that are accurate others that are not. For instance, we are not averse to crosses or garlic, I actually like garlic. We have to sustain massive damage, like being torn limb from limb, or burned in order to be killed. The last vampire that had to be killed was bled, dismembered and burnt." He purposely left out the fact that this was the vampire he had killed recently, the one responsible for killing her next door neighbor from the slum apartment.

"Humans can pose a very real threat to us because there are many more of them than of us. Most vampires only drink about a tablespoon or two worth of blood every two days or so, which is less than a person would donate to a blood bank. The older or stronger a vampire the less blood they need. I feed about twice a week and need very little. We can survive on animal blood for a short time, or on packaged blood from a blood bank, but fresh living human blood is what we truly need." He stopped when he heard her take a breath like she wanted to say something.

"By *most* vampires, does that mean that there are some that are not drinking just a little bit?" She stated plainly. The mere thought of a vampire draining someone dry gave her the chills.

"As with humans, there are some of our kind that just have to make monsters of themselves. There is a structure of sorts to our society, but it's a long explanation and I will get to that at a later time. Let us just say that this structure allows vampires like me to hunt down and punish the ones that are endangering our secrets." She could feel his breath as he spoke ruffling her hair.

"How come humans don't know about you with the bad ones and even the not so bad ones? I would figure they would catch on pretty quick." She kissed his chin when he leaned close enough.

"Well, we have certain abilities to blank the minds of humans, and before you ask, I have never used that ability on you. Do you have

any other questions before we go get you some food?" He seemed

reluctant to let her go and she was certainly reluctant to leave his arms.

"I've seen you eat, but in all the movies vampires can't eat." She

threw out, just to keep him next to her longer.

"We only get the sustenance we need from the blood we

consume. Our bodies can process food to a very small degree. Just

enough that we can eat and drink normally, but it gives our bodies

nothing useful. Now up you get, I can hear your stomach grumbling."

He shifted to allow her to stand up and then he grabbed her hand as

they walked downstairs. It was about one o'clock in the morning and

Logan was sitting on the sofa with a sandwich in one hand and a soda in

the other, watching a movie.

Michael steered her to the kitchen and helped her fix a sandwich

and got her a glass of orange juice. "It's a good idea, even though we

only take a little, to fuel your body with good food and some sugar

afterward. I would hate to see you get ill because of something I have

done. Speaking of getting ill . . ." He paused looking like a naughty boy

caught doing something he shouldn't be. "I have a confession to make."

"Go on." She said simply, she was sure it couldn't be anything too terrible by the look on his face. It wasn't regret, it was definitely

guilt though.

"Back when you first met me, I had been following you for a

few days prior to that. I slipped something into that last alcoholic drink

you had. That is why you got so sick and why your detox from drugs

went so easily and quickly. I also would break into your apartment to lay

next to you while you slept. Are you angry?" He watched her face for

any sign of anger.

"How could I be angry about that? I just want to know what the

hell you gave me. I don't think I have ever been quite that sick before."

She finished the last bite of her sandwich.

"A vampire's blood is naturally detoxifying. If I were to take any

drug it would pass through my system in a matter of minutes. Alcohol

passes as well, but more like you drinking a large amount of water and

having it pass through in about an hour or two. Yes, we do have to

eliminate like a human, but only if we have eaten or had anything to

drink other than blood. With a human, consuming a small amount of

our blood will heal injuries, or do a very rapid detox if there are toxins

in the system. The drugs and alcohol in your system took the quickest

route out of your body. That tiny amount is also why you started getting healthy so rapidly. If you would like to feel your neck there will be no trace of the marks, because I put a little of my blood on them to heal them." He smiled at her shocked look when she felt her neck.

"It's not even the least bit sore there. I really should thank you for slipping me that; who knows how long I would have been sick and hooked on drugs without it. Are there any other benefits?" She asked putting her empty plate and cup into the dish washer next to the sink.

"Actually yes, there are a great many. If you drink a small amount every so often you will never get cancer, never become obese, and never get arthritis or dozens of other things. That is one of the reasons that some humans become our assistants or as one of my friends calls them willing victims." He turned to Logan. "Are you ready to show her?"

Logan laughed and stood up tossing the soda can into the trash. "You know it. Just to let you know Kayla, Michael is old and strong enough to wipe the floor with my ass. I know you trust him, so you know that he won't let anything hurt you. You may be frightened by my change and I want you to know you're safe." His tone was patronizing and she narrowly avoided slapping him in the face for it.

"Well thanks, but I've seen werewolves on TV before. I'm pretty hardy; I doubt I'll be scared. I'll probably be much more fascinated."

She folded her arms across her chest. "Well, go ahead."

"Uh, actually we should do this outside. I would hate to break something and Marge hates the smell of damp wolf in her house." Logan walked out the side door and Michael and Kayla followed, turning on the outside lights as they went.

"This is the reason that you can't help out with the horses, isn't it?" Kayla stated blandly.

"Yes." Logan crouched like he was going to spring at something and then she heard a strange gurgling growl start deep in his chest. He was facing her and she watched in amazement as his face began to sprout silver and black hairs. His ears slid to the top of his head becoming the ears of a wolf complete with fur covering. His mouth and nose elongated and everywhere she looked on him something was in the middle of a shift from human to wolf. His clothing simply slid from him as he shifted. It took mere seconds and before her stood the most gigantic charcoal, silver-gray colored wolf she had ever seen. His head was even with her waist and if he stood on his hind legs his head would have been over hers. He shook himself and then howled low and quietly, sounding rather sad.

"Uh . . . well . . . Yeah . . . not exactly like in the movies. I

thought werewolves were a melding of man and wolf, not just men that

turn to wolves." She looked to Michael who was shaking his head.

"What?" she asked confusedly.

"You handled that better than I expected, but I hope you handle

the next part just as well." Michael nodded his head in Logan's

direction, and she looked back and saw that his body was changing

again.

This time her fascination was touched with fear and awe. His

back legs were extending but remaining very similar to those of the wolf

he had just been with the toes being slightly longer. As he stood upright,

she could see that his upper body was getting larger and longer with the

front legs now becoming much more arm like. The fur on his chest and

stomach thinned and the human muscles he would normally have were

very much enlarged and very visible. There were claws on the ends of

his wider thicker fingers and he had a much flatter shorter version of a

wolf's muzzle in the middle of his face. The ears of the wolf were still

mostly there, only slightly smaller. When he finally stopped changing he

stood nearly seven feet tall and was wider and more muscled than any

body builder she had ever seen. When he howled this time it was like something torn from the chest of a human in utter agony blended with

the sound of a wolf.

"I can do much more damage in this form, but I am slower than

as the wolf." The voice that came out of Logan was very gruff and she

could feel it rumbling through her body. Kayla found Michael's hand

with hers and squeezed it gently to let him know she was okay.

"I know this may be rude, but may I touch you?" Kayla took a

step forward and Logan tilted his head to one side like most dogs do

when they hear something strange. It was such an odd expression for

such a large and aggressive looking creature that Kayla laughed despite

her trepidation.

"Do you not trust that what you see is real?" Logan asked,

looking as if he was about to back away from her.

"I trust my eyes, but I'm dead curious. It's gotten me into

trouble a couple of times. May I?" She smiled as he nodded yes and

walked forward. The first thing she touched hesitantly was his arm. The

fur was softer than she would have expected, but the muscle underneath

was as hard as stone. She ran her hand across his chest that had very

little fur on it and saw him shiver, but was not exactly sure why. "Lean

down please." Kayla asked and he obliged. She reached out and felt his face and then gently rubbed his ear. She giggled as he sighed and closed

his eyes. "Wow, I thought that only worked on dogs. I know there is a

pressure point in the ears that is calming. Thank you for allowing me to

do that. I bet you have one hell of a time scratching your back in this

form." Logan nodded and she happily walked behind him to start

scratching. His left paw, foot, started twitching almost immediately.

"Oh Gods that feels amazing. You have a year to stop." Logan

chuckled and it rumbled the ground beneath their feet.

"Okay, I want my girl back now." Michael said. He didn't look

jealous at all. In fact he was smiling like he was happy that Kayla had

taken this so well and was glad to see two people he cared about getting

along.

"I never had her to begin with." Logan stated as he finished

turning back into his normal form. He was completely naked and Kayla

blushed, turning away, thinking Nikki really would faint if she saw all of

him. "You don't have a twin or a friend just like you, do you?" He asked

Kayla as he tugged his clothing back on.

"I have a best friend, but as to her handling things the way I do,

I have no idea." Kayla said as she and Michael followed Logan back

inside. "Now that we are all together maybe you two can explain more things for me. Michael and you spoke of turning, please explain how

that works for you." She tucked her feet up on the couch and leaned

against Michael who obligingly draped his arm across her shoulders.

"Well let's start with vampires. It takes an exchange of . . ."

Michael stopped. "I hear a cell phone ringing upstairs in your room

Kayla."

Chapter 10:

"Shit, my phone! I'll be right back." She dashed up the stairs and dragged the phone from her purse, answering it in a rush and sounding completely out of breath. "Hello?"

"Kayla, girl, where in the hell are you?" Nikki's voice crackled across the line. Kayla knew she was worried by the way that she sounded, a touch of exasperation mixed with anxiety.

"I'm with Michael." She knew Nikki would remember him.

"Michael, is that the jerk from the bar?" There was so much sass in that question that Kayla cringed, waiting for the talking of a lifetime. She knew she needed to head Nikki off quickly before she got a good start.

"He did a lot of explaining and things are not exactly as they appeared. I'm fine." Kayla answered. She knew she wouldn't be able to tell Nikki everything, but she wanted to make sure that her friend was not worried about her.

"So he's not married?" Nikki asked, sounding interested, like she always did with a good tidbit of gossip.

"Nope, recently split. I'm sorry I worried you." Kayla sighed.

"He took me out of town for a bit. Work thinks I had a family

emergency. I'm not sure when we will be back."

"So *did* you?" There was a giggle from the other end of the

phone. "Give me the juicy details; he looked like he would be a God in

bed." Leave it to Nikki to get straight to the naughty part of any

conversation. She switched gears faster than a drag racer on speed.

"Nikki, you are such a perv, and yes, we did and yes, he most

certainly is. How did your date with Mr. Kenneth go?" Kayla wanted

her own set of juicy details. They always swapped gossip.

"It went nowhere quickly. He talked about you the whole damn

time. Girl, he is totally crushing on you." Nikki laughed out loud,

showing Kayla that she wasn't mad about the bad date.

"What did you call for, other than to track me down?" Kayla

was happy to hear Nikki's voice; she was a comforting presence even

across the phone line.

"I got a strange call from some man asking about you last night.

I tried to call you but my phone died out and I had to wait for it to

charge." She sounded concerned, not something Kayla was used to

hearing in her voice. Now she was wondering if Michael's enemies had tracked her down and how much danger her friend Nikki would be in.

"What did this person ask about?" Kayla came back down the stairs with the phone against her ear and her purse in the other hand. Michael saw the concerned look on her face immediately and knew that something wasn't right.

"He wanted to know your name, where you work, where you live and a whole list of things. I told him he would have to ask you and hung up. He was creepy cold sounding. I don't like it one bit. Can you come home?" Now there was a hint of fear in her voice; another thing that Kayla wasn't used to hearing. Nikki was a very strong young woman, and there had been days when Kayla had leaned on her for strength. If she was scared then that man must have really gotten to her.

"I don't know. I'm out of town with Michael. Do you want to come here? I would feel safer if you were away from there for a while." Kayla's main concern was anyone tracking her down and hurting Nikki to get to her and Michael. Logan and he both nodded when she made the suggestion.

"I can get some time off from work. It's the slow season. How will I get there?" Nikki sighed as if her shoulders had just relaxed a bit. She must know that getting out of town would make her a good bit safer.

"I can send Michael's friend to come get you. Look, if we can get you here can you bring me some of my things?" Kayla saw Logan getting up and gathering his things to leave immediately. It was just after 2 in the morning, and for Nikki to have tried to call her at this time it must have been a very unsettling phone call.

"No trouble at all I know where your key is. I miss you girl and I was worried. Anyway is his friend cute?" Nikki only seemed to think about one thing, hunky men.

"Yeah, he is, not sure if he's your type though; former navy seal." Kayla heard Nikki giggle.

"Ooh a military man. Tell me about him?" Nikki's voice went up in pitch, which told Kayla she was interested and excited.

"He's less Adonis and more Hercules. You should see him without a shirt; you would faint." They laughed for a little while. Kayla noticed as he was leaving, that Logan had a very smug look on his face and Michael was pointing at him with a scowl on his face. "Michael's friend is leaving here now. Call the boss as soon as the office opens, Michael's friend should be there to get you at about then. I need to go for now. Kisses love." Kayla said in their normal goodbye over the phone.

"You get some rest, you sound tired. Kisses to you too lovely."

Nikki hung up the phone and Kayla put hers back into her purse.

"I do not like this at all. If that call came from who I think it

was, your friend is in almost as much danger as you are." Michael

hugged her hard for a moment, his face a mask of concern. Kayla only

hoped that they got to Nikki in time.

"I gave Logan her cell number. He'll call and tell her when he

gets there." Michael said as he walked her back up the stairs holding her

hand. She wondered how he had gotten Nikki's phone number. "There

are some things I can do to help take your mind off of your worry if

you would like." That husky sound in his voice told her all she needed

to know about what was on his mind. She fell backwards into his arms

without warning him, knowing that he would catch her. He carried her

all the way to her room.

"I think I am in need of a lot of distracting." She said and

wrapped her arms around his neck planting a fierce kiss on his lips. The

door to the room swung shut with just a thought from him, but Kayla

was already too distracted to notice.

Nikki walked down a couple of apartments to Kayla's and

packed her a bag and then went back to her place to pack one for

herself. She made sure to put a couple of cute night things in there in

case this friend of Michael's was as hunky as Kayla told her he was.

Then she cleaned up her apartment and dropped her Siberian

husky, Tundra, at a neighbor's house. She was way too worried to try

and sleep and the neighbor was nice enough that when Nikki told her it

was an emergency, she didn't fuss about being woken up so early. The

neighbor had a boxer named Lovey and the two dogs got along very

well.

She got back to her apartment and waited, somewhat

impatiently for this friend of Michael's to arrive. It was almost eight in

the morning when she heard a vehicle pulling up into the parking space

in front of her apartment. She had already called her boss and left word

that she would be out of town for a while. She grabbed both bags as she

went to the door.

The man standing there with his hand raised to knock was

certainly the spitting image of Hercules. He was tall and muscled like a

God. His reddish brown hair was shoulder length and wavy, and he had

the prettiest green eyes she had ever seen. He did seem to be a tad bit on the unfriendly side with a slight scowl on his face, but maybe he was

just shy.

"Nikki, I presume." He nodded, picked up both of the bags and

tossed them into the trunk of the car. He then opened the door for

Nikki without saying another word. She locked her front door and then

got into the car with him.

"Kayla didn't tell me your name when I called." She said lightly,

hoping to help him get over his shyness.

"Oh, uh, sorry, I'm Jason." He was backing the car out and

turning to leave the complex where she lived.

"Like you said, I'm Nikki; it's nice to meet you. So what was it

like being a Seal?" She smiled her most charming smile. She wanted to

make a good impression on anyone this damned cute.

"A what?" He looked uneasy and that feeling seeped across the

car and latched on to her. She didn't like it at all. The uneasiness made

Nikki's stomach twist up and she felt slightly sick.

"A Navy Seal, Kayla told me you were a former Seal?" She

swallowed hard and started wondering if this was not the friend that she

had been told about.

"Oh, yeah, um, it was difficult and I can't talk about it." He went silent, making her feel even more ill at ease. She looked at the

roads around them for a time and didn't like that her instincts were

cranking up into high gear.

"How far are we going? Where are we going for that matter?"

She was starting to get very leery and all of her instincts screamed for

her to run.

"South." He looked at her out of the corner of his eye and

sighed, and then he began digging in his pocket.

Nikki just knew at that point that things had gone terribly wrong

and she was in very real danger. She didn't really know how much

danger until he had stabbed her with a needle and the feeling of floating

washed over her and her eyes fell closed of their own volition.

"Michael, are you sure I got the right address and number for

that matter? No one answered the cell when I call." Logan spoke into

his phone as he stood on the tiny front porch of the apartment that he

had been directed to at just after eight A.M. There was a very faint

lingering of Kayla's scent and that of another female. He didn't think he

could have gotten lost, and he was starting to feel that something had

gone very wrong. He thought he could smell a male, but it was very faint, he would have to turn into his wolf form if he wanted a better

sniff. This was not the place to be switching forms.

"I gave you the right address. Maybe she is inside asleep."

Michael answered him. Logan could hear Kayla asking what was up

from over the phone.

"I don't hear anything. It sounds and smells like no one is home.

I'll go in and check. Ask Kayla where the spare key is for this place and

her own." Logan was not happy about this, he knew something was

wrong. He had tried to call Kayla's friend and hadn't gotten an answer

and now this.

Once he got that information, he hung the phone up and went

to Kayla's apartment first. He found nothing amiss and went back to the

apartment where Nikki was supposed to have been waiting for him.

Once inside it looked like everything was as it should be. There was no

sign of a struggle.

It was as he was leaving that he caught a good whiff of the male

scent that made him very worried for Kayla's friend. Whoever it was

that had come for Nikki had been a willing victim, someone who

hovered around real vamps, let them drink, and prayed to one day, be

turned. There was the faint scent of vampire overlaid on top of his very human scent. He would have missed it had he not gone inside; it was

just at the doorway.

Michael held Kayla close knowing how much she was worried

about her friend. He nearly broke his own cell phone when it rang and

he pressed it to his ear. "Yes?"

"She's been taken. It seems they probably tricked her. I have no

clue where they went, but I have the scent of her, the bleeder and his

vehicle. Would you like me to follow it?" Logan's voice was tense and

there was the low growl of anger underneath that Michael had grown

accustomed to.

"Not alone. I know you want the trail to stay fresh, but they may

have set traps. There is not much we can do without your pack."

Michael held Kayla down in the couch. The minute she knew something

really was wrong she had started to rise and wanted to leave to help find

her friend. "They are likely using her as bait. I do not want to risk them

laying a trap for any of us." He said this while making sure to make eye

contact with Kayla, letting her know that he was not going to lose her to

carelessness.

"What do we do now?" Logan asked tersely.

"Now we wait. They expect us to make the next move, but our move will be to set up a better defense and a much tighter ring of protection around those that we care about." Michael hung the phone up and looked at the fire in Kayla's eyes as she ground her teeth in anger and frustration. "By the Gods, you are beautiful when you are angry."

Nikki came into a very cold and very black room. There was a ceiling above her, painted black with a red light bulb hanging loosely from a dangling socket in the center. It cast a sickly sanguine glow about the room. The walls were draped in some shimmery maroon fabric that made her feel like she was in the middle of a blood cell. The bed she was on was soft enough, but it felt like this room was in the middle of an ice box or very deep in a basement. The damp cold seeped into her bones making her shiver. All of her things had been taken from her and she realized in a sudden rush of alarm that she wasn't wearing a stitch of clothing.

She turned her head from side to side gently to look around better. She tried not to move too much. Whatever she had been drugged with had given her a terrible headache. It pounded with the blood in her veins and she felt tears springing to her eyes in pain and frustration. There did not seem to be a door or any windows to this

room. She didn't like the fact that she had been left unbound. That

meant that they did not expect her to be any trouble, and if she was

trouble that she would be expendable.

She couldn't hear anything outside of the room, so the walls

must be very thick. The silence and stillness only served to increase her

building terror. The floor was carpeted in a thick black rug, and the bed

she was on sat in the very middle of the room, looking far too much like

a sacrificial altar for her comfort.

She tried to clear the fog from her mind by going over

everything she could remember about the man that had come to get her

and when that ran out, her mind drifted on its own to her history.

She had never told Kayla about her past. She knew that Kayla

would be afraid for her sanity if she were to ever hear just what her

friend thought had killed her parents so many years ago. Nikki had only

been ten years old; her family had all lived near a lake in Washington

State. As nature lovers, both her parents had lived the organic all natural

kind of life that most people thought only applied to hippies.

Her father had been a State forestry officer and her mother had

home-schooled both Nikki and her brother. If anyone had deserved to live long full happy lives, it was her family. Fate had taken a bloody

hand in their life and she was still enraged about it, the horror of what

had happened rolling through her and making her ill even to this day.

She had gone to spend the night with a friend in the town

nearby and that left her Mother, Father and her older brother at their

woodland home alone. The call from the police for her to come home

had been a shock at four in the morning. When the friend's mother

dropped her off, at first no one would tell her anything. There had been

wildlife rangers and police cars all around her home. They wouldn't let

her get close until the three gurneys had been brought out with three

closed black zipper bags on them. She wanted to scream, cry, and rip

open the bags to beat on her parents' chest and make them wake up.

She didn't, because somewhere deep inside she knew that they were

beyond help.

She had broken from the grip of the officer with her at that

point and darted into the house. She stopped just short of a puddle of

red on the floor at her feet. The house was a scene of carnage that she

knew would haunt her dreams for the rest of her life.

The furniture was overturned, her father's shotgun was on the

floor not far from his favorite leather chair and it was bent nearly in half at the middle. Curtains were shredded and everything that was breakable

looked to have been broken, chipped, or smashed. The smell of blood

made her gag, and she tried to breathe as little as possible. There was an

overwhelming scent mingled with the blood that was unmistakably the

smell of dirty wet dogs.

"We think it was a mad bear." the officer said turning her and

leading her back outside. "There are no tracks around the house, but it

rained pretty heavy last night, so there might not be. We have trackers

out looking for a bear that has gone off his mind. Your Mother's sister

is going to be taking you in. She will meet you at the hotel after all of

your things are collected. Anything you want from your parent's is yours

to take as well of course." He kept blabbing, and somehow she knew

that he was distinctly uncomfortable. She let his words wash over her

for a moment, before they latched on to what he had said about keeping

things.

"I want my father's rifle." She said simply. She couldn't shoot it

yet, but she had her own .22 that she could practice with. "It smells like

dog in there, maybe they should look for wolves." She sat on the hood

of his car. "And I am going with them before I leave with my Aunt."

The officer stared at her with shock. "Miss, I know this must be terribly difficult, but chasing a mad bear is not a job for a young girl

such as you." He coughed as she turned her eyes on him and he could

see that she was on the edge of tears and sanity.

"I could care less what is and isn't a job for me. I am going to

track down whatever did this and kill it. And it's not a bear!" The tears

started at last, pouring down her face that was scrunched up and red

with anger.

She had made that promise in the heat of anger and desperation

and still had not been able to make good on it. She did follow the

rangers into the woods hunting what they kept insisting was a bear. She

only found one track under the cover of a tree. The low branches above

had been the only thing keeping the track from washing away in the

rain.

Her father had taught her how to track and she knew that she

would never forget this print. It wasn't a bear; it wasn't even a wolf as

far as she could tell. It looked like no other print she had ever seen

before in her life. There were parts that seemed human and yet others

that looked very much like a wolf.

She tried and failed to drag herself out of her memories, but at

some point in her mental wanderings, she fell asleep. She hoped that when she woke again that her head would not be hurting and that she would be able to think clearly enough to try and find a way out of this trap.

"Distract me." Kayla said as she paced the entire length of the living room back and forth. Michael knew she meant him to distract her in a non-sexual way. She had chewed all of her fingernails down to the nail beds and she was now frantically twisting strands of her hair around her fingers.

"I can go back to explaining changing if you like. It's enough to get your mind working." Michael sat on the couch waiting for Logan to return with his pack. That was something that had surprised her. She didn't think Logan was the type to be in charge of anything, but it seemed that Logan wasn't just any werewolf. He was the head of a large pack of eleven other werewolves. Most of the pack had military training of some sort, but others had drifted away from other packs that were too rough and aggressive for their tastes.

"If you think it will help." She sat on the couch next to him for all of a few seconds and then stood up again to pace.

"This is going to be graphic." He stated simply.

"I think I can manage." She said with a glance and a smile. He looked way too calm. She was sure he cared about her and Logan, but other than that, how much did he really have invested in helping others?

"I'm sure you can. Okay, so with vampires, in order for the change to take place, a human has to be drained to the point of death, just before the heart gives out, and then they are fed the blood from a vampire to replace what they have lost. As long as a human has more of their own blood than that of a vampire's in their system they will remain human. If that ratio is reversed then the disease, virus, whatever it is, takes over. I've heard a rumor that they did one change completely by machine. They hooked a vampire up to one side and a human to the other and as they drew the blood out of the human into the vampire, the vampire's blood was being pulled and pumped into the human. It seems possible, but certainly not preferable." There was an odd sound in Michael's voice and Kayla was wondering what it was there for.

"You're not expecting me to run screaming yet, are you?" She asked stopping in front of one of the windows to look out at the dark.

"Well, to tell you the truth, the more you find out about my kind and Logan's, I do keep expecting you to lose it and take off." There was a long pause and silence from him before he spoke again. "I am getting the feeling that you are highly resilient, flexible, and open minded. The humans that we run into the most are usually from two different types. You have the horror fiction fans that can't stand how non-threatening we are. We also run into the Goth crowd. Those are truly bothersome. You know the ones that are totally infatuated with all the stories and myths about vampires. They are so excited to find out about us that they nearly shove their throats under our fangs. It's a bit disturbing really." He shook his head.

"Yeah, I think that would be rather unsettling. So tell me about those that are not from those two groups." She asked while she took out her cell phone for the tenth time and checked it.

"When you are turned you are no longer capable of being able to reproduce. That would be one of the unhappy side effects. Some of us have never had children of our own before the change, others have. Those like me often adopt children from terrible situations. I rescued a little boy not long ago whose mother was thinking of selling him for more drug money. He's now safely tucked away in one of our human assistant owned boarding schools, being much better cared for and even making friends." Michael smiled, remembering the little boy in tears of joy over having a bed of his own with actual blankets.

"You rescue children and then tell them about yourselves? I'm sure they turn out well adjusted." Kayla said sarcastically.

"We don't always tell them. We adopt out some of the children to completely human parents and they never know anything other than that they were orphans and got adopted. Others that seem strong enough to handle the truth are told when they begin to ask questions. Both Marge and Henry were raised by vampires. Marge was raised by my cousin Carmen who is the only member of my family to have actually been turned, besides myself. Henry was rescued from an abusive father. We have contacts with some of the clerks and courts; we get the needed papers forged and then the children are safe. Before you ask, I have NEVER taken a drink from anyone under the age of 18 or from anyone not able to make an informed decision on their own, unless they were criminals. Also, I have never killed a human while drinking. None of the vampires is my sector would."

"Sector?" Kayla asked quietly.

"There is a breakdown of groups in our world. First you have the neutrals who are vampires who refuse to swear loyalty to any other vampire. Some of them hunt like I do, from the shadows and leaving not a single body in their wake. Others are much more violent, they drain their victims in an act of gluttony that is frankly disgusting. Half of

that section is at least aware enough of possible troubles to cover up

what they have done. The rest are truly uncontrollable, and that is where

Logan and I sometimes end up hunting down my own kind. There are

vampires, like myself, that feel they should live peacefully with humans

in the shadows, only allowing select humans to know about us. We do

sometimes need someone capable of spending large amounts of time

outside in the sun to help with certain aspects of everyday life.

"Unfortunately there is another group that feels that vampires

should rule over humans and use them as slaves and food. Thankfully

those fight among themselves as much as they fight against us. Most of

my enemies come from that section; one enemy in particular is

Nicholai. He is angry that one of the women he wanted for himself

chose me over him. I should never have been with Eliza. She went

behind my back and had another vampire change her. It has been a

nightmare with that woman ever since.

"Sometimes when you turn people, it brings out the worst in

them. Eliza is like that; for now she remains loyal to my sector, but

Nicholai is winning her over. She would kill you if she knew about you,

probably out of jealousy." Michael stopped and took a sip of wine from a glass he had sitting on the table next to the couch.

"Well that explains about you, but what about werewolves, how does that work?" Kayla stood up and began pacing again. "Do you know how much longer it will be before Logan gets back with the others by the way?"

"They should be back any time now. Logan will send a few off with Nikki's scent to try and track it, but with her being put into a car, it will be much harder. They can at least figure which way they went. That should tell me if they are going where I think they will.

"Let's get back to turning someone. I've only seen the werewolf change done once. Before that I had no clue how they were changed. He was actually half dead when he was changed; it saved his life." There was a strange pause here and Kayla wondered what it was for. "The werewolf doing the changing must be in their hybrid form, the one halfway between wolf and human. There is something in their saliva that carries the virus. It is only present in large enough amounts in that form. As the wolf there is very little and as a human there is almost none. The person getting changed must be bitten several times and the bites must be licked by the one or more doing the changing. It takes much more time for the change to sink in. With vampires once the transfer is made the person is almost immediately different. With werewolves, even after they are infected, it takes a day or so until it is complete. They are not able to change forms unless it is completely finished. They are at their most vulnerable during that phase. Once they are finished changing though, they are much stronger than a vampire of about the same age, but slower and less resilient.

"Werewolves are a good bit easier to kill; all of the stories about silver are mostly true. It's corrosive to their bodies. It makes cleaning a silver made wound extremely difficult. A silver bullet is always a major problem especially because the bullet doesn't come out quickly. All in all, I would say that vampires are like wine, we get better with age, and werewolves are like explosives, powerful from the start. The only reason I can wipe the floor with Logan is due to my age and the age of my blood parent. You can also strengthen someone already a vampire by having a blood exchange with a more powerful vampire. My sire was strong because her sire was strong and very, very old. If you decide to make the change, I will have my sire do it so that you and I will be equals." Michael stopped abruptly as Kayla pulled away from him and gave him a strange look. "What, now your bothered? What was it?"

"Your sire was a female? I think I may be very jealous." She had a touch of a frown on her face.

"Don't be; she's like a mother to me, or an older sister. I have never had a true love . . . until now." He said the last brushing his fingers across her cheek, making her blush.

"So have you ever changed anyone?" She asked secretly hoping that he had not and yet fearing more jealousy if he had changed a woman.

"No. I have facilitated the change for others. Getting them acquainted with those of my kind that wished to change them, but I have never felt the need. Like I said, I will have my blood parent change you so that we can be equals, or as close to as possible given that I was changed a long time ago." He held out his hand to her. "Please, come, sit a while, you are wearing yourself down and making me nervous all at the same time."

"Fine, but only because you asked me to." She sat down squarely in his lap curling herself up so that she could still kiss him. He certainly did not mind her kisses and he even drew one out into a rather passionate beginning to more that was interrupted by the sudden appearance of Logan.

"Gag me, you two get a room." Logan snickered as he walked

into the living room from the garage.

"Glad to see you are back. Where is the rest of the pack?" Michael asked Logan as he dropped down into a chair looking rather tired and wind-blown.

"Oh, I have them out running the perimeter. I did leave three of them behind at Kayla's place just in case there are any . . . visitors. Plus the three I sent on the trail. They'll come back as soon as it goes cold and let us know which way. I also got a message from Jenna a while ago. You need to call home and make sure that everything is set up for you to be out hunting for a while. You know how they get when they don't know where you are and how long you are going to be gone for." Logan stood back up. "I have to tell Marge about the extra mouths to feed. You know she'll want a few of us to help her go for a grocery run. She knows we are always starving."

Chapter 11:

Nikki woke again in that same strange room, but this time she was not alone. There were three people standing over her and one of them was a large muscular black man that wasn't wearing a stitch of clothing. She blushed and turned to look at the other two people in the room.

On her left stood a tiny blonde woman with a wicked smile on her face. She looked like an ice princess, and Nikki couldn't control the feeling that she wanted to be as far from her as possible. Next to the blonde stood a man that if anything was even more frightening than the woman.

He was so pale and his hair so light that Nikki thought he may be an Albino, but his eyelashes gave him away. They were a darker golden blonde that told her he probably bleached his hair for the startling effect. If the woman in the room with her could be compared to ice, then this man was liquid nitrogen. There was no expression on his face and his pale gray eyes had an almost dead look to them.

"I am glad to see that you are awake. I do hope you have

enjoyed my hospitality. I think maybe it is time for you to repay me for

that hospitality. Marcus, please see that our dear friend here repays us

for all of our kindness. See that you don't forget the *change*." The man

and the woman left the room laughing as the dark skinned man

approached her. There was no way she was going to be able to outrun

or out fight this man, but she would be damned if she went down

without at least marking him. In the end he had her pinned to the bed

and was snarling as he tied her with ropes so that she could not get

away. He had a bloody lip, a bloody nose, a bunch scratches and a nasty

bite on his hand. She had a busted lip and a long list of bruises including

one on her right cheek where he had back handed her across the room.

Once she was secured, he stepped back from her and his body

seemed to shift and twist, mutating in her vision; she thought that she

had been dropped into the middle of a nightmare. When the smell of

him hit her, she knew she had found the thing that had killed her family.

She was screaming before he even touched her and when that

thing leaned its mouth in to bite into her right shoulder, she thought for

sure she was going to pass out. She didn't pass out, and when he

speared her on his manhood while licking the wound in her shoulder

she desperately wished she had.

Thankfully after what seemed an eternity of brutality, and at least four more bites she did black out. Her body had taken way too much at that point and she was almost glad to seek oblivion.

Her head felt like a jackhammer was going to work on her temples and any movement made her stomach churn. Nikki now wished she hadn't woken up. She was alone in the room again. This time her only company was the pain and sickness. Everything hurt, she was sure even her hair hurt. She was untied now and there was dried blood, "dog" slobber and other fluids all over her. She rolled to her side and saw a bucket with water and a rag hanging over the edge. Next to it was what looked like a bowl of meat scraps and bottled water.

When she was finally able to stand up, she kicked the meat scraps into the corner and chugged the bottle of water as fast as her stomach would allow her to. She then set about washing off as best she could with the rag. She was in tears and hissing in pain every time she touched one of the bites, but she wanted to make sure all of "him" was off of her.

She felt like she was getting a fever for some reason and really hoped that thing hadn't had rabies. Her skin felt too warm, her eyes felt hot and she had that all over ache and chill that spelled impending

illness.

She found the door behind one of the red curtains and of course

tried to open it to no avail. She was naked and cold so she tried to pull

down the curtain. The longer she tried the angrier she got and the more

she felt flushed all over with heat. She finally gave it one last giant tug

with a growl escaping her and yanked it free from the wall. She took a

good look at it and saw that it was just long enough to wrap around her

like a toga. She tied it in place and then looked behind every other

curtain for any possible way to escape since the door wasn't an option.

She found nothing but more blank cold walls.

She wanted out before that thing came back around for another

go. There was only that one door and up in a corner she would never be

able to reach was an air vent that was too small for her to crawl

through. She turned her attention back to the door, shoving her hair

back out of her face so she could get a better look.

It must have a heavy lock on the outside of the door because

there was no visible way to use anything to try and pick the lock; there

was no opening for a key on this side. She wondered if there was a way

to slide something between the door and the frame and pop it open that way, but nothing in the room was suited to that purpose.

She finally gave up because her head was pounding so hard and she was getting dizzy. She lay back down on the bed hoping this terrible feeling of illness would subside soon. She was asleep in moments.

She woke again some time later to the sound of the door opening. It was a different man this time. He watched her warily and set down a plate with a sandwich and another bottle of water. He stepped away from the food and leaned his back against the doorway out. She was too hungry to care that he was there so she just snatched the food and water and scarfed it down as quickly as she could without choking. She noticed while she ate that someone had come in and cleaned up all the nasty meat. They had even cleaned out the bucket they had left her for her personal needs.

The man just stood there watching her the whole time never saying a word. His only distinguishing feature was that his brown hair was long enough to put into a tail at the nape of his neck. Everything else about him was so bland and normal that he would disappear into any crowd as a total non-entity.

When she was finished he tossed a small jar of some kind of pink ointment or salve onto the bed next to her. "It's for the bites. It really helps." He said and then turned and left her in the room all alone

again. By this time she was getting really crazy with being trapped and if

it wasn't for the flu like symptoms that she felt creeping up on her, she

would have been beating on the door. As it was she was starting to get

the shakes and chills, so she yanked down another curtain and curled up

in the bed with it, wrapped around her. She was asleep before her head

had even found the pillow.

"Wake up. Psst, can you hear me?" The voice shoved Nikki

roughly from her sleep and her eyes flew open. She nearly jumped from

the bed, but managed to stay put with only a minor amount of flailing.

She felt worse than ever, every sound seemed magnified and the light

was so bright her eyes hurt. When she rolled her head to the side as the

dizzy spell settled, she saw the man who had brought her the sandwich

before.

He stood just inside again with his back pressed against the

door. "You haven't used the ointment. Do you need help? I promise, I

mean no harm. I went through the same thing you are going through

now, a couple of months ago. Well, without the sexual assault thank

God." He didn't move, just waited patiently for her to muddle things

through in her head.

"Help?" she asked her mouth and lips dry and her throat raw.

"Yes, help put the ointment on the bites you can't reach. It will help them heal faster and ease a good bit of the pain and sting. Maybe even take down your fever a notch. I also left another sandwich and two bottles of water. You probably have a raging thirst at this point. I did." He still stood there just watching. He seemed like the absolute last thing he wanted to do was startle her or heaven forbid anger her.

She nodded as she grabbed the sandwich and bottles and pulled them back onto the bed with her. Now he moved over to the bed slowly, his hands always held open facing her. He picked up the jar and opened it. She got a whiff of honey, mint, lavender and blood. She had no clue why blood would be in a healing cream, but at this point her bites hurt so bad she would have done anything to help them. A small part of her mind wondered why she could smell everything in the ointment that well.

"Would you mind taking off the toga, I need to be able to see all of the bites." He stepped behind her and waited while she adjusted. The first touch of cream on a bite made her wince and shake in pain, but it quickly numbed and then that whole area of her back that had been on fire numbed out and started feeling like normal skin again instead of seared beef. She sighed in relief as he dabbed the stuff on the four

wounds she had on her back and shoulders.

"Dear lord, he mauled you terribly. I had three bites on my arms

and that was it. You've got to have at least seven or eight, and those are

the ones I can see." When he finished he handed her the jar and walked

back to stand at the door. "I figure you can reach the rest of them. The

stuff is kind of sticky but that goes away quickly. The relief should last

for at least a couple of hours. Here," He tossed her another bottle of

water and a small pill bottle. "There are four Tylenol in there, it's not

much, but if it takes the edge off, then it will be worth it, right?" He left

her alone and closed the door behind him. She heard the lock slip into

place and then his footsteps retreating.

She downed the pills and the water and then went to work on

the rest of her bites. Once she was done her exhaustion caught up with

her and mixed with the relief from the pains of her bites she was able to

sleep really deeply for the first time since being drugged.

It was voices out in the hall that brought her around the next

time. She kept still and strained to listen, making her ears pop until the

voices became much clearer.

"Is it working?" This was a deep voiced man, that didn't sound like anyone she had heard before.

"Yeah, she has the fever and the aches. Her senses are cranked

up, I can tell by how she winces at the light and loud noises. She hasn't

gone off her mind yet, maybe she can make it through." This voice

belonged to the man who had been somewhat nice to her.

"I don't think Nicholai expected her to be strong enough to

handle the change. He wanted to dump her raving mad on the doorstep

of Michael's little tramp. What do we do with her now? He won't want

to keep her, and killing a werewolf isn't easy, even if they haven't

completed the change yet." The deeper voice sighed.

"We could blind fold her and throw her out in the woods

somewhere. She won't likely know how to track us back. Not like she

would want to come back anyway." Her helper said.

"How much longer before she can fully change?" Deep voice

asked.

"Today, tomorrow at the latest. I'll figure out something, you

just go make sure that all the blood suckers are down for their daily

naps." That was the nice guy again. She kept her eyes closed as she

heard his boots coming towards her door. The door opened and closed

and she rolled towards it opening her eyes.

"Still feeling badly?" he asked setting down another sandwich and more water. He stood waiting again while she ate.

"Better, some. What is happening to me?" She asked after the sandwich was nothing but a memory.

"They are turning you into a werewolf. That is why you have felt so sick. Are you seeing, hearing and smelling things more intensely?" He walked around behind her. "Here let me check your bites again. They should be mostly healed now." She untied the toga again.

"How long have I been here? How long before I . . . well you know?" She didn't even flinch when he touched where the bites had been.

"These look so much better. Most won't even leave a scar. You're on day three of the change. If you heard us talking, which I think you did, you will know that you should be able to change either today or tomorrow. I would wait if I were you. The longer you hold off, the easier it is on your body." He finished checking her bites and then sat with his back to the door. "You want out of here?" She nodded. "So do I. I was forced into the change too. I stayed because I thought I had no other choice. It has been hell and I have been trying to find an excuse to get out of this place. You are my ticket out." He sighed. "Now for the hard part, there is no cure for what they have done to you. You will

have to either learn to live with it or get killed by something bigger than

you are. You are going to have to learn to control your emotions, which

now that you are changing, are going to be much more intense. You

seem calm now, and I don't know how much of that is shock, or you're

still getting over the change. Do you think you can make it if we try to

escape?"

"I can manage. So, what's to stop me from going up there and

killing those maniacs right now?" She growled and shuddered and he

stood back up. If she started getting volatile he would have to change in

order to keep her from killing him.

"Take it easy, lady. Those maniacs would turn you into a big rug

on the floor in a matter of seconds, especially the really cold blond guy,

Nicholai. I'm going to try and get you back to what Nicholai calls the do

gooders. From what I've overheard, your friend is with them. If I can

get you there, they will protect you. They may even accept me, but I

doubt it." She was still shaking, but at least she was staying human for

now. "Will you trust me?"

Nikki was silent for a very long time trying to calm the vibration

she felt rolling through her. Trust him? How could she trust him? He was here in the place with the people who had done this to her. He had

been kind though, and he did seem to be her only way out of here. She

nodded her head, not wanting to trust her voice for some reason.

"Okay, you stay here and I'll bring back the things we need to

get out of here. If anyone else shows up but me, then I got caught. I'll

do my best; like I said, I want out of here as much as you do." He

turned and left, still locking the door behind him.

By the time he returned she was nearly crazy with worry that

somehow he had gotten caught. He came in now wearing black military

pants and a gray t-shirt with combat boots. He had the two duffel bags

that she had packed for going to see Kayla; one for herself and one for

her friend. He also had a back pack strapped across his back and a

handgun on his hip.

"I got everything of yours that you had, including your cell

phone. Keep it off until we can get out of range. I have my Harley

pulled around and ready; you just have to get dressed." He tossed her

both bags and she caught them without thinking, something she

probably would not have been able to do prior to whatever this change

was doing to her.

"Good, your reflexes are coming in nicely. I'd show you exactly how a change takes place, but the main house is asleep right now, being

daytime and the vamps being what they are. Most of the wolves are out

scouting and tracking. We need to move quickly." He certainly looked

nervous.

Nikki tugged on a pair of jeans, a t-shirt, socks and boots. Then

she dragged her blonde locks back into a pony tail at the nape of her

neck.

Once she was dressed, he pressed his finger to his lips for

silence. "If anyone speaks you say nothing. I'll handle things. I've

already told them you are showing signs of not making it. Sometimes

the change is too much and the human body starts to fail. I'll carry all

the bags. You just shuffle your feet and stare at the floor. Act like you're

really weak."

"Got it." she said already bowing her head.

"They think I'm taking you back to kill you on your friend's

doorstep." He put his hand on her shoulder and she didn't pull away,

she just looked down at it then back at him.

"I'm not like them. I can't do the things they want me to do

anymore. Let's get out of here." He turned and led her out of the room

and through the house to freedom.

"But Nicholai, you haven't given me enough time. I'm sure I can draw him to our side, he is just stubborn and it will take more time." Eliza pleaded with the pale blonde man before her. He seemed so pale as to be almost translucent. His eyes were a terrifying ice gray and he kept his white blonde hair cut just to the shoulders and brushed back off of his face. Eliza shivered as he turned those eyes on her.

He was across the room standing in front of a fireplace of charcoal colored stones. His white hands cupped around a mug of fresh warm blood. He sipped at it as if it was just a cup of coffee or tea. The lights in this grand room, with its floor to ceiling windows draped in lavish red silk curtains and the two separate fire places, were turned low. Even Eliza who was eccentric and very dark spirited was put off by the creep factor here at Nicholai's home.

"You, my dear, have had more than enough time. If he has not fallen for your considerable charms by now, then he is not going to. I will be sending my hounds out for him this time. Those of the council fear it is asking for trouble to tangle with Michael. I will show them that he is no greater or better than any of us, no matter who his blood parent is." Nicholai turned away and whistled sharply. There was a huge amount of scratching and clicking as three large Dobermans and a

Rottweiler came hurtling around the corner into the room. They

immediately sat at his feet looking up at him for instructions. "My

dearest pets, I need you to find Michael. Track him down and show me

where he is and who he is with. Do not approach him and do not harm

him." The dogs took off like rockets scrambling to get through the door

and out into the wild to track down their prey.

"Why do you not want them to approach?" Eliza asked her face

alight with curiosity.

"That is for me to know and you shall only find out if you break

with him and pledge to me. I will not have him forcing the truth out of

you. As for our little guest downstairs, I am sure that the transformation

will unseat her mind and having the only friend she knows go stark

raving mad will certainly make Michael's pet to rethink her priorities."

He smiled, but there was only cold calculation in it. He brushed his

fingertips across her cheek and leaned in to smell her skin. "Let us retire

to my bed to discuss that shall we." His next movement was to grab her

by the back of the neck and force her to precede him into his bedroom

where he had his way with her slowly, with his hands around her throat

nearly choking her, all the while smiling down at her in cold viciousness.

Michael slid into the bed next to Kayla as the morning sun began slipping up over the horizon. She snuggled in close to him but did not truly wake up. His body was telling him that he desperately needed the rest. He knew without a doubt that Logan and the pack would watch the house and surrounding area and only wake him if there was no other choice.

He refused to tell Kayla, but he was almost sure that her friend Nikki was dead by now. Nicholai would probably display the remains in such a way as to cause both Kayla and Michael the most amount of pain.

He was starting to have a hard time keeping a coherent thought so he wound his arms around Kayla and let the sleep he truly needed take over.

Logan was out on the perimeter with two of his pack mates when he heard the sound of the intruders. There was no question in his mind as to what had been sent. Obviously Nicholai now knew where they were. His mates had already changed form and were hunting down the Dogs. The Dogs were created much in the way that a true vampire would be, but something in the virus did strange things to any animal's

mind.

Dogs were much smarter than normal and had much greater

endurance, strength and speed. They were also mentally bound to the

vampire whose blood was used to create them. In this way, the vampire

who made them could see anything that the Dogs were looking at and

to some degree send them commands over great distances. Unlike

vampires, Dogs were not harmed by sunlight.

These particular Dogs had the stench of Nicholai all over them

and Logan had no intention of letting them carry any information back

to their master. With a screaming growl he ripped into his blended form

and tore after the filthy beasts.

Chapter 12:

"Kayla it's time to get up." Michael shook her shoulder gently but she refused to let go. Instead she twined her arms around his neck and let him pick her up. "Logan and his pack just took out a group of Dogs that tracked us."

"What's so bad about some dogs?" She asked still groggy.

"Dogs, capital 'D'. They have been altered by the same virus that created me. They are fast, fierce, and completely loyal to the vampire that created them." He sat her down on the edge of the bed. "We are going to have to leave. They will follow us away from here if Logan and his pack haven't killed all of them. I'm leaving a few traps and Logan has some friends that are not part of the pack that are willing to stand guard. No one knows that these people are close to me. They think they are simply workers that I have hired. Once we are gone they should be safe." He hugged Kayla close for a moment when she shivered.

"Those enemies really aren't that bad are they?" She said feeling very frightened for her friend Nikki.

"Yes they are. I will explain more once we are safely away from here." He stood up and began layering on clothing, including gloves and a fedora.

"Why do you need all the extra clothing?" She stood up and began stuffing things into the gym bag she found at the bottom of the closet and tugging the jeans she had been wearing back on.

"It's daylight and I'm not hanging around until dark. Nicholai's vampires refuse to run in daylight so it is safer for us." He took out a bottle of sunscreen and covered any exposed skin in the SPF 100.

"Are you going to be safe?" She touched his arm lightly and time seemed to freeze with the two of them looking at each other. She could smell the sunscreen and feel the thick jacket under her hand but the only thing in her mind was the way his eyes looked. Two blue rings of absolute shock. He simply stared at her as if he could not even begin to understand the words that had just come out of her mouth.

"You are worried for me?" The tone of his voice matched the disbelief in his eyes.

"I love you, and no matter how bad-ass you are, I will always worry." She leaned up on her toes and kissed his cheek, then went back to getting things together for herself.

"I'm old enough and strong enough that with the extra clothes and sunscreen I'll be fine for very short distances. The windows in the

SUV have a special sun filter coating. I'll still have to lay in the back

undercover. The less stress to my body now, the better off I will be, if

there is trouble later." He picked up a second gym bag with his own

things in it. "I'm ready if you are."

"There's just one last thing." Kayla tossed her bag on the floor

and walked over to him her eyes amber flames in the shadow of her

hair. Michael's breath caught in his chest as he watched her move.

There was something in her motion of a predator already and he felt his

body stir to it.

She leaned against him; her whole form pressed against his and

she kissed him full on the mouth. He kissed back at first but pulled

away in bewilderment at the taste of blood on his lips. She leaned in

again and he saw that she had bitten her lip and was offering her blood

to him again. He knew she was trying to give him strength to help him

and it broke his heart with joy.

He was not going to squander this gift. He pulled her to him

and fed from her lips until she moaned against him, his hand caressing

tender places through her jeans. Her pleasure built until she pulled her

lips from his and let out a moan that left her panting and shaking in his arms.

"Would you like me to carry your things to the car, my lady?" He asked her with his eyes aglow with passion and mirth.

"And me as well. My knees are rather weak." She squeaked as he scooped her up and grabbed both of the bags. She wrapped her arms around his neck and curled into him. "Every woman needs a man like you."

"Not every woman…" He laughed. "I can only handle one and you are the only one I want." He kissed the top of her head and smiled.

When they reached the bottom of the stairs he set her on her feet and held her hand as Logan pulled the SUV into the garage and closed the garage door. They heard it sliding down into place and then walked out waving to Marge and Henry as they left.

"You smell like a beach bum." Logan said as both Kayla and Michael climbed into the back of the SUV where the seats had been lain flat.

"There happens to be a good reason for that you know." There was a black tarp attached to rollers on the sides of the SUV that pulled back over the flattened seats. It covered from the back of the front seats all the way to the back gate of the SUV and there it clipped into place leaving Kayla and Michael in almost complete darkness.

"Where are we going?" Kayla asked as she lay snuggled with Michael. The space in the back was cramped and she was sure there was some kind of buckle or clamp digging into her hip bone, but she couldn't think of anywhere she would rather be at this moment.

"I think Logan decided to take us in a direction they wouldn't immediately think to look for us. We are going towards where I live. Am I right, Logan?" Michael tried to shift a bit to give her more room. He had removed his hat, gloves and sunglasses and tucked them above his head within easy reach.

"Right, you are. Boston sound like fun to you Kayla?" There was a chuckle from the front seat that she barely heard through the covering.

"Where do you live anyway?" Kayla asked him.

"Harrisburg, Pennsylvania. Yeah I know, so very un-vampire like. It's actually a decent place to live." He laughed and then continued. "Well it's really on the outskirts but that is the closest big town. When I took over this sector my biggest concern was getting away from all the temptation of New York."

"Took over, you mean, you are in charge of, well, of whatever you call a group of vampires?" She was astonished all over again. It

seemed like the more she found out about him, the more unlikely it was

that this man would be satisfied with a women like her.

"My blood parent had the job before me, but she was running

into some of the problems with advanced vampiric years. There is a

weariness that can come over us where we really do not want to interact

with others, humans or other vampires. Most get through it with the

help of a lover or with some family, so to speak. The vampires that face

it alone usually end up willing killing themselves." He sounded very

familiar with this subject.

"So she was tired of living? Does she have someone special?"

Kayla wanted to know that this woman was happily taken by someone

else. Jealousy wasn't one of her good points, but that didn't mean she

didn't have it.

"She has her husband, Roland, now. He was my tour guide in

Romania when I went there. We became close friends. He was human

at the time by the way. I'm the one that encouraged him to talk to this

tiny little woman at a bar; it turns out that was of great benefit to both

of us. That woman was Jenna who was soon head over heels in love

with Roland. I think she turned him less than a week later. I was still bouncing around in Europe when they both tracked me down to tell me the good news about their marriage. That is when the accident happened." There was a catch in his throat as he tried to speak. Whatever had happened, Kayla guessed it must have been traumatic. "I went with a new guide that was doing climbs at this one ridge; I can't even remember the name now, it's been that long. Well the ropes he had were old and worn and I couldn't tell that one of mine was wearing out. I trusted my weight to that one rope alone for just a moment and fell. I don't know how I survived the immediate damage but it was clear to me that I was not going to live out more than a day or two. Jenna came to me in the hospital they sent me to that night, I thought most of it was hallucinations from the pain killers I was given. She changed me right then, as a way of thanking me for bringing Roland into her life. Talk about the most excruciatingly wonderful experience I have ever had. Turning hurts, I won't lie, but as the pain ebbs and the new sensations take over it makes you feel alive like never before."

When he stopped speaking, she was silent for a while, forming the question that had invaded her mind. "Do you have that weariness?" She thought he may have when she first met him. So many times she had seen sadness in his eyes.

"I thought I was getting it, and then Jenna insisted that I go to Savannah. That is where I found you, and do you know, now that we are together and you know everything, all my weariness has disappeared." There was a snort of laughter from the front seat. "Logan, how much farther, its cramped back here and I'm sure Kayla would like to stretch her legs."

"Not much farther until the first stop, maybe an hour or so. Once we get there you can cover up and get back inside the safe house until dark. It will be easier to travel by night at that point." Logan called from the front of the vehicle, all traces of levity now out of his voice.

Kayla was getting drowsy from the long ride like she always did, so she snuggled up against Michael and was quickly asleep. She seemed to sleep a lot around him and wasn't sure if it was from too much excitement or something he was doing to her.

Nikki clung to the back of her rescuer as his Harley sliced through the sunlight patches on the road. Her heart was thumping in her chest and the blood was an audible sound in her ears. *So now I will be the monster I have hated for so long.* She thought to herself. She wondered if this would make it easier for her to track down and kill the specific monsters that had killed her family. She knew that she was a long way from her home state and that she might never find them. Maybe she could somehow take her revenge by killing those that murdered other families? Maybe even find a way to prevent such horrors from happening to anyone else. Maybe that was why she had been spared so long ago on that night.

The Harley rumbled beneath her and she wished desperately that she had ear plugs; the noise was excruciating. The man who had rescued her, she didn't even know his name. Not that it mattered at this point. She was feeling weak and jittery and was just praying that she didn't fall off the back of his bike. How was she ever going to face Kayla after becoming a monster? How was she going to let her know that she really and truly did not blame her for what had happened? How was she ever going to find a decent man? Could she handle being with a man after what had been done to her? Could she even have children now? These thoughts chased each other around in her head making her sick. She latched her arms more firmly around the man's waist and hung on for dear life, hoping just to make it through the next few minutes.

"I take it you are still sleepy?" Michael asked kissing Kayla on the top of her head.

"I can be persuaded to wake up." She mumbled nipping at his chest through his shirt.

"I think now is not the time for that sort of thing. We are at the safe house." He chuckled as she rubbed her eyes while he pulled his hat and gloves back on. "Logan you have the garage door down yes?" Michael asked.

"Yep, just got it closed all the way. You're good to go man." Michael pulled the cover open and he and Kayla crawled out of the back of the SUV. She was very stiff and Michael actually picked her up to carry her inside. The whole picking her up thing was nice at first, but she was sure that she needed to remind him that she had two functioning legs.

This house was a lot like the house she had grown up in from what she could see. It looked like your standard sub urban house. They entered into a small laundry area and that led to an eat-in kitchen. By the time her legs were done with the tingling they had made their way to the living room and hallway.

"I set up safe houses every so often. I also switch out which houses that I own are safe houses. As you can see all the windows have light blocking curtains." He looked around to find the nearest clock.

"It's still about three hours until sundown. I'm going to go get some

actual rest. Kayla go ahead and make yourself at home, take a shower,

watch a movie, whatever you want. There should be frozen stuff in the

freezer and some canned stuff in the cabinets. I don't like to keep stuff

that will spoil in these houses, but I don't want anyone going hungry

either." He said that with a look at Logan who was already pulling a

couple of frozen pizzas out of the freezer.

"I think I'll take a shower and grab a bite, then maybe join you

for a short nap." She poked her head into each open door until she

found the bathroom. There was a very nice Jacuzzi style tub and she

decided a really long hot soak would make her feel ten times better. She

ran the water as hot as she could stand it then stripped down and

slipped in. There were a few different specialty soaps on a nearby stand

and she picked the one that was labeled "Amber" it smelled absolutely

wonderful.

She was finally able to fully relax some of the muscles that had

been all knotted up. She actually had to catch herself as she almost

started dozing off. Kayla felt like her arms and legs were made of lead,

she just didn't want to get up out of the tub, but she forced herself to anyway. That was when there were angry words and yelling out in the main part of the house. She quickly wrapped a towel around herself and ran to see what was going on.

"And I told you to stay clear of that place!" Logan was enraged and she thought he looked pretty damn scary too.

"I caught her scent leaving the place with another of our kind. I didn't get anywhere close." This was a new male voice that Kayla didn't recognize.

"They could have followed you here anyway. With it being daytime who knows what kind of wolves they are sending our way." Logan kicked a chair and it literally punched a hole in the wall and stuck there. "You may as well tell me which direction they were going in when you picked up the trail. We need to rescue her friend."

"They looked like they were following the trail out to that farm you guys were at. I tailed them for a bit, where they couldn't scent me." He started to continue but Logan put a hand up.

"They, she's human, what do you mean they?" He looked at Kayla standing there in just a towel and then back at the other member of his pack.

"She's in the middle of the change. She's been bitten by one of our kind." He had this kind of apologetic look on his face like he really

had not wanted to say anything in front of Kayla.

Her heart felt like it had plummeted into the floor. She suddenly

needed Michael more than ever and then he was there behind her with

his arms wrapping around her holding her close. "It will be okay, Kayla.

We will find her and Logan can help her transition gently. Logan, send a

few of your men after them. Don't let them get away and don't let any

harm come to Nikki."

"I'll go myself. I failed to bring her here to safety and I feel this

is partly my fault. We need to have a long conversation, outside now!"

He pointed at his pack mate and then at the door. The two of them left

shortly after.

Michael led her back to the bedroom that he had been using and

they sat down on the bed. She didn't even think about being strong at

this point, she just burst into tears and let him hold her until the flood

of emotions past.

"This is entirely my fault, isn't it? I mean if I had stayed away

from you this wouldn't have happened to my friend. I can handle me

being in danger, but she didn't deserve this. She's more than just a

friend; I have family members that aren't as close to me as she is." Kayla had finished crying but her eyes were still red and her nose was stuffy.

"I'm a real wreck when I cry."

"It isn't your fault at all. If any blame should be laid, it should be on my shoulders. I just couldn't help myself; I had to have you with me. If your friend is still able to function enough for an escape at this stage of the change then there is hope that she will make it through alright. We just have to hope that Logan finds her before the other side. We also have to figure out who rescued her and why." He pulled her down into the bed beside him and held her as close as he could without hurting her.

The motorcycle rumbled to a stop at the beginning of a very long dark dirt road. Nikki was about as sick to her stomach as she could get. Her head was pounding and she was chilled all the way through.

"Can we stop now? Where are we anyway?" She asked the man who had rescued her. He had told her his name was Todd when they had stopped once for her to be sick.

"We are where we need to be. I can't go any farther without the wolves protecting this place thinking it's an attack. So we wait until they come to us." He turned the bike off and pulled a thin blanket from one of the side bags and handed it to Nikki. "Here, I can feel you shivering. You've just hit the last stage of the change. You should start feeling better over the next day. Look down the road, I think we have company." He nodded his head in that direction and she turned to look.

There were three pinpoints of light, probably flashlights. That meant that at least three people were coming out to meet them and that also meant that at least that many were probably hiding in the woods to either side of the road.

"I smell . . . I smell more. Like you, they are like you." Nikki could smell them for sure and she could tell that there were a total of six different ones. She assumed that the extra sense of smell was something that came along with being turned into a monster.

"Yes, they are like us. Now be quiet and let me do the talking. I'm hoping to keep us both alive, since we smell like we just left the house of the bad guys." He went silent and held both of his hands palms out, up in the air. She just sat on the back of his bike gripping the blanket around her shoulders and feeling like she was dying.

"Why are you here blood pawn?" The man who spoke was still a good ways off but Nikki could hear him as clearly as if he was standing right next to her. His voice sounded like he was being insulting

"Pawn no longer, I saved this one, a friend of a friend to you. I only want protection for her and at the least safe passage for myself." He didn't move. "I know where your watchers are and I appreciate the strength with which you approach this delicate situation." Nikki was shaking so hard that she nearly tipped the entire bike over, him included. "Look, they started the change in her and she needs help. Can you at least help her?" He stopped trying to be political.

"Is that the girl, Nikki?" The voice asked, sounding worried and shocked for the first time.

"It is. She just hit the final stage of the change, and its coming on stronger than with most. I really think she will need help. I've never helped with this sort of situation, and I am not qualified to assist." He sounded worried, but to Nikki at this point everything was a blur. The voices became muddled and the shadows reached out to grab her and then there was this light shining into her eyes blinding her. She howled and lashed out feeling the skin peeling from her arms and hands as she did.

There was no stopping the transformation at this point; all she could do was hang on to a tiny portion of sanity with a death grip and hope she made it through. Her flesh burnt and twisted and her muscles were tearing loose from the bones beneath. Everywhere on her body felt like molten metal had been injected into her veins. She started screaming and then her ears perceived that the scream became an agonizing howl ripped from her chest. There were hands all over her pinning her down holding her in the mud there on the dirt road. She wanted to bite them and fight them off. She knew she had the teeth for it now, knew down deep that she was the beast and could make them pay for what they were doing.

A voice broke through the night, it started as a howl of dominance and she felt it in every fiber of her being, she must obey. That howl became a man yelling, she could not tell what just yet, but his voice held a calm authority that broke through her panicked aggression.

"I said leave her to me. I will handle this." Her head cleared marginally as the hands left her and her eyes adjusted now that the flashlights were no longer blazing into her face directly. She stood up, shaking the mud off. She hunched her shoulders and looked down at her hands seeing the true form of the beast she had become for the first time. She saw the claws on her hands the pale white and cream fur that now covered her arms and legs.

Her clothing had fallen away and now lay on the ground at her feet, she wasn't even sure she could call them feet at this point. They

looked like exactly the kind of thing that would have left the print under

that tree all those years ago when her parents had been killed.

It wracked her heart with agony to know that she had become

the thing she had most wanted to hunt and kill. It hurt so much that she

began an anguished keening. Then there was a very large hand much

like her own transformed hand resting gently on her arm. She saw it

through the tears rolling from her eyes and down into the fur on her

face. She touched that face with her other hand and keened harder.

"Beast." She managed with her much changed mouth and face.

She looked up at a darker black and gray version of what she must have

become. The one before her shook his head.

"Beauty, strength." He said to her softly. "Run with me." He

held her hand and pulled her along until they were running freely under

the cover of night. She felt the wind through her fur and it felt

wonderfully cool against the fever hot skin. His hand was warm and

strong in hers and somehow he made her feel secure.

There was no need for words, just having someone there to help

her run out the extra baggage and emotion gave her a sense of release

and freedom. She tried to match him stride for stride seeing a new kind of beauty in the strength of his muscles under his fur. There was no

path through the woods where they were running, but somehow, she

saw everything clearly and knew that if she did stumble this new friend

would catch her.

When she finally began to tire she slowed down to a walk,

panting heavily with her sides heaving and her pulse throbbing. She was

feeling very strange, almost like she needed to shed this new fur

covering and just be herself once more. She had no clue how to begin

to change back; she wasn't sure how she had changed in the first place.

Her companion stopped a ways ahead of her and turned back to look at

her, his head tilted slightly to the side. He was panting, but not as

heavily as she was.

"Tired?" He asked and then walked back to her when she

nodded yes. "That was your first change; changing back hurts a whole

lot less and is simple." She wasn't sure how he formed so many words

with what was essentially a muzzle. "Think, remember how it felt to be

who you were, how it felt to be in your human skin. Picture yourself

how you always see yourself and hold that thought strong in your

mind." He put his massive hand on her shoulder. "You can do this; you

own your body and soul. You are a strong woman." He said everything she needed to hear, and how he knew exactly what she needed, she had

no idea.

She closed her eyes, a soft whimper escaping her from between

her teeth. She forced everything she had just experienced from her mind

and thought back to how she had felt right before she had been

kidnapped. How she had taken the time to shave her legs, her best

feature in her opinion, and how she had made sure to choose clothing

to show off her athletic curves. How she had brushed her long blonde

hair until it shimmered. Part of the way through those thoughts she felt

a tingling sensation all over her body, it was warm and almost pleasant,

like muscles that are sore after working out. When she opened her eyes

she was nearly blind in the dark, but she could feel that she was back in

her original body and she wept with thanks.

"I'm me again! Um, I'm naked, aren't I?" She put her hands to

her skin and found that she was indeed naked. "I can't see very much."

"It's okay. I've kept the form to get you safely back to the farm.

Can I carry you?" She looked up and up at the sound of the voice and

could make out only the eye shine. He hadn't seemed that huge when

she had also been transformed.

"You can still see in the dark." She made it a statement and covered her chest with one arm and her privates with her other hand.

"I can look away if you would like. To be honest, I was enjoying the view." He watched her blush a very pretty shade of pink.

"Can't someone just bring me my clothes?" She still refused to move any closer to him or to uncover herself. This was becoming very awkward.

"The others have taken your things up to the main house. I can make sure that the parts you want covered are hidden by my arms if you allow me to carry you in. Besides that, the bugs out here are going to start descending on you shortly as the smell wears off." He sounded amused, and she knew he was probably right.

"Fine, but I don't want you getting grabby." He picked her up as if she weighed nothing and cradled her delicately in his hairy arms. It was amazingly warm and comfortable and she was so very tired. She wasn't sure when it happened but at some point she fell asleep with him carrying her.

Chapter 13:

"So you have her?" Michael asked Logan over the phone. He had just put Nikki into the bed that Kayla had so recently used and covered her up to allow her to sleep.

"Yeah, I got here just as they were confronting her rescuer. She was right at the brink and all the stress set her off. The pack didn't even get a chance to change so that they could handle her in the hybrid form. You should have seen her! She was amazing and so strong for a first change." Logan sounded like he was in awe, not something that Michael was used to hearing in his voice.

"How did you get her changed back? I know that can be an issue with first time shifts, especially under stress." Michael asked him, hoping he had not resorted to the "Taser". It was a sure fire way to bring a wolf down temporarily, but it was very hard on their system.

"I was already shifted and I pulled the pack off of her. She started keening and I knew she was scared and in shock. I finally got her to run with me. I knew if she could exhaust her body that she would think more rationally and be able to get herself changed back. Thank goodness I am in amazing shape. After a first time change, she nearly

ran me to exhaustion." There was shock evident in his voice.

"What was that, Kayla?" Michael asked and Logan could hear

her telling him that Nikki had been a high school track and field star

and still kept up with a lot of running.

"I heard that. No wonder. She is a marvelous piece of work. I

haven't seen legs like that in I don't know how long, human and

blended form. She nearly had me drooling." Logan and Michael both

laughed at that statement.

"You did ask for a strong woman of your own did you not?"

Michael asked him, still chuckling.

"Be careful what you ask for you may get it. I know how the

saying goes. I've dealt with plenty of male turnings, but this is the first

female change I have ever seen. I'm not sure what I should do

differently. I know I have to be careful with her; she's not going to want

to see herself as a monster. How can I let her know that all three of her

forms are power, strength, and beauty? I can't even begin to tell you

how amazingly gorgeous she is in her hybrid form. Her skin just a touch

darker than normal, her fur all beige and cream with white tips, oh gods

and those blue eyes like glaciers. I'm rambling aren't I?" Logan stopped and heaved a deep sigh.

"Yes, my friend, you were. I can understand completely though. Once you find a woman that grabs your attention, not much else floats through your mind." Michael reached out and grabbed Kayla's hand as he said that.

"I think I hear her stirring in her sleep. I want to be there when she wakes up. Tell Kayla that what happened to her friend wasn't her fault and that I will do everything in my power to make sure she comes through this in the best way possible."

"I will Logan. You take care and I will see you both when you get here." Michael hung up the phone and Logan put his cell back into his pocket. Now he could go watch her in her sleep and make sure he was there with food and water for her when she woke up. New wolves were always hungry. Hell, all wolves were always hungry. He made sure that he had a few extra sandwiches for himself on the tray that he made for Nikki.

He carried the tray up silently not wanting to wake her from her sleep, but she cracked her eyes open the minute the door handle turned. Seeing her now, her hair tousled from sleep, her eyes bright with a touch of fear, he felt his heart skip for a second. She looked so beautiful that he wasn't sure, how was he even going to speak to her. She had a different kind of beauty than Kayla, who was just a touch on the exotic side.

Nikki looked like home grown American goddess. A face that was strong and cute at the same time with golden hair like honey and ice blue eyes that cut you deep. He had never seen anything that he had ever wanted more.

"I'm Logan, Michael's friend. I was the one who was supposed to pick you up from your place. I am so sorry that they got to you first. How are you feeling?" He sat in the chair away from the bed once he had placed the tray of food on the bed next to her. Sometimes, with the newly changed, you had to treat them like a skittish pup.

"Hungry." That was all she said as she snatched the bottle of water off of the tray with a sandwich and began eating at top speed. He noticed that she still did it delicately, like a lady, making sure not to leave crumbs everywhere and even using a napkin from the tray to dab the corners of her mouth between bites.

"That happens a lot in your situation. Do you remember anything from last night?" He was really hoping she did, because that meant that there would be a lot less explaining and that her mind was accepting the change better.

"I remember everything, from the moment those two ice cold lunatics left me in the room with a monster until I passed out being carried by . . . wait, that was you, wasn't it?" She held her third sandwich forgotten in her hands.

"Yes, I ran with you and talked you through changing back and then carried you inside. Two ice cold lunatics? You didn't possibly get any names did you?" Logan sat forward, he assumed that she had been taken by Nicholai's followers and names could confirm that suspicion.

"The maniac that bit me, licked me and raped me was named Matt." She was growling under her breath as she spoke her hands clenching so hard that the knuckles all cracked, her sandwich was beyond ruined.

"Easy now, just breathe, we can't get to them yet, but I will give you first shot at him when we can. I know who Matt is, he works for Nicholai, Michael's biggest complication. I figured that is who must have taken you. Please breathe, now is not the time to stress your body. You've been through hell and you need to heal." He really didn't want to have to use the tranquilizer pistol in the back of his waist band, but he also didn't want her going ballistic, changing, and tearing the house apart.

For her part, Nikki hardly noticed that she was naked and that she was sitting in the room with the most amazing piece of man flesh she had ever laid eyes on. It was that realization that really brought her around and got her thinking about what she needed to do to get back to as close to normal as she could. She closed her eyes and did some of her Yoga breathing, and when she had calmed down enough she brushed the crumbs from her hands back onto the tray and pulled the sheet up to cover her breasts.

She almost smiled at the hint of disappointment on Logan's face. "I'm sorry, I just have so much going through my system, and I can't keep my emotions balanced out. It's making things hard to think."

"Yeah, it's like that at first. You should start getting used to the extra influx of adrenaline and emotion pretty quickly though." He stretched and leaned back in the chair again, and now Nikki got a good look at just how well put together he was. She could clearly see the outline of his abs and pecs; dear lords above what a magnificent piece of work he was.

"I guess I should thank you for helping me." Logan heard the husky tone her voice had dropped to and he knew it was time for him to leave the room. He was not about to let *that* sort of thing happen until she was in complete control of her emotions and her shifting. A shift in the middle of sex could be awkward at best and deadly at its worst.

"I've got to check and make sure everything is ready for us to leave to meet up with Kayla and Michael. You finish your food. Your bags are at the foot of the bed. No thank you is required." He saw a flash of pain shoot across her face. "I'll be back to check on you later. Can't leave a pretty girl alone too long, some strange man may come along and snatch her out from under your nose." He said, it knowing that it would show his interest, but still diffuse a potentially dangerous situation. The pain vanished from her face to be replaced by the most adorable blush.

He left the room repeating in his head that he could not have sex with this woman. On the seventh repeat he added to himself, *yet.* Then he started whistling happily as he made sure all of his pack mates were doing what they were told and that they all had complete orders. Now it was time to go and speak with this Todd character and find out what his story was.

"So what am I going to do about my job?" Kayla asked. She and Michael were sitting on the roof of the house watching the stars and moon above them. He had spread out a blanket for them to lie on and there was a picnic basket with food and drinks in it just to one side. They had been in this safe house for a few days now and as happy as she was to spend time with Michael, Kayla was starting to get restless. She missed her home, her work even, and she definitely missed Nikki.

"You could always quit work and let me take care of you, but something tells me you would not be happy with that situation." Michael really did seem to know her well.

"No, I don't want to be just a kept woman or anything like that. I like taking care of myself, but I meant for the immediate emergency. Do I call them and tell them that I need more time off or do I just go ahead and quit and find another job after all this dies down?" She sighed and twisted some of her hair around her finger. "I don't like feeling dependent on others for the things I need." She already hated the fact that Michael had taken her away from her home and her work, but it was for her own safety and she liked living more than feeling self-reliant.

"Well that law firm has a main branch in Harrisburg. I'm sure we can get you transferred there. You could still live on your own if you wanted, or you could move in with me. I could make you pay rent if it would make you feel better." He laughed and she rolled her eyes.

"I still have not wrapped my head around the thought of changing, but if I did, how would I work at a law office then? I thought I'd never want children, but what if I change my mind and then it would be too late. There are too many things to think about." She shook her head trying to clear the cobwebs of confusion out.

"This is not a conversation I expected to have at this stage. It feels like I am rushing you into a choice, and I do not want to do that. You have time to make a decision based on all the facts. I think you should probably talk to some of the other vampires I know, mostly the females and get their perspective on things. I can't tell you about the mothering instinct and the need for children as I can never experience that as a woman would. I do feel the need to protect children; that is why I rescue the ones I can." He sighed; this was becoming much more than a complication of safety issues.

"Michael, do you hear anything? I feel like I'm being watched. I used to get these feelings sometimes when I was alone. It's like there are eyes on me." She went silent and he closed his eyes turning his head from side to side and listening intently.

"I think we have worn out this safe house. Do you want to make a run for it or make a stand, there only seems to be two of them, both are younger than me by the smell." He stood up and picked Kayla up to jump down onto the back deck causing the deck lights to flash from over their shoulders out into the yard. This gave them the advantage of being able to see the intruders and having the intruders partially blinded by the lights.

"I'll follow your lead here." Was all she had time to say before a young man, maybe 18 at most and an even younger girl of about 15 walked up to the porch, but kept their distance.

"Hello there young ones, what brings you to one of my homes?" Michael's voice had taken on a tone that stated he knew he was in charge and was used to being obeyed.

"We didn't mean to intrude. We're being chased. I caught your scent and the . . . lady's, and well if you were friendly, three are safer than two." The boy spoke and the girl just hung on to his arm as if she was drowning.

"Yes, three are safer. I'm only friendly if you are. Who is chasing you?" Michael put his arm around Kayla saying without words that she was spoken for and not to be touched.

"Some crazy tiny blonde woman kidnapped us and changed us. She tried to get us to start draining people, but Penelope and I don't want to hurt anyone. We aren't like that. My name is Johnny by the way." He patted the girl on the shoulder. "He won't hurt us Penny. He's like us, you don't have to be scared."

"I'll help, if I have your word that you will not feed on anyone without taking each and every precaution. No killing, you must wipe the memory, and no permanent injury; also no feeding on anyone that has been claimed by another Vampire. Do I have your words?" Michael's voice crackled with some unknown power that made both of the others bow their heads.

"We swear it, my lord." Both of them spoke, though the girl's voice was just a whisper of sound.

"Come on inside then. We seem to have a common enemy. I know this woman you spoke of and I can assure you that you are very lucky to have gotten away. I'm hoping that she did not trick you into running in order to follow you to me. Michael opened the back door and everyone filed inside. There was a tense moment when Penny brushed against Kayla and stiffened, pinching her nose closed. The poor thing stood shivering for a minute. Michael shook his head sadly. "She's refusing to feed isn't she?" he asked the boy Johnny.

"Yeah, she did once when she was first turned and almost killed a man. She didn't mean to, she didn't want to; she just doesn't have the control part down. I told her it was an accident and the man lived, but she hasn't fed in over a week. I tried to help her but she literally ran away from the last person I fed from. Can you help her; I don't want her to die." Johnny held her close. Kayla didn't know if they had been boyfriend and girlfriend before being changed, but they were certainly inseparable now.

"Yeah I keep a cold storage of prepackaged blood here. She won't get the same nutrition as if it was fresh but it will keep her going and suppress the Hunger. I'll grab two packs now and heat them up." Kayla went into the living room with Johnny, a skinny boy with a scruffy face and a Mohawk of bright blue and she could see the blood red dyed locks of Penny as she stood behind the corner leading into the hallway. She kept Johnny in sight, but she refused to get too close to Kayla.

After a while in the silence Johnny looked at Kayla. "I figure he told you about us. You have the right smell for a willing participant. Is he going to turn you?" He was watching Penny out of the corner of his

eyes.

"He will if I ask for it. I'm still learning and have not made my

choice yet." Kayla watched the boy grimace.

"All choice was taken from us. We never wanted this. We just

wanted to run away from our parents so that we could be together. At

least now no one can keep us apart, If we can just help Penny get

through the trauma of all of this. She really is too sweet of a person for

this kind of thing. I think once she realizes she doesn't have to hurt

anyone that she will be okay, it's just going to take time." At that

statement Michael returned carrying a thermos with a straw poking out

of the top of it.

"Here you go, sweet. This will be easier on you. This was

willingly donated and no one was harmed. It's not as good as fresh, like

I said, but it will help." He handed the thermos to her and she nodded

her thanks. Her first sip she rolled her eyes and moaned. She sucked

down the entire contents of the thermos in no time and then handed it

back to Michael. After that she crawled into Johnny's lap and curled up,

quickly falling asleep. She was a tiny little thing barely over five feet tall

and Kayla seriously doubted that the girl weighed more than a hundred pounds.

"How long will this hold her for?" Johnny asked hugging her to him possessively.

"I'm not sure, but she needs to start learning to feed properly. I can take her out while the Hunger is satisfied and teach her how if you would like. I can't leave until one of my friends comes here to watch over Kayla. She isn't changed yet and therefor my enemies pose a great risk to her." Michael was standing between the kitchen and the living room.

"We are pretty exhausted, is there some where we can sleep safely through the day?" Johnny asked standing up still cradling Penny.

"I'll show you a room." Michael waved for Johnny to follow him down the hallway.

Kayla sat in the silence of the living room hoping that Nikki was doing alright and that Logan would bring her here soon. She was very worried about her friend and also scared that Nikki would blame her because it was Kayla's involvement with Michael that had caused her to be kidnapped.

Logan had sent the new werewolf Todd out of the area. He was still a threat to the safety of the people under his protection. He

wouldn't kill him, yet, but he certainly was not going to trust the man.

Nikki was out in one of the empty fields with Scott, a little tiny guy who

was changed just short of his 50th birthday. He was the most calm,

centered individual that Logan had ever met, which made him the best

teacher for a frightened, possibly volatile, student. He cast a glance at

the two of them sitting in the shade of an oak tree.

It looked like he was teaching her meditation. Nikki had told

him that she did Yoga a lot and he hoped that would help her to get a

handle on her emotions. He couldn't help but contrast her with the

almost cold calm resolve that Lily had shown when she was alive. Then

again, Lily had been changed into a wolf back in around 1910. She had

years of practice, and poor Nikki had been a wolf for all of maybe two

to three days.

He sat down on the top of a fence rail and let his mind wander

for a bit. The sun was up in the sky and it was comfortable outside. He

knew his perimeter was secure and he let a bit of relaxation wash over

him. It wasn't long before he slipped into a memory of Lily.

"So this is the newly changed is it?" The woman looked like a dream come

true to him. He was certainly impressed with her beauty. Strawberry blonde hair braided down her back and blue green eyes that held a touch of merriment behind the tough facade.

"I figured you could take in another stray." Michael laughed and shoved Logan forward slightly. "Say hi to the nice pack leader, Logan.

"Michael, I'm not sure about this. I've been running solo for over three months now. What can I learn in pack life that I haven't learned already?" Logan was not thrilled to be pushed into the role of a follower. He had been the leader of his seal team and he wanted to remain, if not a leader, then at least independent.

"You can learn to follow, pup. Then, and only then, can you learn what it truly means to lead." The woman had spoken and the tone of condescension was thick in the air. He had never felt the urge to bow before anyone like he did to her. She was in complete control and she knew it. What would it be like to make love to a woman like that?

His mind flashed forward ten years to when Lily and he had been joint leaders of the pack, to the time when Nicholai had taken her from him.

"I have your running mate, wolf. How will you save her and your friend Michael? Don't forget you also have to save yourself." Nicholai held a poison coated silver dagger to Lily's breast, right over her heart. Michael was in a room full of

blades and pockets of sunlight. He hadn't fed in weeks and Logan stood on a ledge

hands tied behind his back over a pit of silver daggers. If he changed he would fall

into those daggers and likely die there.

It had ended with Michael saving himself and Logan getting to

Lily just in time to save her. Then he started fighting Nicholai and she

stepped between him and the silver dagger aimed at his heart and had

died in his arms. Nicholai would never be forgiven, and one day Logan

would make sure that he took his last breath.

He shook his head leaving the memories in the past. They still

ached like old wounds, but the pain wasn't nearly as sharp. He turned

his attention back to Scott and Nikki. It looked like he was ready to

show her how to change at will and into each different form. He had

that crouched over pose, that most wolves got in the beginning of a

change, but he was gesturing with his arms and speaking to her.

Logan wasn't quite close enough to catch his words, but as he

had been through this kind of training before, he was pretty sure he

could guess what was being said. He watched Nikki closely, she was

dressed in very lose clothing, the best thing for practice, but he could

see the muscles in her arms where her sleeves ended. The change had

already enhanced her natural physicality. He thought she was beautiful beyond words and the strength it had taken to make it through her

forced change still sane enough to escape, simply blew his mind.

There was a shiver running through her now and he knew she

was on the verge of shifting so he paid close attention to her for a little

longer. It took her mere seconds to shift from human to the full wolf

form, an extremely impressive feat for a first try. She still had that

amazing coat of cream, white, and beige, and even from here when she

turned to look his way he could see a flash of her blue eyes.

He waved and nodded his approval knowing she would see him

and he saw her nod her head in return. She didn't have any of that

hardness that Lily had. She was softer somehow but just as tough and

strong as anyone could want. She caught his attention right from the

start and it had been ages since he had considered looking at a woman

in that way.

She was shifting again, this time into the hybrid form, the first

time he had laid eyes on her had been in this form and it still gave him

chills. Not many wolves had coat colors as unique as that; even Lily had

just been a slightly reddish shade of brown. It was almost like Nikki was

born to be a wolf and the gods were rewarding her for finally becoming

what she should have been all along.

The one other strange thing was the fact that she retained her natural eye color. Most wolves actually shifted eye color when they turned.

Nikki felt him watching her even as she shifted back to human, and she turned pink in the face. She scrambled back into her clothes. Only then did she turn to look back at him, but he was staring off into the distance as if remembering something. Scott waved her off, saying that he would show her more later, but she was well on her way. She needed to speak to Logan, but was leery of disturbing him. Need won out over worry, and she jogged over in his direction. Coughing gently to attract his attention, she walked up the hill to where he sat.

"I see you are doing well with your shifts." His mouth smiled, but there was a haunted look in his eyes. Nikki wondered what he had been thinking about.

"It's not as bad as I had feared. Knowing that I can shift back easily makes it better. I'm not trapped, you know?" She crossed her arms rubbing the upper arms as if she was cold even though he knew she wouldn't be.

"I do understand. It was hard on me, and I made the choice to transition. I wanted this, you didn't. Still you are doing very well. How are you handling the emotional influx?"

Logan mentally crossed his fingers. If she was doing better with

that, then they would be able to move her to meet up with Kayla.

"The meditation now, and yoga that I used to do, have helped

tremendously. I don't think I would have made it through otherwise.

When can we go see Kayla? I want to let her know that none of this is

her fault. Also, I think I need to tell you more about my family history...

it is important now more than ever considering my . . . state." She

heaved a sigh and plopped down on the ground.

"Okay. You can tell me all about it on our way to meet up with

them tonight." He stood up and offered her his hand. She took it

without any reservation and he helped her stand. "For now, I think you

need food, a shower, and a nap. In that order, come on."

Nikki was exhausted, and her muscles burned like you wouldn't

believe. "Is all this really necessary?" She asked, wiping sweat from her

forehead with the back of her sleeve once more.

"It's life or death, little wolf." Scott grinned at her again. He had

taken to calling her that, and she had to admit it was cute, and made her

feel less like a monster. "Silver blades are usually the weapon of choice for vampires and other wolves. If you do not learn to fight with something that can block those blades then you will be in very big trouble."

"Well, I don't feel like I'm getting better at anything yet. Give me a gun, for goodness sake; I know how to use that." She pulled the two daggers she was using; blunted of course, back up into a guard position with arms that felt like lead.

Scott leapt into the attack with more energy than should have been possible for a man of his age. It seemed there were many benefits to being a wolf. He thrust and she parried, he made an overhand chop and she blocked and dodged, he sent a slash at her face and she dived under it to bring the blunted point of one of her daggers into his ribs.

With an expulsion of air from his lungs, he went down in a tangle and winced when he put his hands to his ribs.

"Oh my gods, I am so sorry!" Nikki dropped both blades and ran to his side. "Is anything broken? Are you okay?"

"I'm fine, little wolf, fine. That was just a bit harder on old ribs than I was expecting. I am impressed after only three days you do very well, very well indeed." She helped him to stand up and handed him one of the many small towels hanging on the tree limbs around them.

"I took some karate as a kid, but that's been so long ago I doubt it has anything to do with what I'm learning." She flopped on the floor.

"Something in the change makes learning new physical skills much quicker, both for wolves and vampires. Take me for instance; I was a school gym teacher. I knew kick ball like nobody's business, but next to nothing about any sort of fighting. I was trained by the previous pack leader, Lily, and then by Michael some too, once Nicholai had killed Lily. Poor Logan." Scott stopped realizing that he must have said something he should not have.

"Poor Logan? Were he and Lily together?" She hoped she didn't sound too interested. She just couldn't help herself around hunky men.

"Yes, they were together for quite a while and were co-pack leaders for a time. I haven't seen him as content as he has been lately in a very long time. You joining the pack has meant something to him." Scott tried to stretch a bit while Nikki let those thoughts roll around in her head for a while.

After a few winces of pain and even one sharp intake of breath he sat back down on the ground and shook his head.

"I guess this means we take a break?" She asked pointing at his ribs. She heard footsteps behind her and smelled Logan's cologne.

"For me, yes, but you my dear need to change forms. Logan will be taking over for the next part of your training." Scott laughed as she stood up and groaned.

"And I will not be nearly as gentle as Scott here." Logan said, stepping into the cleared area holding a practice sword fit for a barbarian warrior in his hybrid form paws.

Chapter 14:

"Sir, I think she needs to go out to feed. She isn't doing well."
Michael turned to look at the boy Johnny and Penny, who was moaning
and crawling on the floor unable to stand.

"I think you may be right. The person who turned her must
have been very young indeed, for her to need to feed again this
quickly." He turned to Kayla. "Johnny has pledged to me and will obey
any of my commands. Will you feel safe enough with him here to watch
you until I can return?"

"I'll be fine. You worry too much." She kissed him on the
cheek. "Take care of her, she looks awful."

"Okay then. Logan and the others will be here later this evening,
maybe even after midnight. Johnny, I command you to be sure that she
comes to no harm."

"I will sir, you can count on me." He sat down on the floor in
front of where Kayla was sitting.

"Okay, Penny, dear, let's get you taken care of. I'll carry you to a
place where you can feed safely." He picked her up and disappeared out

the door.

Kayla stood up and went to the kitchen, noticing that Johnny had followed right behind her. "You can't follow me to the bathroom, okay, other than that thanks for watching out for me."

"I'll take good care of you." He said quietly and she went about getting herself a snack. She felt a sharp pinch in her right shoulder and turned around to see him holding a syringe that was empty. It took only seconds for the sedative to black her out.

There was the sound of tires on pavement when the drugs released their hold on Kayla. She was in a vehicle of some kind and she was bound hand and foot behind her back. This position caused her shoulders an undue amount of agony and she tried to shift to ease the cramping. She couldn't see anything and she tried to tell with her other senses what was going on. By the smell of things she was on something that had recently been used as a litter box for cats. It was somewhat soft and she thought it may be a used filthy mattress. She tried to breath shallow and avoid getting sick due to the smell.

She remembered exactly how she had gotten to this point and her anger flared at the lying bastard that had tricked her and Michael.

Johnny would pay for his lies as soon as she figured out a way to get out

of this mess. She wasn't sure, but a stake through the heart of that jerk

might kill him.

Whatever he had bound her with was tough enough to cut into

her wrists; probably zip ties. There was no real way to get out of them

especially with her feet trussed up to her wrists from behind. She

stopped moving for a little and tried to listen carefully. From the sound

of the echo she was in the back of some kind of moving truck. The cab

must be separate or he would have noticed her moving around by now.

There were no cracks of light so it was still dark outside, and by the

sound of other cars around them she figured they were probably on an

interstate of some kind.

Had Michael noticed her missing yet? Had the weakness of

Penny all been a ruse to get her alone and unprotected? She knew she

was in very real danger and unless there was some way Michael could

find her, she was not likely to get out of this on her own.

The house smelled different. It was missing the warm, almost

spicy scent that he had come to recognize as Kayla. Michael knew in

that instant that something was terribly wrong. He had taken the young vampire out to teach her how to feed and it had gone extremely well.

After she had properly fed she had asked for some alone time to wrap

her head around what had become of her.

It had not seemed an odd request to Michael, knowing that the

girl had been forcibly changed, so he left her in a public park not far

from the safe house. The minute he knew that Kayla was missing, he

realized that everything had been a ruse.

He snatched his phone out and hit the speed dial for Logan.

"Yes?" Logan asked in a muffle that sounded like he was

stuffing his face with food again.

"They've snatched her. I can't explain now, I have to try and

track them. You need to get the pack together and head this way now.

Bring the new one with you. We need all the power we can get."

Michael hung up the phone and grabbed all of his daylight gear. It

would still be night time for some time, but he didn't plan on stopping

until he found her, daylight or no daylight. He made a detour from the

trail to grab the sun suit that he had left stashed at another location.

He followed the scent that was on foot at first and then he

smelled the truck that they had climbed into and followed that. It hit the

interstate, muddling all the smells and making tracking that much more difficult. He assumed that they would be taking her back to Nicholai's

home, but they took a different direction all together. His heart was

nearly crushed when he lost the scent somewhere and was unable to

track them further. He put in another call to Logan and told him where

to meet. Then he sat in the dark of the hotel room he had rented to

meet in and cried until he felt weak.

The truck had stopped, but Kayla didn't hear anyone moving

around outside. It was still very dark and she didn't have a clue as to

where they were. That's when she heard a vehicle door open and close

and the truck shifted. She closed her eyes and tried to still her pounding

heart as she heard someone walking around to the back of the truck.

The back rolled up noisily and she kept her eyes closed and held

very still. No one was talking but at least one person was moving

around in the back of the truck with her. Then there was a blinding pain

as she was kicked in the ribs.

"I know you're awake, bitch, time to take you to Nicholai." She

recognized Johnny's voice and flinched as he grabbed her and tossed

her literally out the door to someone else who caught her, hanging her

over his shoulder. All the movements made her shoulders scream in pain and her ribs where she had been kicked felt like they were cracked at the very least.

Strong or not, that kind of pain causes automatic body responses, in her case, tears streamed down her cheeks as she gritted her teeth against a gasp.

"Take her to the holding cell. I'm sure he will be along shortly with that bitch of his." Johnny walked away and whoever it was carrying her trundled off with her bouncing excruciatingly on his shoulder. At least at some point one of them had clipped the strap holding her wrists to her feet so she was able to relieve some of the cramping.

She tried to look at everything around her to remember which way was out, but it was just too dark for her eyes to adjust. She started feeling sick with the pain and the rocking motion, especially with her head hanging upside down against the man's back. She closed her eyes and kept repeating in her head that Michael would find her.

The cell he dumped her in was all metal and bright lights. It looked alarmingly like an operating room. There was a small cot with very white sheets in one corner and even a stainless sink and toilet behind a short half wall. The man dropped her onto the cot and the flash of pain was so bad that she didn't even get a chance to try and see

Holmes/ Blood and Fate/ 313

what he looked like. All she could do for quite a while was lay there

trying to breathe through the pain. She almost wished she could pass

out.

"I'll find the scent where you left off, Michael, I promise."

Logan patted his friend on the back as they were leaving the hotel room

the next evening once the sun was low enough in the sky. The whole

pack was there along with Jenna and Roland. Logan had called in all the

favors he had to get so many here to help.

"I know you can track better than I could, but it's been a cold

trail the entire night." Michael had never felt so depressed in all his life,

both mortal and immortal. It helped to have Jenna there, but not much.

"Take me to the place the scent dies out." They all filed out of

the room and took to the streets. Michael did the mental cloaking where

it was needed, but otherwise he let each wolf or vamp take care of

making themselves unseen.

The scent trail stopped just past a rest area on the side of the

interstate. Logan walked into the area with his nose to the wind trying

to pick up any faint scent he could find. Nikki was nearby hunting the

ground for any clues. In the trip from the motel to here they had discovered that she had the best night vision of any of them.

"I think they may have changed vehicles here." He pointed to a couple of parking spaces off in a dark corner of the rest stop. Nikki came over and without even a flash light took a look at the scuff marks in the loose dirt.

"Yeah, I can see where the new truck must have been stashed here sitting for a while. The new one pulled up next to it and only one person got out, went to the back of the truck, then two moved to the second truck. You can even see where there was a rope or something dragging the ground between the two. Can you follow the new scent?" She looked over at Logan.

"Seriously? I can track anything that touches ground." He put his nose to the wind again and then shrugged. "But I think I may have to change for this one. Hey, doll face," He looked at Nikki. "Carry my clothes for me, please?"

"Only because you said please." Nikki stood waiting while he handed her each piece of clothing. There was a blush on her cheeks and a smile on her face in spite of the dangerous situation. Kayla had been right; he was certainly a well put together man.

Once he was changed, it didn't take him anytime at all to locate the new trail. He looked up at Michael with his wolf eyes and nodded in the direction the path went.

He loped along at a sedate pace that they all could keep up with; his nose to the ground. They didn't go back out onto the interstate; they went to a back gate and a small road that ran behind the rest stop. Nikki noticed that the lock on the gate had been broken and the chain removed so they took themselves out that way and Logan quickly led them to the left.

The road was narrow, winding, and seemed to be rarely used, making it that much easier to track the scent. They followed it for quite a while before there were any roads to the right, and on the forth one they found that the scent turned down that way.

"I think I know where he is going." Jenna spoke up and Nikki squeaked not having expected it. Everyone turned to face her. "Your ex let it slip that she had been in this area in an abandoned jail. That sounds like the kind of place that he would take up residence wouldn't you say, Michael?"

"Yeah, that sounds like him. I'll get the car if you know where and how far it is from here." He nodded at Jenna.

"I'm sure I can find it. Run Michael, I get the feeling that he is going to try something very bad." Jenna patted his arm as he turned and

blurred down the road as fast as he could.

As soon as Michael was too far to be called back, all hell broke

loose. Each wolf in the pack was tagged with a dart that quickly led to

unconsciousness the only two left standing were Roland and Jenna and

they found themselves surrounded.

"Well, well, if it isn't the "Mother" of my dearest enemy. What

are you doing here in the midst of a pack of piddling pups?" Nicholai

was smiling, but there was nothing pleasant about it.

"You stole something that does not belong to you Nicholai.

You really should give it back. It does not prove anything that you can

capture a simple human female." Jenna said quietly, she knew that she

and Roland had better find a way to talk themselves out of this

situation, even as old and strong as she was, there were too many for

them the take out.

"I will do as I please, as I told you so many years ago when, well

long ago." His eyes flashed with hate. The years since that had

happened had not been kind to his mental state, and Jenna was sure that

not finding his "one" had sent him over the deep end. "I see you are

still with this piece of trash." He nodded at Roland.

Roland spoke up then. "I don't care how much you hate me, you know that Jenna must survive to rule Michael's area, since you are so intent upon killing him."

"Ah, so true... but you aren't needed are you?" Nicholai took a step forward, but tiny Jenna blocked him with one hand.

"He is mine and I will not allow you to hurt him. Attempt to and I will call challenge. You know you cannot best me one on one." There was steel and fire beneath the calm, quiet voice and even Nicholai's anger could not stand before it.

"Then you are all free to leave. Take the mutts with you and go. Do not return and there will be no fights." He turned to the woods surrounding them. "Stay and watch them. Make sure they leave." After he spoke he took to wind and was gone as quickly as Michael had been.

They slowly started removing darts from the pack and hauling them back down the road. "They used wolfs bane in the darts, I can smell it. They are going to be out for some time and come to with a raging headache." Roland spoke to Jenna as he did most of the work, to allow her to stand guard, since she was the most capable fighter.

He was halfway through moving the wolves back to a place to meet with Michael when both Jenna and he realized that Logan was not among them.

There was something going on outside her cell that Kayla was pretty sure she didn't want to find out about. There was snarling and howling and then cursing and screaming. She sat on the hard cot feeling very human and fragile. All she wanted was to find a way out of this and back to Michael. She had already been through the room twice looking for a way out or a weapon of any kind. There was nothing.

The sounds died down abruptly and she could hear the door to where she was being held, unlock. This was just not turning out to be a good day for her. They tossed a large bundle to the floor. It looked like a human wrapped in a drop cloth of some kind. *Guess it's not their day either.* Kayla thought.

She didn't feel safe sleeping with the new arrival in the room so she sat on the cot and watched them. They were obviously breathing, but they may have been injured. She seriously debated going over and checking, but not knowing how they would react to any touch kept her glued to the spot.

Finally after what felt like hours of going over all her mistakes in her head, the bundle of whoever was starting to moan and twitch. She could tell by the sound of those moans that it was a man. This made her

even more leery and she waited in fear. When the person in the bundle

finally pulled it away from his head and face she breathed in a deep sigh

of relief.

"Logan, how in the world did they catch you?" She asked quietly

as she rushed over to help him extricate himself from the drop cloth.

"I was tranquilized. I am glad they grabbed me and not your

friend. I think they meant to hurt Michael more by grabbing me." Kayla

looked at him strangely and he wondered how garbled that had come

out.

"How is Nikki?" She attempted to shake him into speaking, not

that she moved him any at all.

"She is fighting with the change, some, but is doing much better

than expected. She doesn't want you to think she is a monster." He was

speaking much more clearly now.

"I don't care about that, she's alive! Is she okay? Does she blame

me?" Tears started trickling down her face when she thought she may

lose the only real friend she had in a very long time.

"She is coping, and no, I don't think she blames you. She was

with us when we set out to rescue you. How long was I out?" He rubbed his palms against his forehead trying to alleviate the throbbing in his skull.

"Before or after you got here? Wait, she was with you on the way here? Where is Michael?" She grabbed him by the front of his shirt and shook him as hard as she could.

"Whoa, one thing at a time. Michael called in the whole pack and his blood mother to try and find you, and since Nikki is now part of the pack she came with us. She was fine when I last saw her, but I got tranquilized and I don't know what happened after that. How long have I been out since they brought me in?" He gently pried her fingers out of his shirt and she plopped down on the floor next to him with a sigh.

All she could think about was Michael getting hurt trying to save her. She knew she wasn't worth half as much trouble as she had already caused. Finally she remembered to answer Logan's question.

"Oh, it's only been an hour, according to the clock on the wall over there. They dumped you off and I didn't know who or what it was wrapped in that cloth. I would have helped you out sooner if I had known it was you." He swore colorfully and smashed his fist into the floor making her jump. "What?"

"If they used what I think they did, that means they had me for about five hours before dumping me here. There is no telling what they

could have done to me in that amount of time." He swore again.

"What would they have done? Like experiments?" She lifted his

shirt without asking to search for needle marks.

"Yeah, but you won't find any marks. I heal too quickly. You

may want to stay on the other side of the room. They may have

contaminated me or who knows what else." She raised one eyebrow at

him.

"I'm stuck here with people who want to kill me. You are my

only chance of escape at this point. I'll take my chances. Now let's find

a way out of here."

Michael screamed for the second time, forcing those around

him to plug their ears again. "They have my love and now they have

taken my brother. I will not stand for this any longer. I will challenge

him if I have to." He smashed his fist through the trunk of the nearest

tree leaving a round hole all the way to the other side.

Jenna's small hand landed lightly on his shoulder and he went

still instantly in her calming aura. "You cannot beat him that way,

Michael. He is too old and strong for you. We have to find a way to do this either diplomatically, which I do not hold out much hope for, or

stealthily." She had a bit of a wicked smile hovering at the corners of

her mouth that Michael recognized all too well. Things were about to

get interesting.

There were four of them left of the main party that had set out

to rescue Kayla; Jenna, Michael, Roland and Nikki. They piled into

Roland's giant Hummer, that when Roland bought it, Michael

laughingly called it the Land Barge. Michael knew where they were

going, but did not feel up to answering any of Nikki's rather frustrated

questions.

They were going for the "gear" shed. Logan's pack was keeping

a perimeter around the abandoned jail. Just far enough out to not alert

the sentries, but close enough in to be of help when Michael called

them in.

He could not stop the racing of his thoughts and he knew that

he was seconds away from a killing rage, like he had never had before.

Nicholai would not survive this if he had anything to say about it.

Somehow, someway, that man was going to go to his final grave as soon

as Michael got the chance. He had caused too much pain and anguish to

be allowed to live, and if Eliza got in the way and went down with him, so much the better.

They pulled into what looked like an old abandoned factory with the fence rusting to ruins all the way around it. What nobody knew was that security here was through the roof. All of Michael's security personnel where trained here, and he kept the bulk of his military style weapons and gear stored here as well.

Roland and Michael had both gone round eyed when Jenna said softly that they needed to go to the "shed". They knew immediately who and what they were after.

As they were pulling through the gate, now being opened by a pair of black and gray street camo, wearing vampires, with loaded AR-15's, she spoke again. "MVM should definitely know about this. Nicholai has overstepped himself. Now if we can just get M to get out of torpor we should be fine."

"Who is MVM?" Asked Nikki quietly.

"Trust me on this youngling, "Roland said, "I know who it is, and most of the time I wish I didn't. Just pretend like you are along for the ride. Stay quiet and in the background. Maybe he won't notice you." Jenna punched him in the arm.

"My blood father is not that bad for goodness sake. Frightening, sometimes, but he certainly never hurt anyone we liked." She sighed.

Chapter 15:

"They are coming back." Logan stated. "I don't know how much more of those wolfs bane tranquilizers I can handle." He was hugging the toilet as it was, and the few crackers they had shoved through the steel door of what looked to be a prison cell, came raging back up out of his stomach with a vengeance.

The sound of him being sick so many times had killed any appetite that Kayla had. She had given him her set of crackers as well, only keeping one of the bottles of water for herself.

He had explained to her that the plant aconite, or commonly known as wolfs bane had an anesthetic effect on werewolves. It was the only known plant or drug capable of putting them under.

"I mean, hell, why would they call it wolfs bane in the first place, do you think?" He said after a moment of hacking and spitting into the bowl of the toilet again.

"What do they want with us? I've been drugged and taken out twice now, and I have no clue what they are doing with you while I'm out. All I know is that each time I come back, my gut hurts like it's that time of the month. I don't want them to kill any chance of me having

kids!" She stood up and waited for the door to open, panic making

havoc with her thoughts. It would be a few minutes more, considering

how far away he could hear them down the hallways.

When the door did open they shot him with another dart and

she watched him collapse. They didn't inject her with anything this time,

but they brought in a gurney with lots of straps and at gun point forced

her down onto it and strapped her in.

"Where are you taking me? What are you doing to me?" She

asked, but the silent man and woman behind surgical masks said

nothing to her, just wheeled her off down the long hallway. She

watched as lights passed over her head and the cell doors changed to

what appeared to be office doors.

That is when the smell of antiseptic and medical cleaning

solutions hit her nose. Her heart jerked around in pure animal panic.

She wanted out and far away from anything that seemed like medical

procedures around these monsters.

"Ah, my patient at last." The voice sent spears of ice into

Kayla's heart. She knew that this person only wanted to hurt others and

cared for no one but themselves.

Her only thought, *I am going to die without ever seeing Michael again.*

Then they gave her a very light dose of meds, something that left her fully aware, but unable to fight back. She was lifted from the gurney and placed onto a table that looked like it belonged in an alien horror film.

Her legs were spread wide apart and her feet were strapped into a pair of stirrups. She knew, just knew, that nothing good could come of this. They literally cut her clothing away from her, not bothering to cover her nakedness with anything. Her arms, legs and chest were all strapped down to this table as well.

That was when she got her first look at Nicholai and she did not like it at all. He was wearing a white lab coat and a pair of surgical gloves with a headlamp on his forehead. He looked like he had wandered away from a horror film set.

"I hope I need no introduction, but I will be kind enough to do so anyway. I am Nicholai and I will be making sure that you never get back to Michael. If you do somehow survive what I intend to do, he will certainly never want you again, though why he would want a human in the first place I will never know. You are all the same to me, bleeders for the taking." He sat on a stool at the foot of the table putting him at the right height to invade her most private places. "Now just so you understand what is going to happen to you, I will explain. You see we

are not capable of having children, but you my dear are. What I want to

know is if we can conceive in the presence of an acceptable womb. I

have taken your eggs in previous procedures and taken sperm from

Michael's dog. I tried combining them alone, but failed miserably. Then

I had a stroke of luck that Eliza here had a small vial of Michael's blood.

I added that to the mix and finally success. Two of the eggs survived

and I am now going to implant them into your very human living

womb. You will hopefully carry what will be the first hybrids to term

and I will take them from you and leave your corpse for the carrion

birds."

She almost couldn't speak. The thought of what was about to

happen to her was almost too much for anyone to bear; only the

knowledge that they would be her children no matter what kept her

from losing all connection to sanity.

"What makes every two bit criminal think they have to have a

giant speech about how they are torturing others?" She said to thin air.

"Seriously, next time knock me out, save me the evil genius

monologue." She rolled her eyes and almost laughed when he sputtered.

She could not imagine that sound coming out of a man so cold and hateful, it was just too preposterous.

"You continue to act strong, but we will see who will be the corpse when all is done." And he began the procedure, making her feel very violated and very frightened.

"So where are they keeping the vampire Popsicle?" Michael asked as they entered the hidden basement of the factory above.

"He is in sub-basement 3 I believe and don't call him that. In order for torpor to be healthy you have to drop the temperature." Jenna responded as she led them down the halls to an elevator.

The elevator was almost silent as they descended two more levels. The guard at the door nodded to them as they entered a very dark hallway with doors to the left and the right.

"What are all these doors?" Nikki asked as they passed many of them, all with keypad locks and a look of frost about them.

"These are the Sleepers. These are the vampires that have grown tired of the world and needed a time of rest to become alive again. My blood father is one of 30 that we are housing here." Jenna said quietly.

"Some of them are still somewhat aware of what goes on around them. I try to come here every so often and read aloud or play soft music. I hope they find it soothing. Ah, here we are. This is his chamber." She

indicated a door with more than a keypad lock. There was a thumbprint

scan and a retinal scan as well. "As far as I know he is the oldest living

one of our kind. I have never asked him, but he may know of others."

She was talking while pushing in a long line of numbers then she

scanned her thumb and eye and typed in the list of numbers again.

Finally the door dinged and a wash of ice cold air shot out from around

the edges as it opened.

There in the doorway stood a man in his early forties with very

short salt and pepper hair. He had soft brown eyes that he was rubbing

at stubbornly.

"Is it the apocalypse yet? I told you I wanted to sleep until the

end." He looked up and noticed who was standing in front of him. "Oh

no, he's gotten out of hand hasn't he?"

"Kayla, hey snap out of it girl." She could hear someone talking

to her, but the voice wasn't clicking with a name. She was crammed into

a corner, a very cold corner and she was shivering as her bare skin

pressed against it.

"Come on sweets, you have to come back from what they did,

for Michael's sake." That snapped her head around to stare only

partially sane still, at the speaker.

"Michael?" she asked stuffing her hand in her mouth.

"Yeah, Michael. You can't go off your rocker when he is busting

his butt to save you. What did they do to you?" Now the name came to

her, this was Logan, Michael's friend.

"I hurt, Logan." she moaned as she held herself. "I'm cold." She

looked around. "I'm naked."

"I've been trying to get this gown on you for about ten minutes

now, and I have a blanket." He helped her get dressed and wrapped

himself up around her with the blanket to try and warm her faster.

"What did they do to you?" He asked again, letting his anger

slightly free so that it would increase his body temperature.

"They . . . they impregnated me!" She wailed and pounded her

fists into his chest. "They used stuff from you to do it!" She shook even

harder and then went limp against him.

"Oh dear gods! How? How did they get it to work? We've tried

that before with, well, with willing participants. It's never worked." He

rubbed her arms and could feel her warming up.

"They used vampire blood in the mix, Michael's blood." She

stopped and pulled away from him taking the blanket and wrapping

herself up with it. "I don't know how to feel about it. The violation of it

all, but it's my child no matter what, and in a way Michael's too, even if

they used your DNA." Logan looked half horrified and half like he

wanted to rip someone's head off. In an odd way that made her feel

better.

"Michael is not going to be a happy camper. Do you know for

sure that it took?" He started pacing. His shoulders so tight he could

almost feel the muscles ripping off of the bones out of shear tension.

"If anything I've read about pregnancy is true, I won't know for

sure for a few weeks. How in the hell am I going to get out of here?"

She sat on the edge of the cot and hugged her knees to her chest. "All I

know right now is how much it hurts. I don't think he did it the way a

true doctor would have. He may have ruined me." She said with tears

running down her face.

"I'm sure Michael will figure something out." Logan said feeling

intensely awkward. "He is likely half killing himself to get you out of

here. Look, when they come back again, which they will have to, if they

are going to keep a check on you, try and be hiding down behind that

half wall there. I'm going to stand behind where the door opens and rush them. If they go down, I'll grab you and we can make a run for it.

You think you can handle that?" He wasn't sure just what she was able

to handle at this point.

"I have to. If it that is what it takes; I have more than just me to

look after."

"And that is where things stand with Nicholai at this point."

Michael finished. The whole group was sitting in a big room on the next

level up from the chambers. There was a small kitchen and a bunch of

tables and chairs. They sat around one of the tables with Nikki

devouring a huge sandwich.

"I told you when you asked me to turn him that being your birth

son would not change who Nicholai would become with the blood,

didn't I?" Jenna's blood father asked.

"He's your son?" Michael squawked, a totally undignified noise

out of a vampire.

"Neglected to mention that to them didn't you? And you guys

please stop with the whole MVM thing and just call me Maximus. It is

my name you know." He laughed a rich baritone that rumbled

pleasantly.

"Nicholai is your son? Why didn't you tell anyone?" Michael

stared at her like he had never seen her before, like she had become a

stranger to him.

"I couldn't tell anyone, I felt so ashamed. How could someone I

loved so dearly have turned into a monster? I was very young when I

was married off to a Baron from a nearby kingdom. The man I was wed

to was nearly three times my age. I think I was all of 14. It took 10 long

years for me to become pregnant with Nicholai. My husband refused to

bring in any midwives to help with the pregnancy or the birth. Thank all

that is holy that Maximus was there. You were going by Valerius at the

time I think. He was staying in our basement, posing as a mad scholar. I

went in to labor a few days after my husband left me pretty much alone

in his home. Maximus and one female servant were the only help I had.

He heard my screams all the way from the basement and came

to help. He knew immediately that something was not right and that I

was not going to be able to deliver the baby naturally. He grabbed a

dagger from a nearby desk and slit me open to pull the baby out. That

was when he shoved the baby to the servant and shoved both of them

out the door.

I was fading quickly as he cut his palm and shoved it into the wound and all over the opening. Then he drained me and changed me.

We left that night. I was only to see my baby from a distance. I guess

growing up without me and with his father the way he was, turned him

sour." She went silent for a while.

"Tell them all of it my dear." Maximus prompted her.

"I got sick of watching, heart sick, so Maximus took me away

for about twenty or so years. When I came back, my husband had died

and, my son was now ruling in his place. He was dying from something

I had never seen before, but Maximus said he had about two or three

months left to live. I couldn't bear to abandon him again. I couldn't just

let him die. I begged Maximus to change him and Maximus, being the

father I did not have as a child couldn't bear to see me in pain. He

changed him and to this day it has been the worst decision I ever

pushed onto anyone. I will always regret it, but I cannot rectify it either.

I can't kill my only child." She broke down into tears at this point and

Maximus, like a father, held her while she cried herself out.

"I will not try to kill him, for your sake Jenna, but I will not let

him harm any more people I care about." Michael said quietly. "My only

idea is to capture him and force him into torpor. It's been done before;

I see no reason why it won't work again." He stood up to pace for a while not saying anything.

"When do we leave?" Nikki asked around a mouthful of food.

"Pup, you are not ready to handle what he can throw at you."
Maximus turned a very hard gaze at her and she shrank back."

"We will drop you off at the perimeter on our way in. Hook up
with Scott. All of the rest of the pack will attack the outside positions
on our word." Michael turned to look at the doorway as three men with
armloads of gear came in. "Alright everyone lets gear up. Maximus take
charge if you would please. Jenna has told me you were once a general,
and I am sure you are more suited for this than I am."

Maximus nodded his head with a curious smile on his face.
"Son, I was commanding armies before the birth of the Christian God."

Kayla crouched down behind the half wall around the toilet area
and shook with adrenaline and fear. She had ripped the sheet into a few
pieces and turned it into a very short, but serviceable skirt by tying the
pieces together. Then she ripped the gown apart to make a shirt that
would actually stay closed. Being poor makes you really creative. Logan
had laughed until she pointed out that she would be next to useless
running around naked or in a hospital gown with the back flying open.

At least she had her shoes and socks from when she was kidnapped.

Logan was behind where the door opened and he looked like he was ready to bash someone's skull to bits. He wore a snarl that turned his rather handsome face into a mask of rage. If she didn't know he was on her side, she would have been terrified.

When they heard the key in the lock outside click he twitched but made no other signs. She jumped and had to bite her tongue to keep from squeaking. The men coming through the door didn't know what hit them. The door that Logan was behind slammed them square in the face and they went down in a heap. Only one of the two managed to scramble back to his feet, but by that time Logan was all over them both, tangling them further with the straps of their weapons and with their clothing.

He took both of the rifles from them and slammed the men into the walls a few times. It looked like this time Nicholai had failed to take enough precaution. These two guards were purely human, and not nearly enough to handle one very big and very angry wolf.

Kayla really didn't like the sound of both of their skulls cracking against the wall, and she doubted they were alive if the blood leaking from their heads was any indication.

Logan passed her one of the rifles. "You know how to use this?"

Kayla shrugged. "Point it at the bad guys and squeeze the trigger gently." Her voice only trembled a little bit, for which she was very grateful. She didn't want to sound half as scared and pathetic as she felt.

"Good enough. If you run out of ammo or it jams, point it at the ceiling and step behind me. Got it?" He dug through the guards' clothing for more ammo and took the small radio one of them was carrying. "This will tell us if they know we are out. Grab the keys and lock the door behind us." She grabbed the keys as he was dragging the men completely into the room where they had been locked up. Once the door was shut, Kayla blindly followed his lead and they made their way into the hallway.

He pointed out the directions as they walked. He was silent; she thought she sounded like a particularly drunk horse on hard tile. She even saw him wince when she stumbled a bit and she knew that she was the weak link here; it infuriated her.

I don't ever want to be the weak one in need of protection again. I will train day and night if I have to. I may have kids now that need my protecting. Never again will I be incapable of protecting myself. She vowed to not be a burden to anyone ever again.

They slipped around corners and finally he held his hand up in the air in a fist. She assumed that meant that he wanted her to stop behind him, so she did. He backed up and pointed around the corner and mouthed the word "Humans" to her. She snuck forward as quietly as she could and saw the loading dock that she had been brought in on. There were three guards all standing around talking like there was nothing important going on.

Obviously their absence had not been noticed at this time. She didn't know if that was a good thing or a bad thing. She backed up and let him go back to the corner. He stood there for a while and watched the men and she stayed behind him shivering in anticipation and pent up nerves.

She almost tapped him on the shoulder since he was taking too long, but he turned around and pointed at himself and then to the guards. Then he pointed at her and then towards the big rolling door. She knew that he was going to take out the guards, more humans again, while she was to open the door so they could get out.

It didn't sit well with Kayla that all that they had encountered so far were human guards. She knew that the place should have been full of vampires and wolves. Why had none of them been on guard? From

inside the building she could not tell if it had been day or night, but her

first sight of the loading dock showed no outline of sunlight around the

big rolling door, so it must have been nighttime.

Logan held up three fingers and nodded at her and she nodded

back. When the third finger dropped he tore around the corner of the

hall and straight into the pack of guards. Kayla took off across the

loading area to punch the big red button that opened the rolling door.

She stepped back to the side behind a pillar as it rolled slowly open and

she bit her lip to bleeding as Logan made sure the guards would not be

getting up again.

When he grabbed her arm as he walked up she jumped about a

mile, but still followed him out the quickly opening door. She was just

standing up from ducking under the door when he stopped dead in his

tracks and she ran smack into him.

"I see you have decided to join us at last." It was Nicholai; she

would know that voice anywhere. Lights flashed on from every angle,

lighting the place up bright enough to hurt her eyes. Before them stood

Nicholai, backed by an entire legion of vampires and wolves already in

their hybrid form. Logan let out a growl the likes of which she had never heard before. She knew he was going to do something dramatic

and in this situation, terribly stupid.

She put her hand on his bare arm and he felt scalding hot. He

twitched once and looked back at her. She shook her head and said

softly, "I need you, and Michael needs you. Please don't do this."

"Listen to the whore, wolf pup. She knows you would die for

nothing here. Die on my blade like your lover did all those years ago."

The smirk on Nicholai's face would have infuriated a saint, and Logan

was nothing close to saintly.

Logan let out an agonized howl and started to crouch down like

she had seen him do before he changed and she squeezed his arm as

hard as she could. "Don't! Please!"

He shook her off and snarled at the forces facing them. "I will

see you dead this night." He growled deep in his chest.

"I seriously doubt that my furry little enemy. You and what

army could possibly stop me?" Nicholai laughed but a voice cut through

his maniac cackle like a hot blade through snow.

"I don't know about the army my son, but I surely can stop

anything you can do." A new voice joined the conversation.

Chapter 16:

Michael, Jenna, Roland and Maximus all landed at the edge of the field surrounding the abandoned jail. They had made the long high jumps that vampires could; it covered an amazing amount of distance in a very short period of time.

Nicholai's look of utter shock and bewilderment was almost enough to start Michael laughing. Then he saw Kayla's frightened bruised face and he nearly lost all control. He was vibrating with pure rage and homicidal thoughts; he could care less what he had told Jenna. He wanted Nicholai's head on a stake and his heart burnt to ashes in his hands.

"Blood father," Nicholai bowed slightly in his direction. "I had not thought to see you here, or awake even."

"You have not thought of a lot of things it would seem. I have been awakened early because of your foolish actions. Something must be done Nicholai. You know this kind of infighting will lead to trouble with the humans. Someone will notice something, and then where will we be." Maximus walked to within a few feet of his blood son. "Send your army away, Nicholai. We should talk just you and me."

"I have nothing to say to any of you. I respect that you are my blood father, but that whore is not my mother and never will be." Nicholai walked away and back to the front of his troops. "If they try to stop me from taking her back, kill them." He shouted. That was when all hell broke loose.

Kayla watched the exchange between the newcomer and Nicholai, but their voices were too low for her human ears. When Nicholai told his army to kill anyone trying to save her she knew things were going to go bad and quickly. She stepped back on instinct, knowing that Logan would have made the change. What she did not expect was for him to grab her and toss her over his shoulder, rifle and all. He wasted no time trying to get her out of there. He charged to the left and around the side of the building without waiting for her to see what was going to happen.

She screamed at him and pounded on him to take her back to Michael, but he ignored everything she did. She pushed herself up with one hand, still clinging desperately to the rifle and saw unknown vampires racing after her. She propped the weapon up as best she could and started firing off shots in short little burst in the general direction of

the vampires.

Only luck and a high volume of bullets and many vampires in a

small area allowed any of the shots to hit home, but the vampires that

got hit did slow down or drop out of the chase.

Logan took a second between bursts of shots too look behind

them and then patted her on the bum, shouting "Good job!" as he

turned another corner and ran away from the building into an oncoming

pack of wolves. She turned her head just long enough to see them

coming and screamed. Logan waved at them and she knew these must

be his pack members.

Two wolves were in the lead as they overtook Logan and her, a

very dark gray werewolf that was smaller than the rest and an odd cream

and beige colored werewolf. This one had ice blue eyes unlike all the

rest. Somehow she knew without asking that this was Nikki. Her heart

plummeted into her stomach and she ached for the chance to tell her

how sorry she was about what had happened to her, but there was no

time.

The pack passed them and hit the vampires like a loaded freight

train. The snarls and screams were terrifying and she pointed the rifle at the ground so as not to shoot any of her rescuers by accident. That

many bodies moving that quickly in so many different directions, one

bullet was all it would take for the fire to become unfriendly.

Logan crashed into the woods surrounding the place and kept

going for a bit. It was like he was looking for a particular spot to stop.

He stumbled into a clearing with a couple of downed trees and he

stopped to look the place over for a bit. When he put her down he

pointed at her and said "You stay here." He dropped his rifle next to

her.

He turned and raced back to the fight as fast as his hybrid form

could run. He didn't even wait to make sure she was going to listen. For

her part, she at least waited until he was out of sight. Once he was truly

gone, far enough to not hear her, or so she thought, she grabbed the

rifle he had dropped and headed right back out towards the fight. She

may be able to shoot some of the bad guys, if she could tell them apart

from the good guys.

Michael leapt at Nicholai only to find an arm and hand like

hardened steel blocking his way. Maximus had his other hand wrapped

carefully around Nicholai's throat. "I told you, I would handle him.

Nothing is worth losing your life to him, nothing. Your lady is safe, go

to her, and comfort her. I will take care of this." Maximum's voice was

quiet, but carried a command that Michael was unable to refuse. He

turned to track down Kayla, but was immediately drawn into skirmishes

with other vampires and Nicholai's werewolves.

The first to step into his way was Eliza. She had her hands up as

if she were going to surrender. He "commanded" her to move and she

stood there. He knew then that she had gone over to Nicholai and that

there was no way he was going to leave her alive at his back.

"Eliza, why must you always be in my way?" Michael waited for

her to make the first move, but knew in his gut that she would always

wait for the chance to make a sneak attack. It was just the way that she

worked.

"I want you back. I've always only wanted you. Let us leave all

this. I'll prove that I can be loyal to you and only you." She tried to

move towards him and he stepped back.

"You have proven were your loyalties are very clearly. Now get

out of my way, before I remove you." He took a step back towards her

and she snarled. There was a flash of movement in her eyes as she

looked left and right. He knew at that point that she had back up.

Before he could make up his mind as to which direction to move first

she launched herself at him. She hit him low in the gut like a football

tackle, just as two wolves took hold of his legs. Little did she know that

there was no way that the three of them were enough to take him. He

had done a blood exchange with Maximus before leaving the "shed",

and now only Maximus, Jenna, and possibly Nicholai, if he got lucky,

could challenge him.

There was anger in him that burned so ferociously that he

almost scared himself with its intensity. He grabbed for the closest wolf

and literally tore its head from its shoulders sending the two pieces

hurtling in two opposite directions. The other wolf received a punch to

the chest that tore a hole through him just like the tree that he had

punched the night before. Neither wolf could survive that amount of

damage. He would deal with Eliza next; she had her arms wrapped

around his midsection and was trying to hold him in place for her thugs

to attack. She didn't realize that her help had been removed until it was

far too late. He still had his hands free, so he reached down and twisted

free of her arms, slamming her to the ground.

Michael's hands held her pinned to the ground by the shoulders

and she squirmed in terror. "Michael, no, don't please?" She begged, but not well enough to save her from her fate.

"You plotted with that maniac to kidnap the woman I love. You injured her, frightened her, and who knows if she will even have me now that she has been tortured because of my enemies. I have put up with years of your treachery, your plots, schemes, and lies. I will put up with no more!" He screamed and began pulling her limb from limb. He bit into her space between her neck and her shoulder and drained her so quickly he thought he would be sick. He spit most of it out of his mouth and pulled the metal spike from his belt loop where he had kept it and staked her. Then he leaned down to where her shriveled face held her very much alive and very frightened eyes. He whispered into her ear. "I'll be back to burn you to ash once I have found my love. Don't go anywhere, I'll be right back."

A strangled, terrified moan escaped her lips as she lay there unable to move; too injured to run, too drained to heal.

Logan scanned the fighting as he charged back into the thick of things. He kept his eyes slightly unfocused in order to catch any movement on his flanks. It was a good thing he did, because some of Nicholai's remaining Dogs came tearing out of the tree line to his left and ran straight at him. To a full pack of wolves, a few Dogs were

hardly a blip on the radar, but six or seven Dogs to one lone wolf could

prove problematic; unless that wolf was Logan. When he trained, he

trained with the hopes that he would leave nothing to chance. He knew

how to handle an entire pack of Dogs. He saw his choice of weapons

lying off to the side and leaped, tumbling in that direction to grab it and

roll back to standing in one fluid motion. A metal fence post that had

been twisted in half, It was about three feet long and the twisting had

left one end jagged and pointed.

He dropped into a crouch and waited for the first Dog to take

its turn in their normal strategy of tag and run. One would dash in and

make an attack and just as it was turning to run the second would be

charging in to replace it. If you let them get into a rhythm you were as

good as mutilated, or dead if you were human. Logan would ignore the

first attacker, allowing it to score possibly if its rush was more than just

a fake. He would keep his ears and eyes open for the second to come in.

If he took that one out the others would have to back up and regroup,

or they would get vindictive and all charge in at once; either way, he

won. The minute they stopped thinking like one single being, he could

pick them off as individuals, one by one.

The first Dog in was all a ruse to grab his attention, so when he ignored it, he came to no harm. The second one in tried to get at the back of his thigh, only to be met with the sharpened end of the fence pole. It took the Dog square in the chest, and as the other Dogs howled and backed out of range, Logan took the time to kick the now dead beast from the pole. One of the Dogs stepped forward, hate written on its face. It snarled at Logan, all teeth and slobber.

"Bring it Fido." Logan growled deep in his chest and went to work with the pole. Dogs began dropping like flies around him.

Lost in the whirl of battle he didn't realize at first that all of them were down until he made three full turns and saw only bodies and no attackers. That is when he looked up and saw Nikki facing off against a vampire. He was not going to stand there and let her face that alone. Grass and dirt went flying up behind him as he rushed across the field digging furrows with hands and feet in his hybrid form.

Nikki tore into the enemy lines like a wild thing, hoping that instinct and what little training she had done over the past few days would keep her alive long enough to take some of them out. She lashed out with claws and teeth; somehow knowing with a deep feeling in her chest which werewolves were her pack mates and which were not. She

knew Logan would be coming back to the fight as soon as Kayla was

safely out of range. The pack leader would never let the pack fight

something like this alone.

There was a slightly disturbing amount of joy in killing the

enemy wolves. She pictured each of them as the group of wolves that

had killed her family. There were three dead wolves behind her and a

fourth in her grasp when Logan came into her field of view. He was

surrounded by Dogs, but she knew they would be no match for him.

She had been watching him train almost as much as he had been

watching her. There was a feral grin on his face that made her heart,

already pounding with adrenaline, creep up a few notches even more.

She knew she wanted him and as soon as they got out of this alive she

was going to get him, no matter what he thought about it.

The vampires were starting to take a toll on the pack. One wolf

was down and may not be getting back up and her teacher, Scott had a

bad silver blade gash along his ribs. He had dropped back to try and

deal with the downed member and his own wound at the same time. He

was the only wolf among the pack to have any sort of medical training

anyway. She knew there wasn't anything she could do to help that situation so she put it out of her mind as quickly as she could.

There was a werewolf with its back to her and she knew it was the enemy. It had its great paw hand wrapped around the throat of one of the younger pack members. The enemy wolf raised her pack member by the neck, the feet dangling and kicking. That is when the enemy turned just enough to the side for her to see the face and the features that still haunted her nightmares.

This was the werewolf that had changed her, making it as miserable and vile as he could. This was the monster that had chewed on her, slobbered on her and taken the last bit of her humanity from her. All at once the only thing she could see was red. She dug in her toe claws and charged without thinking straight at the enemy. This was one enemy she wanted dead more than any other.

The big dark hybrid had no clue that she was bearing down on him like a runaway freight train, but somehow he stepped to the side just in the nick of time to avoid her claws sinking into the meat of his back around his spine. Instead she clamped hands and teeth around the arm holding her pack member.

He let out a howl of pain and surprise, his hand jerking open and releasing the other wolf. Nikki held on like her life depended on it and she was pretty sure it did. This wolf was bigger, stronger, and better

trained than she was. She knew her only chance was to get very lucky,

but it was a chance she had to take.

The wolf tried to pound her head to make her let go, still she

hung on. He tried slinging her around and she clamped down harder,

getting another yowl of pain from him. Then he dug his thick strong

fingers into her mouth and started prying at her jaw. She yelped with

her teeth clamped down and then kept yelping as he twisted her lower

jaw almost to breaking. At that point it was either let go or risk having

her jaw torn out of place or off completely.

She dropped down to the ground in a crouch, ready to spring.

He went to move towards her and then stopped looking over to the

side where Logan was mauling the pack of Dogs. He shook his head

and took off running into the woods as fast as he could go.

Nikki turned as if to chase after him, but it was then that a

vampire dropped down right in front of her. She stood up to her full

height in hybrid form, noticing how small this vampire looked to her

this way. She was nervous, but also itching to take something out. All

the anger of seeing her rapist had to go somewhere, she may as well

wear out her fury on this enemy.

"Dog, you will not take me down so easily." This vampire was a black man with his head shaved into intricate swirls. He wore combat clothing like the rest and he had a silver coated Katana in his hands.

"I'll do more than you think." She pulled the long daggers she had been given by Scott from the sheaths on her hips. Sheath and blades had been fitted to her body in this form. The handles were just large enough and thick enough to be easily held by hybrid hands. She waited for the vamp to charge her, which he did almost immediately. She slashed out with both blades leaving slices in his shirt, but not quite reaching the flesh.

"Quick for a newborn pup. I'll not make that mistake again." He tangled weapons with her for a moment leaving a nasty cut on her off hand shoulder that burned like acid and made that arm weak. She held onto the blade in that hand, but just barely.

"Quick for a mosquito," Nikki jibbed back. "I'll not make that mistake again." She dragged her furry arm across her eyes where dust had blown into them. She watched the vampire for any signs that he was going to make a move, and she was ready when he did.

The vampire went to lunge at her again, but was stopped dead in his tracks at the sight of Logan stepping up next to her. He looked windblown and there was slobber and blood all tangled into the fur of

his hybrid form, but she would have known him by his smell alone.

"Need any help with this one, Lovely?" He asked, still breathing

heavily from his fight with the Dogs.

"Nah, I got this. Want to watch?" She panted with her muzzle

slightly open.

"Oh certainly." He watched her flanks for any incoming attacks,

but here was no one else to attack her as each enemy was currently

dead, disabled or occupied with the other members of the rescue force.

The vampire started circling and she matched him step for step.

He was distracted, certainly not trusting Logan to keep out of the fight.

He glanced away for one second to check Logan's location and Nikki

pounced shoving the blade from her good hand straight down into the

top of his skull and the blade from her off hand through his chest into

his heart. The vamp fell flat on his back and lay there in a quickly

spreading pool of blood. The twitching and gurgling coming out of him

was rather disturbing. Nikki pulled out a squirt bottle full of fuel and a

lighter, and she pulled her blades free of the body before setting fire to

the whole bloody mess. Thick black smoke began pluming out from the

body as it quickly burned down to ash.

"Eh gods, that smells terrible." She tried to cover her muzzle with the back of her fur covered arm, only to notice that she was covered in blood and scratches. They stung a little, but the cut across her shoulder still felt like it was on fire. She grimaced as she moved it and turned to look at it. It wasn't deep and would surely heal on its own, especially if she shifted back. She wasn't going to do that until she knew for sure they were safe. She turned to look at Logan.

"That was nicely done." Logan rumbled to her as he stepped up next to her. He was a good five inches taller than her in his hybrid form versus hers. For the first time in the entire fight, she found she was trembling. He placed his paw hand on her arm and looked down at her.

"Thank you." She dropped her head slightly and then looked up at him, her ice blue eyes sending a shock wave through him. He wanted to drag her off into the woods to find a quiet place to shift back and enjoy each other. He knew that there was too much left to do, and too many enemies around.

He leaned down to her and gently licked the blood from the side of her muzzle. "We have much to discuss later. For now there are more where that one came from." He pointed at a group of vampires attempting to corner a few of her pack members. She growled in anger and launched herself at them. Logan followed her, an evil deep

rumbling chuckle rolling out of him.

Chapter 17

Kayla held the rifle in both hands and pressed against her shoulder like she had seen in all those movies and video games in the big chain store near her home. She had taken Logan's rifle hoping it had more ammo than hers, since he had never fired it. She made her way through the trees where Logan had left her. She never quite left the tree line, keeping to the shadows for as much cover as she could get. She stood on the edge and looked left and right, the rifle moving to point in the same direction she was looking in. She kept her eyes up as she moved, using her feet to feel her way around the edge of the clearing, praying that she didn't turn an ankle and become an even easier target. Again she thanked any deity she could think of that she had her shoes.

She couldn't see the main part of the fighting from this side of the giant jail complex. She probably wouldn't be able to see anything until she was close enough to reach the circle of lights that were blazing around the side of the building with the loading docks. She saw a scattering of vampires and werewolves either lying motionless on the ground or crawling as fast as their injuries would let them to anything

that could be considered cover or escape.

A vampire hissed at her as it ran up to her and then past her. It

had happened so quickly that she didn't even have time to fire off a

shot. She was sure it was one of Nicholai's followers, but at least it had

left her alone.

There was a large bulk of something up ahead that looked like it

was right against the tree line. She would either have to go out and

around it, making herself more visible or she would have to go back

into the woods and hope that there were no enemies hiding in there. As

she got closer she was able to make out what it was that was piled up

there. It looked as if all of the fencing that should have been around the

place had been ripped up and piled to the side of the field. There was

chain link, razor wire and all the metal poles just piled like a personal

injury lawsuit waiting to happen.

She shifted to go out and around the pile, but she tried to stay

close to it so that the bulk was there to use as partial concealment. She

felt helpless and totally exposed even though the pile was mostly still in

shadow. She was totally out of her depths and felt even a tad bit

ridiculous carrying the rifle. *I am not a soldier, I am not a warrior, I do not know what in the hell I am doing.* She tried to be as quiet as she could, but if

it were not for the howls, screams and snarls of the battle, she knew that

she would be making enough noise to bring them all down on her head.

The circle of light was closer to the edge of the field to her left

once she had passed the pile of fencing so she went that direction,

hoping to be able to see what was happening and keep from being seen

at the same time. She could hide in the tree line and take shots at the

enemy when a target presented itself, well, as long as her ammunition

held out. She slipped into the tree line again and gave her eyes a

moment to adjust to the dark. She could just make out some of the

shapes in front of her.

There was a tree down just inside the tree line and it made a

perfect spot to scramble up into another larger oak tree. She crammed

herself down into the crook and set the rifle on a large sturdy branch in

front of her. At first, she just sat there not shooting anyone, but as the

fight progressed she started to be able to tell who were the good guys

and who were the enemies. She searched desperately for Michael in the

chaos, but could not see him. She finally stilled her pounding heart

enough to try and concentrate.

She picked her first target, a large red haired vampire that had just come around a corner and went to charge into a knot of friendlies.

She sighted down the barrel of the gun, knowing that this was in no way the best weapon to be shooting at this distance, but it was all she had. She squeezed the trigger with both eyes open and sighted directly on the center of his chest. She prayed for at least a little luck with every fiber of her being. When the vampire went down in a splatter of blood and then attempted to crawl away behind the corner he had just come from she almost gave away her position by cheering. Luck was obviously on her side, and there was one less vampire after her friends.

She picked her next target a tiny Asian female vampire with hot pink dread locks. She aimed again for the middle of the chest and squeezed off a round. Again the vampire went down in a spray of blood and crawled into cover. She guessed that it would at least be of some help to keep them from joining in the battle. The fewer enemies there were the better her friends would fare.

Six more times she sighted on vampires, too scared to make a mistake when it came to telling the good wolves from the bad, and six more times the vampires went down. Only one of the vampires was unable to crawl away. The rest took themselves out of her range as quickly as they could pull their bodies into safety.

She had narrowed her world down to aim and fire and as a new

vampire walked around the corner; she nearly screamed and dropped

the rifle. It was Michael and it was all she could do to try and stay put in

safety, when all she wanted to do was run to him. Michael looked

around at a wolf charging up to him and flung the attacker away from

him with a casual flick of his arm. She was astonished by his speed,

power and grace. She knew he was quick, she knew he was strong, but

knowing and seeing are always two very different things. She sucked in a

ragged breath and scrubbed the tears from her eyes with the back of a

rather dirty hand.

　　With a hit like a hammer striking her chest, his head snapped

around and he locked eyes with her. She couldn't look away; his eyes

were a blazing blue fire that cut right through her. It was only chance

and luck that allowed her to see the wolf sneaking up on his left flank.

She lowered the rifle and sighted at the first target the wolf presented.

The thing's head was just visible over Michael's shoulder. Quickly

before she lost her nerve, she made sure of her target and squeezed the

trigger. A look of unbelievable shock flashed across Michael's face as

he looked down at himself, thinking that she had shot him, but he then

looked behind him in time to see the wolf slump to the ground. He looked closely at the body and the turned his surprised face to stare at

her. She had put a bullet right through the wolf's forehead.

She shrugged her shoulders and grinned, and then she started

trying to climb out of the tree without shooting herself with the rifle.

Michael didn't wait around for anyone else to interrupt him, he just ran

to her across the field with speed only one of his kind could manage.

He was not going to lose her again. Nothing was going to take her away

from him this time. When he reached her, she was just scrambling out

of the tree.

"Kayla, my gods, love, are you okay? What in the world are you

wearing?" She threw her arms, covered in scratches and bruises, around

him and just held on with all her might. He was shaking with rage and

relief and she was shaking with reaction to all that had happened.

"They shredded my clothes, I had to make do." She kissed his

face, neck, any part of him she could reach. She had been so scared that

she would never see him again. She kept him so occupied that he

couldn't speak until her lips finally stopped assaulting him.

"You never told me you could shoot like that." He said holding

her gently with plenty of caution for his new strength. He never wanted

to let her go, but he leaned back so that he could take a good look at her. She was covered in dirt and scratches, but that was mostly from the escape. The one giant bruise on her cheek though was probably from their mistreatment.

"Well, I didn't know I could. I've never used one before." She let go of him to stand facing the field with the rifle raised and ready. She wouldn't let anything sneak up on them to hurt him or her, not after all she had gone through. They stayed that way, him thinking he was protecting her, and her thinking that at least she could slow down any attackers for him.

"Shut up, stupid!" The tiny young woman slapped her companion in the back of the head. "You want them to find us sneaking out of here without joining the fight?" The two vampires were dressed in charcoal shirts and pants, their faces smudged with something to darken them.

"Sorry." He whispered as they crawled, belly down through the thick grass on the opposite side of the jail from the loading docks.

"They don't know who we are, just that we were the trap for that bleeder. If they find out who I am they will never let us live." She crawled a few more feet, the trees and their hidden dirt bikes were within sight.

"But, why would he let them catch him?" The pale young man asked again.

"Why not? How stupid can you be? When Nicholai gets out he will know the location of their secret shed. Can you imagine how much he'll thank us for following him there and springing him out?" The tiny girl hit her companion one more time as they finally made it to the tree line and started walking the dirt bikes far out of hearing range before starting them.

"We seem to be winning." Michael said quietly from the tree line where he stood with his arm around Kayla. He watched closely for any problems, as those that had come here with him chased off the remaining wolves and vampires around the jail. Roland in particular looked pleased and bloody. "Let's get back over there and see how the others are doing. I have some unfinished business." He nodded at the rifle and Kayla finally pointed it at the ground so that she could follow him out to his friends.

Part of the way through the field he pulled her over to the side and he stopped to lean down over the ragged remains of what had been a very blonde female vampire. Kayla stood back, not wanting to say

anything and certainly not wanting to stop him. She recognized the eyes

and the hair, this had been Nicholai's assistant throughout all of the

procedures they had done on her. It was her that had given Kayla the

nasty bruise on her cheekbone.

"I told you I would be back for you. This is not something I

ever wanted to do, but you have forced my hand. Good bye Eliza." He

dropped a bottle of some clear liquid down onto the body and it

shattered splashing everywhere. As he turned to walk away he flipped

open a lighter, lit it and tossed it over his shoulder. There was a large

whooshing sound as the liquid caught and Kayla plugged her nose at the

stench. It was one of the most foul things she had ever smelled in her

life, surpassing the time at the zoo when she had seen, and smelled, a

snake regurgitate its meal.

Michael walked over to a group of two other vampires and two

wolves, one she recognized as Logan and the other she was sure was

Nikki. Both of the werewolves were covered in blood, but they were

standing very close together and there was a tension there that spoke of

something between them. For her sake, Kayla prayed that Nikki had

found someone to love her the way she truly deserved. She hoped that her friend could forgive her for everything that had happened because of her relationship with Michael.

"Where are Maximus and Nicholai?" Michael asked before they had come to a stop near the group. He kept his arm around Kayla protectively, and she was glad he did. It quieted the raging beast of jealousy that surged up her throat at the sight of the beauty standing there. She had long curly red hair that floated about her like magic. Her porcelain skin was lightly scattered with delicate freckles and her eyes were green like emeralds. Standing next to that lady, made Kayla feel spectacularly plain and boring; it was like she knew she would never look that ethereal.

"Maximus is taking Nicholai to be incarcerated. There is a special chamber at the "shed" set aside for vampires just like him." This was spoken by the man standing close to the red haired woman. He looked, aside from the blood covering him, like a teacher. His salt and pepper hair was cut short and he had some kind of muddy brown green hazel eyes. He smiled and it just reinforced the teacher look.

"Not what I wanted to see happen to him, but it will suffice. At least that part has been taken care of. Let me make the introductions after we have made it back to someplace safer than here." Michael turned to pick Kayla up but she stepped back out of his reach. Michael

looked hurt and that tore at her heart, but she knew she needed to get

this out in the open before anything else happened.

"I need to tell you something first. Something they did to me."

Kayla began to shake all over and couldn't make eye contact. She heard

Logan cough uncomfortably as her tears began to fall.

"Nothing they have done to you will change the way I feel about

you. Please let me get you to safety." The others politely walked a

distance away, but she was sure they could still hear everything that was

being said. She didn't care if they knew, but it killed her that she was

going to hurt Michael even more.

"I have to tell you this, I have to. We can't go forward without

you knowing." She shook with tears streaming down her face and his

heart ached for her. He wanted to hold her, to pet her hair, to tell her

everything would be okay, but the words that came out of her mouth

next stopped him dead in his tracks and froze his heart, mid-beat.

"They impregnated me." She blurted out and then crumpled to

the ground, dissolving into tears and sobs.

Chapter 18:

"There is no way in hell I am going to endanger her life and the life of a child that may or may not be part of me, just so that I can be happy. I won't do it." Michael pounded his fist into the concrete floor where he sat. He left a crushed place and looked at the dust on his knuckles almost in surprise. "But sending her away, how can I keep her safe that way?"

"What possible option do you have? If you keep her with you, my son, she and the baby will always be in danger. It's only been a week since we rescued her and some of Nicholai's followers are already sniffing around." Jenna sat like a statue on an overturned bucket, making it look much more like a throne than an abandoned piece of trash.

"I don't know what to do. Where I am, where I go, they will assume she is with me. They know how much she means to me now. I have to make her safe, but if she is pregnant, I will not change her and kill her unborn child. Her scent has changed; it makes me think that the pregnancy has taken." He stood, paced a few steps, punched a hole in a brick wall and then flopped back down on the cement.

"We do not know what the child will be like either. She may not be able to carry it to term, or if she does the child may be too different for her to handle on her own. So sending her off with a new memory now is not the best idea and does not take into account all the possible things that could go wrong. We need to protect her and monitor her during her pregnancy and delivery to give her the best possible chance of survival and carrying to term. We can change her memory after and then send her off with someone to protect her." Jenna sat silently like a statue, which was a clear sign of her level of stress. She was not fond of this idea, but her blood father insisted it was the best way.

"You're right; she has to stay with us during that time at least. It will take Nicholai's followers a while to regroup and to find where we will be hiding with her anyway. I certainly do not want to be without her nearby during this. I would feel much safer with her where I can watch over her." Knowing that he wasn't going to have to say goodbye to the woman he loved just yet, made him feel so much better that he actually smiled a little. He was going to get to see the baby born as well. Somehow it didn't matter to him how she had gotten pregnant with the child, his blood had been used and he felt an emotional connection to it already, as if he had fathered the child himself. It didn't hurt that the

biological father was such a very good friend. He had already spoken

with Logan and while he wanted to keep the kid safe, he didn't want

anything to do with the baby in a fatherly sort of way.

"I think it is what is for the best. I would have Maximus tell you

himself, but he has already returned to his room in the halls below to

finish his rest. I am not sure when he will decide to rejoin our society

this time." Jenna stood up. "We should probably go save her from

herself at that hotel. Who knows what she is thinking by now, since it

has been more than a week."

Kayla lay in the hotel bed of the room that Michael had rented

for her. She was warm and safe and completely miserable. It didn't

matter to her that this was an expensive 4 star hotel with an amazing

view of the Appalachian Mountains, it didn't matter that she had all the

comforts she could ever want or ask for. What mattered was that

Michael had stopped speaking to her the minute she had told him what

had happened. He treated her like spun glass and refused to hold her.

The longer she thought about how he was acting the angrier she got.

She wanted to throw things at him and scream at him and tell him there was no way in hell she would put up with him treating her this way.

Unfortunately he hadn't come by to see her since he had rented her this

room.

She looked at the clock; it wasn't quite night time yet, but the

light seeping around the curtain told her that the sun was going down.

Dinner had been sent up to her room and it sat untouched, the nausea

was back and the smell of food sometimes set her off. She didn't need a

test to tell her she was pregnant. She had all the symptoms and then

some, but she had made peace with that. This baby was part of her and

in a way part of Michael, and it didn't matter how she had gotten

pregnant.

The phone next to the bed rang and she nearly fell out of bed to

answer it. "Hello?"

"Kayla?" It was Michael and before he could say anything she

cut him off. A few curse words and then she actually started talking

coherently.

"Where in the hell have you been? I'm in here by myself,

pregnant, sick as a dog and hormonal and you just disappear for over a

week, no call, or anything?" Her voice cracked and she started crying,

she couldn't even stay mad like a normal person anymore, her emotions were all tangled with hormones.

"I'm sorry. I am coming over. I have things figured out. I will be there shortly." He hung up as soon as he replied, his voice sounding tense and strained.

She threw a pillow across the room and punched the headboard in utter frustration. *Damn that man for being a stubborn pain in my slowly swelling ass.* She threw another pillow and then just flopped back onto the bed and cried some more. She didn't care that she was still in her bathrobe from earlier, she didn't care that her hair was a snarled wet mess from sleeping and crying in the bed. She was too tired and angry to make the effort to primp just for him.

There wasn't even a knock on the door to alert her that someone was here. She just woke up from a fitful dose with a hand shaking her gently. Michael stood beside the bed with the red haired woman behind him.

"What's going on?" She asked rubbing at her tired eyes. The red haired lady must be Michael's blood parent, Jenna. She stepped forward and sat down on the bed next to Kayla putting a very maternal hand on her shoulder. It actually felt good to have someone acting like a mother to her, since she had not had a mother figure in a very long time.

"We have a solution to keep you and the baby . . . oh my!" Jenna stopped speaking and turned her head to the side, leaning closer to Kayla to listen to something. "Oh gods, Michael, there are two!" She turned to Michael who looked like he had been kicked in the gut. His eyes went round and collapsed to the floor, staring at her and shaking. Tears flowed from his eyes, slightly pinkish in hue when they landed on the white sheet next to Kayla. His hand trembling he reached out to place it on her still, for now, flat tummy.

"Two? Two what?" Kayla asked, fear screaming up her spine and making goose bumps race down her arms.

"Two heartbeats dear. You're carrying twins." Jenna patted her hand awkwardly and then looked back at Michael who was shaking his head and crying. Kayla was in too much shock to move to hold him, but her heart ached to see him so distraught.

"What are you here for?" She asked trembling with all the emotions. Twins how was she to handle having two babies and not just one?

"We are going to make sure you are safe. You will be going into hiding. Michael has a few places that Nicholai's followers know nothing of. We can't change you, obviously, so we will do what we can to keep you hidden." Jenna spoke giving Michael the time he needed to compose himself.

"Will, I be alone?" she asked looking right at Michael.

"Of course not dear, Michael will be going with you and I will be taking over his area of the country. It was my job originally and it will be no trouble to take it back from him. After all he has gone through it would not seem unreasonable for him to request some time to gather his thoughts." Jenna tapped Michael with the toe of her very elegant and most likely expensive shoe.

He looked up at Kayla, a small smile on his lips. "I'll take care of you, I promise." His voice rough with emotion, was barely a whisper. He still had his hand on her tummy and she placed her warm one over his rather cold one.

She was so relieved that he would not be leaving her alone any more that she just fell apart and started crying. He finally after so long stood up and pulled her into his arms. Jenna took a little tour around the hotel suite to give them a few moments of privacy. When she came back in Michael was sitting on the bed with Kayla in his lap and they were both drying their eyes.

"We should leave. It's a long way to Canada." Jenna smiled; they would be okay for now. They had each other to make it through the

pregnancy and then they could figure things out from there.

Jenna and Michael helped her to pack her things as she got

dressed, moving slowly so as not to upset her fluttery stomach. She

really wished there was something she could take that would actually

work to stave off the nausea.

"Here sip some of this." She was startled when Jenna handed

her a bottle of clear soda. "It's completely safe, we've done it before

with some of our hirelings that have gotten pregnant. There is just a

drop of blood in there, but it's enough to settle your stomach."

Kayla took a hesitant sip, remembering clearly how sick she had

gotten after Michael had slipped her blood before. She stood there

hoping it would work and soon her stomach did stop churning and

rolling. She was even able to help more with getting her things together

and eat normally for the first time in a few days.

"Nikki and Logan are going to go back to your old apartment to

take care of packing the rest of your things and moving her stuff into

Logan's place, including her dog." Michael said as she handed him the

small bag with all her bathroom supplies.

"Oh, good, I worried about that." She wanted to be alone with him. Having Jenna there made her feel oddly shy, but somehow he

sensed that and grabbed her hand as they walked to his car.

"The trip is going to be a long one. We're going to be driving at

night and sleeping during the day. The bad guys probably expect me to

either stay put where I have the most defenses or to leave and get way

out of the country as quickly as possible. We'll throw them off by

mundane travel and using only cash so they can't trace credit cards. I'm

afraid the hotels won't be as nice as this one, the more expensive places

rarely, if ever, take cash." He held the door for her out to the parking

lot, and when she saw the vehicle he had brought for them to travel in,

she lost it and just burst into gales of laughter. She laughed till tears

poured down her face and her ribs hurt. After all the trials and

complications, she felt she deserved to just let it all out. Then again,

most people would find the idea of a vampire traveling in an RV rather

hysterical.

Michael just handed her a tissue and helped her into the

passenger seat. Jenna took off by herself in a tiny little red sports car

and Michael got behind the wheel of the grand behemoth as she had

begun to think of it. It set her off again to see him driving the thing like

a common family man and it was a long time before she could get herself under control. Michael rolled his eyes and just let her continue, it wasn't going to hurt his feelings any, and once she saw all the benefits of the special features in this RV she would likely stop giggling like a mad woman.

After a time of quietly watching the road she spoke up. "So, Canada, huh? Why there?"

"It's far away, its rural, and most importantly, not even Jenna knows where the safe house is up there. I have an online messenger account that Logan will use to keep in touch that is untraceable. In other words, it's the Fort Knox of safe houses." He smiled at her and went back to watching the road.

"I'm glad you'll be with me. I was worried when you stopped talking to me that you were going to send me away. I don't think I would have handled that well." She was still sipping the soda that Jenna had given her and she felt so much better that she was even contemplating eating more food. "Michael? These children, they feel like they should be part yours." She said it knowing that she wanted him to be in their life like a father figure.

"They are mine, in heart, if not completely by blood. I will protect them and raise them as if they were flesh of my flesh." He said it with such conviction that chills ran up her spine. She looked at him

and his eyes were flashing in the oncoming headlights. She could tell by

the set of his brow, that he was angrier than she had ever seen him, or

anyone else for that matter, before. Nicholai certainly had a lot to

answer for.

"Now what are we going to do?" Nikki asked Logan as they sat

in the shade of a tree at his ranch on the outskirts of Nashville. She had

squealed in delight at the sight of the meadow and nearly fainted at the

sight of the house nestled in among the trees back off of the road a

ways.

"Well, Michael is taking Kayla to a safe house he set up a long

time ago that no one knows the location of except for him. He's staying

with her until she has the baby. Babies actually, in case Jenna didn't tell

you, she is carrying twins. You, my dear, are going to be training with

me from this point on. I see so much potential in you that I just do not

want to leave it in the hands of anyone else." He put his arm around her

shoulders and hugged her close. He could not be happier, that is unless

Michael got all of his troubles sorted out.

"I'm worried about Kayla. There is no way for us to visit her, is there?" Nikki asked leaning into his warm embrace. For her part, Nikki had never met a man she wanted to swoon over as much as Logan. It was a trial for her just to keep her hands off of him when things of importance came up. She was sure that she was depriving him of sleep with her bedtime affections, but she wouldn't stop unless he complained, which wasn't likely.

After the battle they had disappeared into the woods by themselves and let off the rest of their battle nerves in each other's arms. He was totally smitten with her and she was just as head over heels for him. This is what she had been looking for all those years out clubbing. There were no more thoughts of her being a monster, she would be his equal in any way she could. He was her pack mate, the Alpha male to her Alpha female, and there was no doubt that she would soon be a full Alpha in the pack.

"Kayla will be fine, and no, we can't visit. Nicholai's followers know us and would follow us to them." He heaved a sigh that was part contentment and part concern. "How are you handling the becoming a monster problem?"

"What problem? You say that I am wonderful this way, you have never lied to me in the very short time I have known you, what would make me think that you would lie about that?" She smiled up at

him and he kissed her nose.

"You are the most amazing wolf I have ever seen. You are

strong, flexible, quick and intelligent, everything anyone could hope for

in a mate. It's like you were meant to be a wolf. I couldn't be more

proud of the way you handled yourself in that fight." They lay back in

the grass and soon there were clothes flying in all directions as he

showed her just how much he enjoyed her company.

Roland stood in his lab testing the samples he had retrieved

from the sight where the fight had gone down. He kept careful record

of the results of each. He had been a scientist before his change and he

had kept up with modern science as the years progressed. He had

finished testing the samples he had gotten from his allies and even the

sample he had taken from Kayla. The science behind the viruses that

created both werewolves and vampires had taken up most of his time

since his turning.

There was much that he had found out in the past few years,

with the advancement of machines and computers. The genetics

involved in turning were extremely interesting to him. He had found that there were two possible genetic mutations in humans that enhanced

their bodies' acceptance of the viruses. Some humans had no mutation

and therefor made poor choices for the change, as it would cause them

to lose their mind to some extent. Other humans had one mutation that

made them more receptive to either the vampire virus or the werewolf

virus. If they were turned by the proper one, they became an effective

member of that species. If by chance they were turned by the opposite,

well, very few of those survived the turning; those that did were usually

hunted down and killed as a danger to the secrecy of all.

The sample he was working on at the moment was Kayla's. It

was the first one he had ever found of its kind. Somehow, she had both

mutations. He was unsure of what that would mean if she were ever to

be turned, but it definitely deserved a lot more time in study.

He pinched the bridge of his nose as he set the last machine to

run its test. He had about fifteen minutes to spare before the test was

complete. He went for a walk down to check on Nicholai in his

imprisonment. While Roland was much more of a science nerd at heart,

he had learned some fighting from others of his kind and he used it

with skill and finesse.

He took the elevator down to the level of the chambers. This was not one of his favorite places, but he worried that Nicholai would prove powerful enough to escape. He would take this break from his work to ensure the safety of everyone. All of the chambers save for Nicholai's were able to be opened from the inside and the outside. The one he was imprisoned in was only able to be unlocked from the outside.

There was a silence in the hallway outside of the chambers that gave Roland a bit of the creeps. He walked down here every so often now that they had locked Nicholai up. He trusted their guards, but he wasn't going to take any chances.

There were only four vampires in torpor here, not including Nicholai. Maximus had gone back to his chamber and no one knew when he would come back out. Roland did not even know the names of the other two residents, only that they were allies and both were relatively young to have felt the need to use the chambers.

There was a moan of frustration and a scratching noise from the very last door on the right. Roland walked up to it listening very intently. The scratching continued and then a very pained voice whispered out into the hall at him.

"I smell your blood Roland. I will be free again. Soon." Then another moan and the scratching stopped.

"You'll be free just as soon as you can find a way to dig yourself out of solid steel while partially in torpor Mr. Smarty pants." Roland taunted him, but he still shivered in response.

He was halfway down the hall when a noise behind him made him stop in his tracks and turn. Behind him, half in and half out of his doorway was Maximus. He had a pack on his back and he said nothing to Roland. He just strode to the elevator and left, leaving Roland standing in the middle of the hallway in shock. He had certainly not expected this and he would have to tell the others at once.

He took the elevator all the way back to the surface and then made his way back to his lab on one of the top floors. He made it back in time to hear the machine tone that it was finished and a paper printed out. He read the results, nodding his head. It was exactly as he thought, if Nicholai had used any other woman, one with no gene mutation or one with only one mutation, the pregnancy would never have taken.

If Nicholai has his people try to recreate this without Kayla or another dual mutation there is no chance in hell it's going to work. I seriously doubt that he even knows about the genes.

He cleaned up the last of his things in the lab and then left with all of his notes tucked in a folder under his arm. He had to notify the

council that Jenna was putting together of his findings and the fact that

Maximus was now awake and had left without telling anyone where he

was going or why. Things may have seemed to calm down, but he had a

feeling it was just the lull in the eye of the storm.

Kayla loved it here, the nights were longer during this part of

the year and she got to spend so much more time with Michael. The

pregnancy wasn't nearly as much of a burden as she had thought it

would be. Once she got past the stage for all the nausea, that is. There

was a small town nearby, small meaning about 30 people including

them, and the midwife there was taking care of all the medical checkups

she needed.

She and Michael spent most of their time together star gazing,

watching movies or just snuggled up on the couch reading books. It was

a very comfortable time and each day she slept in bed next to him. It

was a bit odd at first how still he was and how cool his skin felt

compared to hers, but it wasn't that hard to get used to. At least he

didn't snore, for that she was profoundly grateful.

Right now he was still resting and she was watching the sun set over the trees with a mug of hot chocolate between her hands. It was so

peaceful out here that she could almost forget that there was danger out

there somewhere looking for her. She shivered; the weather would be

too cold to stand outside on the porch like this much longer.

She rested one hand on her belly and felt the tiny movements

like flutters against her hand. *Soon, little ones, I'll get to hold you in my arms*

and give you all the love you deserve.

Epilogue

There in the darkness, her body pinned in the trap he had set for her, she waited and plotted, hearing the thoughts of those of the blood around her. So long ago that her memory had withered to nothing she thought she could have loved that man, but he had taken too much from her. Her son, killed and her family, torn to pieces; even her tiny infant daughter had been taken from her to be raised by another family. She writhed against the restraints, but lack of feeding had weakened her and there was not enough strength left in her to escape.

I will put an end to that man if it is the last thing I do. Before he begs me to be killed he will lose everything he holds dear, if he even cares enough about anything other than bedding a new woman every night.

A new mind started sending out an almost directed message. He too was trapped and longed to escape, but his target was not the same as hers. She turned her very powerful thoughts his direction and had to pull back some when she felt him wince away in pain.

"Who are you?" The mind voice was direct, but weak.

"I am the enemy of one of your enemy's allies. For now that is all you need.

Prove your value to me and I will ensure that you are free to seek revenge." She sent

back. There was a pause in his mind voice, it was definitely male. It was

as if he was thinking over her statement.

"How?" A smile crossed her face after he answered. She had his

attention and she would be able to exploit him to get to her goal.

"Send me someone to free me, for I am as trapped as you are young man."

The silence from his mind showed shock. *"You do not need to know how,*

yet. It is too hard to speak this way. Send me the image of one I can contact for

help." An image flashed into her mind of a tiny young woman, obviously

of the blood. The man could not keep other secrets from slipping into

her mind along with the image. Now she would surely have something

to hold over him, if she needed to. She broke off contact with him

abruptly and sent out a call to the woman.

She sent her images of her location and the type of confinement

she was in. Along with that she made sure to send her future images of

helping to rescue the man that this young vampire had been worrying

herself sick over. He might not have true love in his heart, but this

young one was loyal to him until death and loved him with every inch

of her tiny frame. *This just got a whole lot better for me.*

It would take some time for her rescue to happen she was very well hidden and the trap had been designed by a near genius level brain.

She had many years of studying the design from where she was bound

and she could guide the woman through it.

Finally her incarceration would be over and she would be able to

take her revenge on the man that had betrayed her, killed her son, had

her turned into a monster and then trapped her here.

There would be no forgiveness for him. He could pretend to be a good

man all he wanted, but she knew the real him. She knew the man that

left a string of broken hearts and broken women behind. She knew the

arrogance that he strutted around with, feeling superior to everyone. Oh

she knew him alright and soon she would put an end to Marcus Valerius

Maximus.

Note from the Author

This is my very first published novel and I hope you enjoyed it. I've been fascinated by the unusual and the odd my whole life, and as such, have always been an avid reader. The more I read, the more my own stories began to develop in my mind. A bit of advice from one weirdo to the next: Never let anyone tell you that your kind of crazy isn't good enough. If you have a passion, follow it with you entire being. Chase it down and tackle that bitch; make it yours!

www.ingramcontent.com/pod-product-compliance
Lightning Source LLC
Chambersburg PA
CBHW072321280626
47159CB00027B/131

* 9 780692 790670 *